DESTINATION WEDDING

AARON STANDER

Writers & Editors
INTERLOCHEN, MICHIGAN

© 2020 by Aaron Stander

Cover photo by Tony Denim

Writers & Editors
Interlochen, Michigan

ISBN: 978-0-9975701-6-8
Printed and bound in the United States of America

FOR BEACHWALKER
AND HAMISH

1
~

Ray Elkins, the sheriff of Cedar County—a narrow peninsula jutting out into northern Lake Michigan—peered out the window of the descending aircraft. As the plane dropped through the clouds, the snow-covered terrain began to take form, first the forests and lakes, then, on the final approach, the topography— rolling hills and deep valleys. Home.

The aircraft made a sweeping turn over Lake Michigan, banking steeply, the right wing dipping toward the water. Ray looked down at the rows of waves marching south on the big lake.

Closing his book and marking the spot with a finger, he shut his eyes, waiting for the reassuring sound of wheels touching earth. After the final bounce, as the aircraft began to slow, he replaced his finger with a folded boarding pass and struggled briefly to pull a small backpack up from beneath the seat in front of him, his body still not fully healed.

He waited patiently in the last row of the slender regional jet as the passengers ahead of him scrambled to their feet, extracted their belongings from the overhead bins, and then joined the long line that slowly plodded toward the exit.

Ray finally made his way up the jetway, grabbing the last piece of luggage from the carry-on cart and started down the long, mostly empty passageway to the main terminal.

"I thought you missed the plane," said Sue Lawrence, the temporary acting sheriff. She pulled him into her arms and held him tightly.

He folded his arms around her, happy to have her close.

"You look good," she said, pulling away. "How are you feeling?"

He gave her an affirmative nod and a weak, sleepy smile. "Happy to be home," he finally said. "I'm glad you're here to meet me."

"Do you have other luggage?"

"No."

"You travel light, Elkins. That's what you left with. I couldn't live for months out of one suitcase. Let me take your backpack," she said, lifting it away from him. "How was Chicago?"

"A short night in an airport hotel. I'm sorry I missed my connecting flight last night. I was looking forward to getting home."

Outside, a cold wind blew against Ray's face. When he took a deep breath, the hairs in his nostrils froze. Spring up north—he wouldn't trade it for all the mild breezes off San Francisco Bay, where the temperature rarely sank below fifty degrees.

Ray could hear the barking as they approached Sue's truck. Simone, a Cairn terrier he and Sue co-parented, bolted from the vehicle as the rear hatch opened, circling Ray and jumping against him until he bent down and caught her in his arms.

"She's been waiting for your return. Today as we headed to the airport, she just seemed to know."

"Have you been feeding her?" Ray asked soberly. "She seems thin."

"Yes," Sue said with a small defensive huff. "Vet prescribed food. No lamb chops, no wild-caught Pacific salmon, no Stilton, no Zingerman's crumbs. She has happily wolfed down every meal." Sue smiled over at Ray. "She probably misses the gourmet enhancements to her diet. I know I do."

As they rolled down the exit road toward the highway, Ray asked, "What's on the agenda today?"

Sue flashed him a playful smile. "The local service clubs have joined together to do a luncheon in your honor. It's a good thing you could get a flight this morning. They've been planning this for weeks."

Ray gave Sue a look.

"You're a hero, man. People love you. I know you hate these things, but you've got to be on your best behavior."

"You're the hero, Sue. I was just the clay pigeon who caught some lead."

"We're going to be presented with a plaque. Don't forget to smile. You want to look good on social media. By the way, the county commissioners were happy to receive documentation that you are fit to resume your duties."

Ray had gotten the all-clear from his doctor in Palo Alto—one of Hanna's new colleagues at Stanford Medical Center—and sent the paperwork on to the Cedar County Board. He had also discussed returning to work with his therapist, whom he credited with guiding him through the dark place he'd inhabited after being shot.

Sue continued, "They asked me to convey to you that you should take all the time you need. If you initially want to work part-time, there's no problem. They passed a resolution to that effect at their last meeting. They also passed a resolution thanking me for my service during your absence."

"I'm sorry all the extra work got pushed on you."

"It wasn't bad, Ray. Everyone kicked it up a notch. Should I remind you of what you've built here? The culture, the *esprit de corps*?" She looked over at Ray, whose expression remained impassive. "Okay, I won't."

Ray had reached out to Sue after leaving California to recover in Florida. He had heard that there were some minor physical injuries at the Cedar County Governmental Center from flying glass, falls, and smoke inhalation, and he wanted to see if everyone was okay. But the psychological damage was devastating. Wendy Morrison, one of the area's most respected psychotherapists and an old high school friend of Ray's, had organized a comprehensive counseling program, and Sue had encouraged everyone to attend at least three sessions. Even so, when Ray checked in during his recovery, Sue told him that a couple of people had resigned and that one had decided to retire. The sudden immersion in that kind of violence had changed everyone. Ray had received many cards, letters, and emails while in Florida and Palo Alto, and he had responded to each one of them, in each case knowing his words were inadequate. Only time would soften the terror to which they had all been exposed.

Ray had also learned during his recovery that Marian Patozak had died of terminal cancer a few weeks after shooting Ray with an old pistol. Her accomplice, Little John, whose real name was Toby Osmann, had been institutionalized after recovering from his injuries and being judged unfit to stand trial.

When Ray had last seen the Cedar County Government Center, it had been on fire. Now, all the damage had been repaired. As Sue gave him a tour of the exterior of the building, she explained that most of the windows on the back of the structure had had to be replaced.

"And then there were all the destroyed vehicles," Sue said. "Everything was covered by insurance," she added quickly.

As they made their way around to the front entrance, Sue asked, "How is Hanna's new job working out? Is she bitter at all about losing her position here?"

Ray shook his head. "Stanford is everything she's ever wanted," he said.

Months before, when Hanna had received an offer of a fellowship at Stanford, she had, in the interest of transparency, mentioned it to one of her colleagues at the trauma center. But then Ray had been shot, and she had taken him to Florida and sent a request to her professional group for extended leave. Their response had been a surprising one: They were not renewing her contract. They were overwhelmed with work and had found a replacement surgeon who could start immediately.

"So the decision has been made for her," Ray had told Sue on the phone from Florida. "She's accepted the job at Stanford."

After a month in Florida, Ray and Hanna had moved to Palo Alto, where Hanna's new group had found them housing, and Hanna had focused on lining up medical and psychological resources for Ray. Then she had started her new job—working long days and often weekends, too, while Ray met several times each week with a physical therapist and a psychologist.

"It was the psychological help, Sue," Ray said now. "That's what I needed the most. It was intense, transformative. I can now see the light at the end of the tunnel. How about you?"

"I've been seeing Wendy Morrison twice a week. She's helped a lot, you know, with things way beyond that incident. I'm changed. And I'm thinking about other possibilities."

Ray's brow lifted.

"Don't panic," Sue said. "No immediate changes."

Sue wanted to ask Ray if he and Hanna were still together, if they were going to work things out long distance as a couple, but she held back. That conversation could wait.

2

~

After the service club luncheon, Ray and Sue lingered, shaking hands and chatting with the many well-wishers. By the time they emerged from the conference center, the parking lot was mostly empty. They took the time to walk Simone around the perimeter of the lot before finally climbing into Sue's truck.

As she guided the vehicle out onto the highway, Ray asked, "Was my behavior appropriate?"

"Oh, Elkins, you constantly amaze me. You were wonderful—gracious, humble, and sincere. That's why this community loves you. Lots of people remember you from way back when, and you're just the same person you've always been. Folks know they can depend on you."

"Enough," said Ray curtly.

"Okay, enough," she responded. "Do you need anything, or would you like me to take you straight home?"

"Don't you have to go back to the office?" he asked.

"I have the rest of the day off, and you're not scheduled to work until next Monday. Half-days for at least the first week—the board insists."

"What's going on?" Ray asked. "Did I land in the wrong place?"

She laughed. "As you pointed out to me, the distaff side took most of the seats on the board in the November election. Turns out these women are smart and curious. They read, research, and have intelligent discussions."

"Fancy that, people who read elected to the county board.

Let's drive to the big lake," he said.

"The Cannery?"

"Yes."

She tossed him a smile. "You're so predictable," she said.

As they drove west, Ray asked a question he had avoided when talking to Sue while he was away. "What's happening with Mike Ogden? How's the fire business?" Mike was the state police arson investigator they'd worked with on the Patozak/Osmunn case. Sue had started seeing him after the investigation.

"He's busy in Lansing. He came up to visit me a few times right after the shooting, but only an occasional phone call or message since then."

"So you're not…?"

"He hasn't stopped by to reclaim his toothbrush." Ray noted the irritation in her voice and wondered at it. He let things go quiet and looked out at the scenery for a few miles.

"Is this what you wanted to see?" asked Sue, pulling to the shoulder at the top of a ridge. "I even got the sun to come out for you."

Ray scanned the panorama—the west shoreline of Lake Michigan running north toward Leland and mid-lake toward the North Manitou Shoal Light Station. He looked south in the direction of South Manitou Island and open water reaching west to Wisconsin. In recent months he'd walked the beach in the Keys and later watched the sun drop into the Pacific. And in the weeks before leaving California he and Hanna had kayaked in the ocean a few times. He loved being close to the water or on the water. But this place, upper Lake Michigan, he loved the most.

"I take it you need to walk on the beach," she said.

Ray nodded.

Sue parked in the small lot next to the Cannery, a century-old structure that now housed a maritime museum. They walked across the frozen sand to the water's edge and started following the shoreline west toward Sleeping Bear Point.

They moved slowly across a thin layer of crusted snow covered with a dusting of sand, Simone loping along near them.

"So what's happening with Hanna?"

"She's settled into the new job. She's happy. Likes her new colleagues. The work is challenging. I think she's in a good place."

"Where does that leave the two of you?"

Ray walked on for a bit pondering his answer. "I don't know. I don't think either of us has figured that out."

"So where are you? Long-distance relationship?"

"I don't know," he answered. Gesturing toward the water, he said, "This is what I need, wild, empty spaces. I don't like living in cities. Hanna's apartment was okay, but that's not for me."

"What does that mean?" asked Sue, stopping and looking intently at Ray.

"I don't know. We didn't say it was over," Ray said carefully, meeting Sue's eyes. "She's doing important work. And she seems to love it out there. And neither of us is good at talking things out."

Sue knew he wasn't going to give her anything more. She shrugged and tried to shake off the feeling of dismay rising into her chest. "I'm starting to get chilled," she said. "The wind has picked up. Simone looks cold, too. I'm going to take her and head back to the truck. But you go ahead, go as long as you want. That will give me a chance to catch up on emails and calls."

"Okay, I would like to keep going, just for a bit. You're sure you're all right with that?"

"Yes, take whatever time you need. We'll be fine."

Ray trekked on, stopping and looking back once toward the Cannery. As he rounded the point, he could see the waves starting to break on the shoal that reached out to the deeper water. He paused and listened to the rhythm of the incoming waves that seemed perfectly attuned to the rhythms he felt in his own body. Looking at the whitecaps advancing toward the beach, he thought about Hanna and the many times they had played in the surf before paddling back to their launch point. He thought about the long evenings that followed, cooking and eating, making love, and waking in the morning, curled next to each other. He hadn't been so close to a woman since his wife had died years before. And now, things seem stalled, their relationship in limbo. Before he'd left Palo Alto, Hanna had said that she might be open to coming back to Cedar County when her fellowship ended, but Ray had no illusions about how things would change between them, living so far apart. He was tired of thinking about it.

He scanned the water slowly from south to north, up past the islands and Manitou Passage, then he turned and slowly started to retrace his steps, eventually seeing Sue's tracks in the snow, too. Then he heard the siren and saw the emergency lights of Sue's vehicle rolling down the frozen beach toward him.

Ray pulled the truck door open and propelled himself into the passenger's seat. As he attached his seatbelt, Sue spun the vehicle around on the frozen surface and headed back toward the Cannery. She slowed, guiding the truck over the low concrete curb stops separating the parking area from the beach, and then accelerated up the highway.

"What's going on?" Ray shouted over the scream of the siren.

Sue hooked her right thumb through Simone's collar and lifted the small dog over the console toward Ray. "Hold onto her."

When she had both hands back on the steering wheel, she said, "Home invasion in progress. Some guy's trying to cut his way in with a chainsaw. Shots fired into the building."

"Where?"

"Elmer Road, Old Mill Creek area." She glanced at the GPS. "Ten miles. We are the closest unit. Backup is rolling. And Elkins, you stay in the vehicle. You're still on sick leave."

Ray started to respond, then held his tongue.

Sue chuckled. "Welcome back to Cedar County."

3
~

Ray worked half-days his first week back at the Cedar County Government Center, most of them at his desk catching up on correspondence and cases he'd missed during his recovery. He and Sue worked the home invasion case and a mysterious case of a car abandoned after skidding off the road, hitting a tree, and bursting into flames.

During his off hours, he took long walks with Simone, most along the Lake Michigan shore or on the trails that crisscrossed the dunes. He did his physical therapy exercises diligently. It may have been that enough time had passed since he'd been shot, but he could feel his strength returning, as if being away had sapped something essential from him that could only be restored in this place.

On Friday night, Sue left a message containing a strange request. She picked him up the next morning in a black Dodge Charger.

"What's with the wheels?" asked Ray, settling into the passenger seat of the black Dodge Charger.

"We're undercover, Elkins."

"Well, your message was puzzling. I take it that's why you instructed me to dress like a weekend tourist?"

"Yes," Sue answered as she eyed his outfit. "Button-down shirt, wool crewneck, Patagonia jacket, Levi's, and newish hiking boots. Yeah, you can pass for a middle-aged guy from the burbs of Detroit or Chicago."

"Okay, so what's this all about?" He looked over at Sue and carefully took in her outfit. "And by the way, you clean up nicely, too."

"My casual date look for the season." She peered at Ray and

chuckled. "We'll probably look like we're on a father and daughter outing."

"Thanks, kid," he responded. As he peered out of the windshield, he thought about her comment. It stung a bit. He had been feeling old, especially since he was wounded. He wondered if he had suddenly become an old man in Sue's eyes.

"And our current destination?"

"Ursidae Winery. By the way, we're off the clock. Marta Franklin, one of the new members of the county commission, asked me for advice. I've known her for lots of years. She's in my yoga group."

"Something going on at the winery?"

"Let me give you some background. Marta manages the tasting room. And there's an emerging problem that they are trying to contain."

Sue gave him a serious look, and Ray wondered what the problem could possibly be. He had never had a problem at any of the area wineries—as a patron sampling their products or as sheriff. Nothing more, anyway, than a customer getting a little tipsy and being cut off by the bartender. He wondered if the problem was an internal one, with the employees.

"Bachelorette parties, Ray," Sue said. "They're mostly on the shoulders of the summer season, spring and fall, when motels still have cut-rate prices. Groups of young women—twenty-somethings, downstaters mostly—come up for weekend bacchanals. Winery tours top the list of daylight entertainment. Fortunately, most of these groups hire one of the bus tour companies or limo services."

"These tours have been going on for years," Ray said. "I don't remember any problems."

"First, Elkins, sheer numbers. The bachelorette party business has exploded. Busloads of young women descend on the tasting rooms every weekend, before the snow is even melted—mainly on Saturday. That's the big business day for wineries on the offseason. By the fourth or fifth winery, the women are mostly sloshed—as in loud, disruptive, belligerent, obnoxious, obscene, combative—"

"Okay, I get the point," said Ray.

"Hold on. I'm just warming up. You remember Liam the Scam?"

Liam Vantini was a local who owned an adult entertainment club, an adult toy store, and a limo service that featured a stretched Humvee. Ray and Sue referred to the vehicle as the lap-dance-on-wheels-by-the-bay. Liam had lost his chauffeur's license after he attempted to deliver a party of revelers to the top of a local ski area one New Year's Eve. "I thought he left the transportation business," Ray said.

"He's back, license and all," Sue said, "with two shiny-new mini-busses for rent. And Liam is just one of many players in the bridal party winery tour trade. But wait, there's more. For a few hundred extra, you can add a male stripper to your tour bus."

Ray thought he caught a whiff of glee in Sue's tone.

"Liam, always the innovator, is credited with originating the idea," she continued. "Several early adopters have quickly followed. It's rumored these guys start in a tux and end in a thong."

"Dressing down, so to speak."

"Elkins," she said with mild reproach.

"I hope they're not driving, too."

"No. They're just the onboard entertainment. The vehicles are properly MDOT certified; the drivers all have chauffeur licenses." She glanced over at Ray pointedly. "There are no legal requirements for strippers other than raw talent."

Ray groaned loudly and then said, "So what's the deal with Marta Franklin. What does she want from us?"

"Just some brainstorming on possible ways to deal with the problem. The bachelorette groups roll in, buy the sample tasting package, toss down the wine, and move on. There's no profit in that for the wineries. Contrast that with their usual customers who leisurely sample a few wines, then buy a bottle or two or perhaps a case if they find something they especially like. In sum, the wineries say their bottom line is being negatively affected. No one else wants to spend time in the tasting room when these groups of bachelorettes are there. They're driving the bread-and-butter customers away."

"So far, it all sounds legal," Ray said, "so I'm not sure—"

"Look at it as a gesture in community relations. We pop in and observe for thirty or forty minutes. And then I'll run you home. Next week we'll do lunch with Marta and talk it through. You're good at this kind of thing. I'm sure you'll come up with some good suggestions."

Sue parked at the far corner of the Ursidae Winery lot. As they walked toward the main entrance, a group of revelers exited the building and headed toward the designated parking area for busses and vans. They were bunched together, shouting at each other, grasping at each other, and teetering awkwardly across the snowy lot on spiky heels. Ray and Sue paused as the women passed them, and Ray saw that their short skirts extended just below their heavy winter jackets. Some of the jackets hung open, exposing glittery blouses with plunging necklines. The tallest and blondest of the group, with a plastic tiara sitting askew on her head and a blue satin sash crossing her torso, trailed the others. The rest of her party waited for her at the bus door, allowing the presumptive bride to enter first. She swayed noticeably as she mounted the first step, and the chauffeur, standing outside the van, guided the rest of her ascent. Several other women required his help, also.

Even in the cold air, the overpowering smell of their collective fragrance lingered. "Way too much perfume," Ray said. "And the choice of clothing, it's gotta be drafty."

"Club wear, Elkins. You need to get out more."

"Do you own things like that?" he asked with feigned credulity.

"I do have a little outfit I wear when the occasion arises," Sue answered, picking up on his tone and tilting her chin up. "Notice anything else about them?"

"Loud," Ray said, "incredibly loud."

"You're starting to get the picture," Sue said as she held one of the two double doors open for him.

4

~

Ray was immediately assaulted by the intense noise in the main tasting room—loud bits of conversation, high-pitched screams, and laughter ricocheting off the tile floor, plaster walls, and domed ceiling. Most of the cacophony emanated from several clusters of young women at one end of the room.

He scanned the interior of the large timber-framed structure. The bar ran the length of one of the exterior walls. Servers—men and women clad in blue Henleys with the winery logo on the right side of the chest—worked the far side of the counter, pouring glasses of wine as they struggled to communicate with the customers in the clamorous chamber. Customers lined the bar, in some places three, four, or more people deep.

As Sue and Ray stood observing the scene, a group of young women trooped past them toward the bar. Sue gave Ray a knowing look.

Ray had seen—and heard and smelled—enough. As he was about to suggest that they make a fast retreat, a woman emerged from the crowd at the bar and walked purposefully in Sue's direction.

"Welcome," she said, giving Sue a quick hug and extending a hand toward Ray. "Sheriff, thank you for coming. I'm Marta Franklin. Welcome to Bedlam." Turning to Sue, she asked, "How can we best do this?"

"Put us behind the bar. I think we can better understand your point of view looking out at the crowd."

Ray steeled himself and followed Sue and Marta, who led them first on a slow pass of the perimeter of the customers crowding near the bar. Then she took them behind the counter where they could see the chaos firsthand. Ray studied the faces of the people queued up for wine. It was easy to separate the partying crowd, mostly occupying one end of the bar, from the other patrons. The customers genuinely interested in sampling the winery's offerings were older, grayer, and more casually dressed—weekend clothing. They were looking at menu cards, toying with partially filled glasses, trying to converse with their servers, or talking with their companions. The bachelorettes were packed tightly together, talking within their separate groups, attending to the servers only when they wanted to sample more wine.

The sound of breaking glass and screaming pulled their attention abruptly back to the cluster of young women partying at the end of the bar. As the three of them moved toward the disturbance, the crowd started to separate, and Ray could see two women in a violent embrace rolling on the floor. A third woman reached in and grabbed two handfuls of long blond hair and yanked the head of one of the combatants back. A fourth woman entered the fray, throwing a punch at the hair puller and connecting forcibly. She, in turn, was shoved from behind and toppled onto the first two. Then several more—pushing, shoving, and throwing punches—joined the melee.

Marta and two other employees moved in and attempted to separate the combatants as Ray and Sue tried to push the crowd back. All of them, however, were quickly entangled in the brawl. Sue was jostled hard from behind, causing her to topple over the squirming bodies on the floor. Ray reached in to pull Sue to her feet just before someone turned into him and pushed him over onto the top of the pile.

"Police!" Ray heard someone shout. "Stop!"

A hand was extended to him, and Ray looked up to see Rory Tate, one of his patrol officers, who pulled him to his feet. Barbara Sinclair, another deputy, a towering woman with a commanding presence, was hauling people up from the floor and moving them away from the area.

And as suddenly as it had started, the brawl was over. The room went quiet, save some muffled sobbing. Ray gently helped Sue to her feet. He could see that she was injured. She was protecting her right arm, holding it close to her body and stabilizing it with her left arm. He guided her to a chair as two more patrol officers, the shift commander, Sergeant Brett Carty, and an EMT crew arrived. He watched Brett Carty quickly take control of the situation, then he returned to Sue's side as one of the EMTs applied an air splint to her right arm.

"Suspected fracture," said the young woman. "We'll run her to the medical center with anyone else requiring treatment."

"That will be unnecessary," said Ray. "I'll take her."

The woman looked up a Ray. "Oh, yes, right, Sheriff. Let me get a sling for her arm. She'll be more comfortable."

Brett Carty moved their way. "Are you okay, Sue?"

"Suspected fracture," she said, her voice reflecting her discomfort.

"Sorry."

"How did you arrive with the cavalry at just the right moment?" she asked.

"We had a 9-11 about an ancient white Lincoln that was all over the road. Tate was in the area and responded. He spotted the old car weaving its way up the drive here. Barbara Sinclair and I pulled in soon after. We were standing in the parking lot when we got the 911 request for what was going on in here."

"So you've got a DUI waiting for you out in the parking lot?" Ray asked.

Carty smiled. "We've got an old dear with her three close friends. Natalie Thompson, ninety-three on her last birthday, according to her license. She was taking her weekend visitors on a winery tour. It's a tradition. She said they do this every spring."

"And she's had a bit too much?"

"Not at all. Thompson says she hasn't had a drop. I believe her. She just shouldn't be behind the wheel. I was just off the phone with her daughter before this all went down. She's on her way to pick up Mom and friends. The daughter said that she will make sure the old Lincoln disappears, and this won't happen again. Just another quiet weekend in God's country."

Ray guided Sue back to their vehicle. As he held the passenger door for her, she said, "The key fob is in this pocket," raising her elbow.

He carefully extracted the fob, then helped secure her seatbelt.

"When we first went in," Sue said after he started the engine, "I thought you were going to bolt back out the door as soon as the noise hit you."

"It was, ah…piercing."

"You and chamber music. Bet you've never been to a rock concert?"

Ray smiled.

Sue started to speak, then halted.

"You okay?" he asked.

"Yes. I just had three ideas hitting my tongue at one time." She looked over at Ray. "The brides and their friends, it appeared that their high spirits quickly morphed into something totally unexpected."

"A lot of alcohol never improves things. Some of those sweet young ladies are going to spend the evening in heartbreak hotel," said Ray. "Their next big date will be with a judge on Monday morning."

"Yes, and I'm sure some of these special memories are already being shared with the folks back home on Facebook," said Sue.

"Your friend Marta," Ray said. "I'm confident that you're now highly motivated to provide some sage advice so she can prevent a recurrence of this behavior."

"Elkins, I still have one good hand, and you're in easy reach."

5

~

Linda Wetherbee, sixty-four, was known around Cedar County as the grand impresario of the flourishing up north wedding industry. This morning, when she heard her assistant, Jennifer Bidwell, arrive in the main work area of her business, Simply Romantic, Linda came tentatively out of her office, feeling self-conscious in a pale turtleneck with a colorful patterned scarf at the neck, wool pants, and low pumps. Linda usually wore jeans, hiking boots, and a down vest, so this getup felt like a costume.

"How do I look?" she asked. Linda had hired Jennifer—twenty-something, plain but pleasant, lanky with an almost adolescent clumsiness—because she seemed wise beyond her years and possessed the technical talents the company needed. Linda knew next to nothing about marketing in the digital age.

"Wow," Jennifer said. "You look nice. What's the big deal?"

"The Ingersolle wedding."

Jennifer's eyes widened. "Yesterday you said we weren't going to do it. I heard you tell the woman on the phone."

"Ms. Ingersolle called me again after you left. She's flying in this morning. Her driver will be here to pick me up any minute."

Jennifer put her hands on her hips. "What about your rules to live by, Linda?"

When Linda had first hired Jennifer, she had joked that she didn't mentor her staff, she indoctrinated them. And rule number one had to do with quality. "Limit the number of events," she had said. "Don't take on more than you can do. Make sure each bride's special day is perfect."

Rule number two was to avoid bridezillas and bridezilla mothers.

"Let our competitors have the pleasure of their company," Linda had told Jennifer.

Now Linda smiled ruefully. "Yes, well, rules are meant to be broken and all that. What's your point?"

"We're fully scheduled for the spring, summer, and fall," Jennifer said. "Much of next year is already booked. If I remember correctly, Ms. Ingersolle wanted early June. That's impossible. And after you got off the phone, you were mumbling about another bridezilla mom. What happened?"

"Our second phone call. We talked for a long time, and she was very persuasive. Maybe I was a bit too hasty when I told her no."

"Why the rush?" Jennifer asked.

"I'm not sure, exactly," Linda said. "I get the impression there's been a battle of wills between the bride and the mother of the bride," Linda said.

"How are we going to find a venue this late?" asked Jennifer. She made a sweeping gesture toward the two whiteboard-covered walls. Starting with May and ending with September, the floor to ceiling calendars were filled with event names, dates, venues, and vendors.

"I explained the problems to her."

"And?"

"Venue is not a problem. The wedding will be at the family estate at Gull Point. And Ms. Ingersolle, Alice, said that for the wedding dinner she will fly in the caterer. The same goes for the hairstylists and the florist. She'll also take care of the music—string quartet for the service and a band for the reception. Oh, and the photographer—she said she already had a national shooter lined up. Get the language, 'a national shooter.'"

"What does she want us to do?"

"On-the-ground coordination, especially the weekend of the wedding. Alice would like everything on the lawn. That said, she wants a tent in case of rain. The tent, folding chairs, a portable dance floor, the setup, we can find people to do that. She will also need servers. No problem. It's not our busiest time. Our vendors will be happy to have some cash flow early in the season. And then clean up. It's the same old routine. We can do this, Jen."

"You're talking about early June?" she asked, gazing at the schedule.

"We settled on Memorial Day weekend."

Jennifer moved left along the calendar. "You've got the Andersen wedding."

"Small, right?"

"Yes. Fifty people, North Shore CC. An outdoor ceremony that can be easily moved indoors if it rains. How many guests for the Ingersolle wedding?"

"About two hundred. And we're being paid handsomely. You'll get a big bonus on this one, Jen."

"What about rule number three?" Jennifer teased. "'Never let money tempt you to forget rules one or two.'"

"Did I say that?"

"How about housing for the guests?"

"Not our problem. Alice said a member of her staff was already working on offsite lodging in the area for their guests."

"Where does this kind of money come from?"

"Art, my dear. Fine art. The stuff we see in museums and will never have on our walls. Google her. Check out her gallery in New York City," said Linda.

Her phone buzzed, and she answered it and spoke briefly with someone before tossing the phone back into her purse. "That was Donald, Ms. Ingersolle's driver," she told Jennifer. "He's waiting outside. I'll probably be tied up the rest of the day. Have a good weekend if I don't get back before you leave."

When Linda returned after six that evening, Jennifer was still there at the office. "I'm surprised you're still here," said Linda.

"Just typing up the final checklist for the Anderson wedding," answered Jennifer. "How was Alice Ingersolle?"

"Want to get dinner across the street?" Linda asked. "I'll tell you about it."

"Sure."

After the waiter had taken their wine order, Jennifer asked, "Were you dressed appropriately?"

"Yes. Same look, but Alice's clothes probably had designer labels."

"You visited the proposed venue?"

"Yes, a peninsula jutting out into the big lake. It's four or five miles south of North Bay, way off the highway. You know, a mile or so on a gravel road that winds through an old farm. Not a two-track, but not much more. There are a couple of dead end signs along the way."

Linda described how the road narrowed as it approached the peninsula, how there was water on both sides. The security gate at the end of this road was not just a bar but an imposing wrought-iron barrier, tall, almost menacing. And the same style fencing ran down to the water on each side. Linda noticed two "no trespassing" signs on the narrow peninsula road and one on the gate.

"Alice said her stepfather is a recluse," Linda told Jennifer. "He's apparently crazy about security."

The piece of land beyond the gate was as big as eight city blocks, Linda estimated, with rolling, heavily wooded terrain. The main house was huge.

"Jen, we're talking fifteen thousand square feet—maybe more. There's another building, closer to the gate, the original house where her mother and stepfather lived. It's tiny in comparison to the new house. I guess her stepfather still lives there. It's a lovely old cottage, looks very English."

"So is it overall a good wedding venue?" Jennifer asked.

"Oh my god, Jen. Beautiful house, indoor/outdoor pool, lawns, flowerbeds. The interior of the house, bright and open, art everywhere, like each room was designed for the art."

"It's ready for a wedding?"

"Not the grounds, not yet. The grass is still kind of dead. But Alice assured me it would be perfect in a month."

"Parking?" asked Jennifer.

"Yes, that's another thing she wants us to look after. She wants offsite parking with a shuttle service. She says we can use an empty field near the highway."

Jennifer frowned slightly. "Did she even mention the bride?"

"Yes," Linda answered, chuckling. "But I'll admit she didn't say anything until I asked about her late in our conversation."

The bride's name was Piper Ingersolle, Linda had learned, and she would be keeping her last name. The groom was Trevor Thornley. They had met at Yale and were both in their late twenties, both lawyers. They lived in New York City. Linda was sure they had had an engagement announcement in the *Times*. The way Alice Ingersolle talked about it, it sounded like a merger as much as a marriage. Piper didn't seem like a typical bride, Linda told Jennifer. Her mother had said that while Piper was happy to participate in the festivities, she wasn't interested in planning them—unlike so many brides who micromanaged their weddings until they were certifiably insane.

Alice had failed to persuade her daughter to have the wedding in New York. Piper insisted that if she was going to be married this year, it would have to be at the Michigan property, so that her step-grandfather could participate. Alice said that Piper had a sentimental attachment to him.

"I think she expected her daughter to cave to her will," Linda said. "And I think that didn't happen and that's why Alice is coming to us now on such short notice. When the step-grandfather—Alice's stepfather—came up in the conversation, there was an incredible change in Alice's demeanor. She got very frosty. We were outside near the lake looking back toward her house when I broached the subject. Her place towers over her stepfather's."

"So what is that all about?" asked Jennifer.

"Alice said that the land had been in her mother's family since just after the Civil War. Her mother passed more than a decade ago, and there was some confusion about the will. She and her stepfather fought over the ownership of the peninsula for years. She ended up with most of it. He was able to keep his cottage."

"Is the bride's father in the picture?"

"Apparently Alice hasn't seen or talked to him since Piper was an infant. I couldn't believe it, but she actually said he was 'not much more than a sperm donor.'"

"The finances? Our standard contract?"

"Yes. Getting that done will be a major goal next week. And one more thing, Jennifer. Before we spend a lot of time on this, run a credit check on Alice Ingersolle."

"But I thought…"

"You know, the rich are very different from you and me, and some of them don't bother paying their bills."

6

~

"Elkins, it's just a wrist," said Sue, sliding reluctantly into the passenger seat of her department assigned SUV. "I'll have two hands on the wheel at nine and three. I'm perfectly competent to do this. If we have to change a tire, you get the honors."

"Sue, I'd rather drive," he responded, starting the engine.

"Remember your old rule," she said. "The person in the passenger seat gets to pick the music."

"Unfortunately, that doesn't apply when I'm driving. Your choice in music would be a distraction." He glanced over and smiled. "So what's going on? A floating foot?"

"Elkins, you got it wrong. A floating shoe with some bones inside," she said, reading from an iPad. "A Beverly Jakes called it in. Do you know her?"

"Not sure. Keep going."

"Her landscaping crew was doing a spring cleanup at a lakefront home. One of her crew found the running shoe on the beach. The man saw what he thinks are bones in the shoe. Dispatch said she sounded freaked out."

"I would be, too," he responded. "I don't think I know her."

"I've read a couple of news articles about this recently," Sue continued. "Seems to be a West Coast phenomenon, California and Washington."

"They're always early adopters," said Ray.

"Elkins."

"So tell me about this shoe phenomenon."

"Bodies go into the water and in time begin to disarticulate.

If the deceased happens to be wearing shoes with a lot of flotation, like some kinds of running and hiking shoes, they float to the surface and are carried along by currents and wind. Over time they can move hundreds or even thousands of miles. Occasionally law enforcement can trace the shoe to the source. So far, all the identified remains are from suicides and accidental deaths. There's no record of criminality connected to any of the bones."

"Interesting."

"Elkins, when you say 'interesting,' I know you're somewhere else. If you had read this in the *Talk of the Town*, you would be regaling me with the exquisite details of phalanges in floating footwear freaking out the beach walkers on Fire Island or West Egg."

"East Egg," Ray corrected. "And they wouldn't wash up in New York. As you said, the prevailing winds and currents carry the shoes to distant shores. New York shoes probably make landfall on the Irish or English coast, or maybe up in Scotland or north to Scandinavia. Where are we going?"

"I plugged the address into the GPS. It's a little peninsula south of North Bay. A private drive runs through an old farm to the site, Gull Point. Do you know the area?"

Ray glanced at the screen. "New one on me. These places set way back from the road, if we've never had a reason to go there, we don't know them." Ray studied the GPS map. "I've probably kayaked past the place, but I don't connect the water view with the land view. You know what I mean. Two very different perspectives."

"I understand," said Sue. "According to the directions Beverly Jakes gave dispatch, we're supposed to look for a large battered mailbox on the west side of the highway with faded or missing numbers and turn left there. There's a mostly dead orchard to the right of the road and empty fields to the left. If we get to the place where the highway does a sharp right turn, we've gone a mile too far."

Ray scanned the monochromatic landscape. "A few days of warm rain would be nice, wash away the remaining snow and green things up."

"Ray, your left turn is coming up," said Sue, looking at the screen.

"Yes, at the leaning mailbox," he answered, slowing and veering onto the narrow trail. They drove through long-fallow fields and orchards, past a decaying house and a barn, the roof collapsed in the middle, pulling the opposing ends toward the center.

Ray slowly crossed a narrow isthmus that formed the neck of the peninsula. He looked at the ribbon of enormous boulders that had been added on each side to protect the road from the high water. Then he braked and waited as the two wings of a massive wrought-iron gate slowly opened. "Gull Point Estate" the placard on the gate read.

"Smile," he said. "You're on camera."

"These people like their privacy," said Sue.

"Which way?" he asked stopping at a Y in the trail.

"Go to the right, toward those pickups," Sue said, pointing.

Ray parked near three pickups loaded with landscaping equipment and red plastic fuel containers. In the distance they saw workers with backpack leaf blowers moving in a ragged line. One of the workers, a thirty-ish woman in jeans and a hooded sweatshirt, broke off from the group, slid the straps of the leaf blower off her shoulders, and walked in their direction, pulling off her gloves and ear protection, a pair of foam-padded earmuffs. Ray held Sue's door as she exited the SUV, then went around to the back of the vehicle and retrieved an Igloo cooler.

"Sheriff," said the woman. "Beverly Jakes." She and Ray shook hands. "And this is Detective Sergeant Sue Lawrence," said Ray, gesturing toward Sue.

"If you follow me to the beach, I'll show you what we found," Beverly Jakes said. As she guided them toward the tip of the peninsula—a vast beach area that opened to the big lake—Ray noticed out of the corner of his eye someone approaching them, moving briskly across the lawn from the imposing mansion to join their group. Beverly Jakes, spotting the tall, slim man dressed in a blue work shirt, jeans, and work boots, paused and waited for him to catch up. "This is Scott Nelson," she explained. "He's the estate manager here." After another round of introductions, they continued toward the beach.

"It's right there," Beverly Jakes said, pointing. "One of my guys, Kenny, uncovered it. Then he saw the bones. I thought he was kidding, but that's what it looks like. He's freaked out." She paused briefly. "I think we're all kind of freaked."

Ray pulled on a pair of rubber gloves and carefully lifted the shoe from the pile of dull brown oak leaves where it rested. He glanced inside and then held it for Sue, who, holding a small flashlight in her left hand, examined the interior of the shoe.

"Yes, looks like bones," she said. "Small shoe. Men's size eight. Air Jordon. Let's get it into the cooler."

"What will you do with it?" asked Jakes. "Is there any way of telling where it came from? We were wondering if we can expect any more body parts to wash up." She grimaced.

"We'll have someone run it over to the State Police lab in Grayling," Sue said. "The shoe looks like it's been in the water for a long time. The remains might not tell us much." She squinted out at the sapphire water. "But I wouldn't worry about other similar surprises washing up." She briefly explained the floating shoe phenomenon.

"So the shoe, the bones, might have come from Chicago or Milwaukee, somewhere on the other side of the lake, a suicide or something?" Scott Nelson asked, looking over at the cooler.

"Yes, most likely," she answered.

"Good to know," Beverly Jakes said.

Ray scanned the area. A dense layer of leaves still covered much of the extensive lawns and gardens. Near the beach, small piles of decaying ice remained. "So where was the high-water point this winter?" he asked Scott Nelson.

"Where you're standing, Sheriff, and probably another ten or fifteen yards toward the house. That last big northeaster we had, the two days of gale force winds, the waves came rolling over the seawalls like they weren't there. Some of the shelf-ice got stacked up here, too. Most of it only started melting the last few weeks. I've been waiting to get Beverly and her crew in here to clean things up. The owner's got a wedding planned here Memorial Day weekend."

"So all this damage is new?" asked Ray.

"Yeah. Last fall the lawns were in perfect shape all the way to the seawall. Right, Beverly?"

"Everything was in top condition," she answered.

"Look at it now," Nelson continued. He indicated a rumpled patch of lawn not far from where they stood. "You can see where some of the grass has been washed out. We're bringing in soil and resodding this whole stretch close to the water. The owner had the seawalls rebuilt a few years ago. And now the lake levels are higher than anyone anticipated. And none of us have seen storms like this. I mean, maybe back in the day, but not in my lifetime."

"You grew up here," Ray observed.

"Yes. Right over there across the bay," Scott Nelson said, pointing.

"I think we have everything, unless there's anything else you'd like to add," Sue said as Ray picked up the cooler. "Ms. Jakes, thank you for calling it in."

"No problem," she responded. "I'm still shaking."

"I understand," said Sue. "We'll let you get back to your work."

As they started toward the parking area, Scott Nelson walked with them, positioning himself close to Sue. Ray thought about the security camera at the gate and wondered with amusement if Scott Nelson was simply a friendly guy or even a guy on the make, or if he was escorting them in the nicest way possible off the property.

"How long have you worked here?" asked Ray.

"Seven years. The contractor hired me as a watchman while the new house was under construction. The owner, Ms. Ingersolle, asked me to stay on after the construction was completed."

"What were you doing before that?" asked Sue.

"Graduate School, University of Minnesota."

"What program?"

"Cultural anthropology. But I was burned out. And even if I

completed a degree, all I had to look forward to was an impossible job market. So I came home for the summer to hang out, do some sailing. I got this job through a friend who thought I needed something to do. I never thought I'd still be here."

"Do you live on site?" she asked.

"Yeah. I've got a great apartment over the garage." He pointed to the four-car structure standing in the woods at the left rear of the mansion.

"Your job, what do you do, exactly?" Ray asked.

"I look after issues like this, general maintenance. However, the majority of my time is concierge kinds of stuff. If Ms. Ingersolle decides to fly in on Friday and spend the weekend, she wants everything in place."

"Like?"

"Like she's not going to Meijer to pick up groceries between the airport and here. She's not going to cook, her personal chef usually travels with her, and she often brings clients and friends. I make sure the refrigerators and pantry are fully stocked, buy tickets for concerts, arrange tours, hire cleaners and any additional kitchen staff, and handle transportation. Everything's got to be turnkey, everything, down to toothpaste and new toothbrushes. Manager. I never liked that title, but that's what I do."

"The security system, I've noticed cameras everywhere," said Ray.

"Yes, lots of cameras. Looks impressive. But the system is dated and constantly in need of repair. The service guy says that whoever designed this stuff didn't know about Michigan winters. I keep suggesting that the system be upgraded, but the owner keeps putting it off."

"Why all the security?"

"During the warm months, Ms. Ingersolle uses this venue as part of her business. She has an art gallery in New York and sometimes brings expensive works here for exclusive showings."

"Who monitors the CCTV?"

"A security firm based in Arizona."

"Have there ever been any problems?" asked Ray.

"No, fortunately. I would have dialed you guys if there were."

They paused near the rear of Sue's SUV. Ray opened the rear doors and secured the cooler to the interior as Sue continued to chat with Scott Nelson.

Ray joined them again and pointed to the other house, standing close to the new building.

"What's the story on that place?" he asked.

"That belongs to Ms. Ingersolle's stepfather. It's a family home from her mother's side. The family's ownership of this little peninsula dates back to sometime shortly after the Civil War. I think that building replaced the original frame cottage. Kind of looks like a cottage you'd fine in an English village, doesn't it? Rumor has it that after Ms. Ingersolle's mother passed, she and her stepfather battled over the property. She ended up with most of it. He has use of that house for the rest of his life. I don't think they've talked in years."

"So if they're not on speaking terms, why did she build next door?"

Scott Nelson smiled. "The view. Before the new house went up, there was a lawn running from that lovely cottage down to the water's edge. The windows and the porch on that side of the building are oriented toward the water. Ingersolle's stepfather is a landscape painter. I'm told he has captured this scene in his oil paintings during different seasons and times of the day. She effectively cut off his view. Need I say more?"

Ray studied Scott Nelson's face. Did Nelson admire Ms. Ingersolle's petty act, or was there some other reason for the satisfaction in his expression?

"The stepfather," Ray asked, "what is his name?"

"Gerhard Talmadge."

"Is he still painting?"

"As far as I know. I see people from time to time visiting Talmadge. I assume those visits have to do with his art. I mean, sometimes I see them carrying canvases to their cars."

"Does he live there alone?"

"Yes," Scott said. "There used to be a couple here, Ilga and Joe. They sort of helped looked after Talmadge, but I think they retired. They've been gone for several years."

"Did you notice the new seawall?" Ray asked Sue as he slowly drove down the narrow gravel road toward the highway.

"What about it?" Sue said.

"It's not just a seawall. There are pilings, tie downs, and a shore power pedestal. You could dock a large cruiser or yacht there."

She nodded, hardly listening. "I'm trying to wrap my brain around building a multi-million-dollar mansion just to cut off someone's view."

"Ditto," he answered.

7
~

S ue worked her way around the grocery store, aisle by aisle, starting with produce and ending with dairy. Even though her approach was thorough, as she moved toward the checkout, there was little more in her cart than a small array of frozen entrees, a bag of organic mixed greens, bananas, yogurt, eggs, milk, bacon, and a box of whole wheat pasta. Lingering at the wall of wine, Sue eyed the aspirational offerings on the top shelf. Grasping a bottle of Sancerre, she carefully took in the label, looked up at the price, glanced down at the much less expensive alternatives, and finally placed the bottle in the cart.

"Good choice," came a vaguely familiar voice.

Sue turned and saw a man she had met before.

"Scott Nelson," he said. "Gull Point? The Air Jordan, the shoe with the bones in it?"

"Oh, yes," Sue said. "Thank you for the context. I trust its mate hasn't washed ashore."

"No more shoes, exactly as you promised. The sheriff got in touch last week to tell me that you've been unable to identify the owner of the shoe—and the foot."

"True, unfortunately. Are the grounds at Gull Point in shape for a wedding?" asked Sue.

"Yes, despite the late-season snowstorms we've had since you were at Gull Point." He studied her. "I think you missed the last few blizzards. I don't remember you having a deep tan when we met."

"You have a good memory," said Sue. "I've been visiting Florida for a month—sick leave and some vacation time."

"And you're still wearing a cast," Nelson observed.

Sue lifted her casted wrist. "It comes off tomorrow morning. I'll be showing off some interesting tan lines."

"Could I buy you dinner at the little cafe across the parking lot?"

Sue hesitated. "Another time, perhaps. I just picked up my little dog. I don't want to leave her in the car." She considered Scott Nelson. He was good-looking and friendly, and the last time Mike Ogden had visited, he'd taken his toothbrush with him when he left. "If you'd like to drop by," she looked toward her shopping cart, "I can offer you a green salad and…your choice of entrees. And some wine, of course."

"May I?" Scott Nelson asked, gesturing toward the frozen containers in her cart.

"Go for it," Sue responded.

Nelson looked through them, then said, "I approve of your choices, but frozen entrees, I don't think so. You've got pasta, eggs, and bacon. Do you like spaghetti carbonara?"

"Absolutely."

"I could make that. And I will contribute a bottle of cold champagne and a fresh baguette. I'll cook, clean up, and be gone. You'll have the rest of your evening to spend with your dog. By the way, your dog, does it bite?"

"She is not an 'it.' Her name is Simone," Sue said indignantly. "And no, she doesn't bite. She is a good judge of character, though. She growls when she finds someone offensive."

"What do you say?" Scott Nelson pressed.

"Is this your usual MO, picking women up at the market with offers of home-cooked meals?" Sue teased.

"Not my usual, but a promising one. What do you think?"

"You've got a deal," Sue responded.

Sue sat in a dining chair with Simone on her lap while Scott Nelson moved deftly around the kitchen, asking occasionally where something was located—a large pot, a whisk, a colander, salad bowls. Simone had been shy with him when he had arrived. She hadn't growled or barked, but after sniffing the grocery bag he carried, she'd sidled behind Sue's legs.

"Hello, Simone," Scott had said, but he hadn't made any attempt to pet her. "I have to admit, I'm not really a dog person," he said with a chagrined expression.

Sue had lost a little respect for him in those moments, but she kept it to herself. Now, she watched as Simone quietly tracked Scott with her brown eyes.

"It must be exciting to be in law enforcement," Scott said as he whisked together eggs and cheese. "I can't imagine you're ever bored."

"Never," Sue said, tearing off a piece of Scott's baguette and buttering it. "Generally, the opposite is true. It's easy to let the job take over your life. When I first got to Florida, I didn't know what to do with myself. But I figured it out: reading, long walks birdwatching, local historical tours, movies, lots of amazing meals that someone else prepared for me." She didn't mention that she'd been staying with her parents, who had retired and now lived part of the year in Naples. "So when's the big wedding out at your place?"

"In a little more than a week—on the Sunday of Memorial Day weekend. Things are getting crazy around there." He added chopped bacon to a hot pan, and it sizzled and spat.

"How so?" Sue watched Simone's nostrils quiver as the smell of bacon filled the air.

"Most of the time out there, it's just me and the squirrels and the birds. The owner's personal chef arrived a few days ago. There's a steady flow of trucks in and out with all kinds of provisions. Workers came and erected an enormous tent in case of rain. And that's just the beginning. After today I won't have a chance to slip away until all the shooting's over." He looked over his shoulder at Sue. "That's just a figure of speech."

She grinned. "I understand."

A few minutes later, Scott carried two salads and then two plates of steaming pasta to the dining table while Sue settled Simone on the couch.

"I set aside a few morsels of bacon for Simone," Scott said. "Is it all right if I give it to her?"

Sue considered the request. Ray was always giving Simone gourmet food, and, while Sue always objected, she had to admit it hadn't done Simone any harm so far. And Scott did get points for trying to make friends with Simone. Finally she shrugged. "All right," she said.

Simone stood up on the couch to receive her treat, her tail a wild metronome as she lapped the tidbits out of Scott's hand.

Scott went to the kitchen sink to wash his hands, and Sue noticed wryly that before joining her at the table, he slid his phone out of his pocket and checked it for calls the second or third time since he arrived. The devices had a way of bringing out people's obsessive tendencies. Or maybe he was expecting a call from a certain special someone. She watched as he paused for a moment this time to turn off his phone before he slid it back into his pocket. *He's taking care not to have an embarrassing interruption to the evening*, she thought.

After her first forkful of creamy, salty pasta, Sue said, "This is splendid."

"My pleasure," Scott replied, and Sue could tell he was pleased by the praise. "You know, with all this wedding planning, and after you and the sheriff had to come out to Gull Point, I started wondering if you've ever had to show up at an actual wedding in, you know, a professional capacity. It seems like there are so many things that could go wrong."

"Not during my tenure," Sue said. "Not the actual wedding ceremony, anyway. We've gotten occasional calls before and after, usually involving alcohol. Weddings are special. Most people are on their best behavior."

"Ever been married?" he asked.

"No. You?"

"Never. Got close once." His tone seemed quite casual for the subject matter. Sue searched his expression for signs of emotional pain but found none.

"What happened?" Sue asked. "If that's not too personal a question."

"She was in Minneapolis, at the university. I left grad school and never went back, and she went on to get her PhD. Oh, well." He shrugged. "That's life."

"So you know the bride getting married at Gull Point?" Sue asked. "I think you said you're friends?"

"Piper Ingersolle?" Scott smiled genuinely for the first time since Sue had met him. "Years ago, when we were kids, we all hung around together. I didn't know her real name then. People called her Twigs, maybe after Twiggy, I'm not sure. She was very petite. She spent the summers with her grandparents in the big old house on the point."

"So she's your age?"

"Yeah, sort of."

"So you were good friends?" asked Sue, tucking another forkful of pasta into her mouth while watching Scott's expression.

"Us kids, we all lived on or near the bay, so it was all about canoes, rowboats, bikes, and hide and go seek. One of the guys had a sailboat. We'd all pile in and sail back and forth across the bay."

"How many years are you talking about?"

Scott looked up at the ceiling and calculated. "I guess from the time I was twelve or thirteen until I was eighteen or so. All those summers blend together in my memory. If I'm remembering right, at the beginning of the summer before I went away to college, her grandmother died. Twigs went back to New York after the funeral. There were no goodbyes. She just disappeared from our lives."

"Did you ever see her again?"

"Yes," Scott answered. "Since I started working for her mother, I've seen Piper a few times, when she comes to visit her mother or her grandfather. When I first knew Twigs—Piper—she was this skinny tomboy. When I saw her again, she had become this sophisticated woman, a Yalie with a Columbia law degree. I could still see the kid in the woman, but she was an entirely different person."

"Did she remember you?"

"Absolutely." He smiled again, but this time it seemed more forced. "But at first there was a distance—like the distance I feel with her mother. Back in the day, the local kids and summer kids, we were all the same. Trophy homes were starting to go up, but not around here yet. Wealth likes to cluster. In this little corner, we were still down market, not like Petoskey or Charlevoix." He added wine to Sue's glass and then his own. "Piper, when I saw her again, I was a family employee, a servant of sorts. I mean, she wasn't condescending or anything, but there was something very different about her manner. Maybe I'm just hypersensitive."

"Maybe when we're kids we don't notice class as much," Sue said. "Or maybe, once she stopped coming here regularly, she grew into her other life."

Scott nodded. Then he rose from his chair and said, "Dessert?"

"As I'm sure you noticed," Sue said, "there weren't any dessert items in my shopping cart. I'm doing penance for—"

He opened the freezer and then turned to her with a half-gallon of ice cream in his hand. "How about a scoop of French vanilla with hot fudge on top?"

"Where did that come from?"

"I smuggled it in with the bread and wine. I thought we might need it."

"That's so over the top," said Sue. "Is that another part of your MO?"

8

~

On Sue's first day back at work after her time away, Ray's eyes were drawn again and again to her pale forearm and hand. He noticed that she kept flexing her hand throughout the day, testing the limits of her new freedom. They spent the morning catching Sue up on what had happened at the government center during her absence. It had been a relatively quiet month, including one silver alert when an elderly woman wandered away from a memory care facility. Fortunately, Ray and his deputies had found her within two hours, wandering in a ditch along 204. There had been a few of the now-common break-ins and episodes of petty thievery that involved the new young drug addicts in the area.

"How are your parents?" Ray asked Sue as they waited for their orders at the Last Chance, one of their favorite lunch spots.

"They seem to be adjusting to retirement," Sue said, "my mother more than my father. Being in Florida for the worst months of the winter is agreeing with both of them, though."

"What was it like being back in the nest again for a few weeks?"

Sue smiled at him. "Interesting that you put it that way. At first, it really was like I was sixteen again. They hovered too much. Fortunately, they pulled back before I threw a teenage tantrum."

"How did you fill your time?"

"Books, Elkins. Am I destined to pick up all your habits?" She rolled her eyes playfully. "Are you going to ask me what I was reading?"

He nodded. "I'm very interested, of course."

"There's a bookstore near their condo, and the bookseller there recommended titles popular with the local book groups. As it turned out, most of the group members are female. As a consequence, I read a lot of women's fiction and memoir. And I have to say, it was inspiring. I even started playing with the idea of writing a memoir myself. All the things that happened to us in December, I thought I had processed them in my sessions with Wendy Morrison, but I realized in Florida that I had been repressing those memories, just filling up my days and not letting myself remember. But when I started getting them down on paper, all of the feelings, the emotions, came rushing back. And lots of details that I had forgotten. I've filled a notebook."

Ray nodded encouragingly.

"I know you keep a journal," she said. "We probably have covered the same ground. It would be interesting to compare our accounts—"

Ray was grateful when their food arrived before he could answer. He didn't want to talk about his own memories of the events in December. It had been relatively easy to remember and process his feelings when he was thousands of miles away from the place where the carnage had occurred. But now he saw the back parking lot at the government center every day, and the scene played out in his head of Sue ramming the van with Marian Patozak and Toby Osmann inside, of the flash of gunfire from the capsized vehicle, the searing pain in his chest, the feeling of his knees buckling and his kneecaps hitting the snow. The worst thing about being shot wasn't the pain, exactly; it was the feeling of being severed from himself, being unplugged from any sense of control over his own destiny he might have felt before that day.

He took a bite of his tofu Reuben and watched as Sue cut her burger in half and salted her fries.

After she inhaled her first bite, she said, "Where was I? Comparing our memories?"

Ray put his fork down and picked it back up again. "When we left, Hanna brought my journal and fountain pen," he said. "I made a few starts, but my heart wasn't in it. And since I've been back, well…I think I wanted to come back healed, but since I've been here, I've realized that I only completed the first phase of healing.

That light at the end of the tunnel seems farther away than I initially thought."

As he spoke, Ray could feel Sue effortlessly reading the mixture of anxiety, fear, and sorrow that had risen to the surface of his emotions.

"I understand," she said.

"I don't think I'm ready to unpack those memories in writing yet." They briefly locked eyes, then Ray looked away, sweeping the room. "I hope you don't mind if we change the subject."

"Of course not," Sue said, and the look she gave him was full of compassion and a flicker of something else that Ray couldn't identify. Ray knew that if anyone knew what he was going through, it was Sue.

"I'm here, Ray," she said, "whenever you're ready." She waited a beat and then said, "I do have something to share, on a completely different topic." She cast her eyes downward coyly, and one side of her mouth lifted in a smile.

"You look like the proverbial cat that swallowed the canary," Ray said, grateful to her for lightening the mood.

"I got picked up last night while food shopping," Sue said. She immediately felt her face redden, in spite of the fact that she had brought up the topic.

"Shoplifting?"

"Come on, Elkins. You know what I mean."

"I'm all ears."

"Scott Nelson, the estate manager at Gull Point. He said hello while I was standing at the wine display. He looked at the contents of my cart and offered to cook spaghetti carbonara."

"His place or yours?"

"Mine—Simone was with me. He cooked. We ate and got to know each other a little bit. He cleaned up and left. He was a perfect gentleman."

Ray smiled.

"Don't even go there, Ray. No interrogations."

"Anything to add to the Ingersolle family history?"

"It seems Scott knew the bride-to-be when they were kids, until Scott went off to college. When Piper's grandmother died, she stopped summering up here. Sounds like the wedding's going to be a major production. You might want to paddle by this weekend. You can add to your encyclopedic knowledge of local lore. There might be enough material for a chapter in your memoir."

"Are you going to see him again?"

"I doubt it. There was no chemistry," she said flippantly. What she didn't say was that Scott Nelson gave her an odd feeling, as though he were studying her. But to what end?

As for Ray, was he simply amused and curious? Sue had always been able to read most people's emotions easily, but sometimes Ray buried his genuine feelings deep enough that she couldn't identify them, and she wondered if he even knew they were there.

"And I had a sense Scott was otherwise engaged at times. He kept checking his phone—and you know how much I dislike that habit."

"So not the perfect gentleman," Ray observed.

"After he finished washing the dishes, he made a rapid retreat," Sue said, sheepishly. "I'm not coyote ugly, am I?"

"Silly question," said Ray, and a flash of warmth passed between them. He rose and said, "Let's get out of here."

9
~

Linda Wetherbee stood before the whiteboard, her eyes moving back and forth from the pages of printed text on the clipboard in her hand to the large color-coded print on the shiny surface.

"Everything is falling into place," she said.

"Amazing," observed her assistant, Jennifer Bidwell. "I had my doubts, but it's happened. A miracle. All the loose ends are neatly tied up. This wedding was almost too easy."

"Where are we on receivables?"

"Up-to-date on deposits and billable hours," answered Jennifer.

"Okay, let's review again, day by day. Forgive my compulsiveness."

"You mean your attention to detail," suggested Jennifer. "That's your hallmark."

"You're a dear. Okay, so currently at the site…?"

"As of late yesterday."

Wetherbee started down the list. "Toilet facilities?"

"Two trailers are in place. Lights work, the air-conditioning is on, and everything flushes."

"Discreetly positioned?"

"Absolutely, they're off at the south end of the lawn hidden behind the tent. Close enough for easy access, far enough away not to spoil the sightline."

"What's the power source?"

"The electrician was able to tap into a source in the maintenance building."

"Splendid, no generator noise. How about the tent?"

"It's up. Extra rigging was added in case of a storm."

"China, silverware, crystal, linen, table and chairs for the wedding dinner?"

"It's all at the site. Mr. Nelson has communicated the client's preference that we lay the tables just before dinner is served, so I've put that on the caterer's checklist. He told me—not in an obnoxious way at all—that his boss wants him to double-check everything I do. I guess Ms. Ingersolle won't tolerate even the slightest slipup. Everything's got to be perfect."

Linda nodded. "That was my impression when I met her. Jen, has Mr. Nelson gotten any easier to work with over time?"

"Did I say he wasn't easy to work with?" Jennifer said with an alarmed look on her face.

"No, but you're always so positive about people, and I've never heard you say anything genuinely nice about him."

"He's all business," Jennifer said. "He's 100 percent focused and seems overwhelmed."

"I thought I noticed some sparks when I first introduced you two," Linda said with a slight frown of disappointment. Jen was such a nice girl, but Linda had never seen a trace of romance in Jen's life in the nine months Jen had worked at Simply Romantic.

"It didn't happen, Linda," Jennifer said briskly. "I don't think he's really my type."

"Okay, okay, sorry for prying. Let's get back on task. Thursday?"

"Thursday, we are scheduled to do a final check to make sure everything we've been contracted to do is completed or at the site. We're ahead of schedule there: it's done."

"Excellent," Linda said, checking off items on the whiteboard and on the list on her clipboard. "Friday?"

"Friday evening, the party starts at 5:00 and is scheduled to end at 11:00. Arrival: The shuttle service from the Manitou Shores Resort begins at 4:45 and ends at 6:15. No private cars will be allowed onto the grounds. It's all about optics. Ms. Ingersolle also doesn't want her circular drive littered with busses, so I've arranged for them to park in the field just on the other side of the peninsula road. The food service starts at 5:00 and continues throughout the evening, an informal dinner on the lawn at Gull Point. Midwestern summer food and drink: steak and brats, chips, slaw, craft beer, wine. Hand-dipped ice cream cones for dessert. The final menu has been reviewed and signed by the caterer, who is bringing everything and is responsible for table setup, meal setup, cleanup, and removal of equipment and food waste. The return trips to the Manitou Shores are scheduled to start at 9:00. Ms. Ingersolle's security team is responsible for gently prodding the guests to leave and for herding the guests to the busses. Of course, I'll be there to greet the first guests and to see that the last bus has left the estate."

"Great," Linda said. "Saturday?"

"Saturday, multiple excursions: Sand dunes hikes, kayaking on the Crystal River, bike rides, and winery tours. From 5:30 to 8:00, buffet dinner at the Manitou Shores Resort. I will be on site there Saturday morning to help match guests with appropriate outings, and I'll return in the afternoon to monitor the buffet setup."

Linda referred to the checklist on the whiteboard. "And then we should both be back at Gull Point by 11:00 on Sunday morning. The wedding is at 2:00. That will give us more than enough time to deal with any unexpected emergencies."

"Sounds like a plan," said Jennifer. "I have to admit, this has all worked out better than I expected. I can't believe I doubted you." She lifted her arms and bowed toward Linda in a gesture of worshipful respect, and they both laughed. "At this point, other than the weather, what could go wrong?"

"Lots," Linda answered. "Remember two years ago when the ring bearer, that darling towhead in the tux, fell off the pier and almost drowned?"

"Thank goodness there are no kids in this service," said Jennifer.

10

Piper slid out of bed, pulled on Scott's faded blue work shirt, and padded her way across the cool wood floor toward the bathroom. He watched her go, the tail of the shirt just covering her rear, her long shapely legs catching the late morning sun streaming in through one of the skylights in his apartment over the garage.

When she returned and sat down on Scott's side of the bed, he feigned a postcoital nap. Her hair tickled his skin as she bent over and ran her tongue over his chest and then lay a trail of kisses up his neck. Scott opened his eyes and smiled. "Slide over," she ordered.

Sharing his pillow, Piper reached over and traced his lips with her index finger.

Scott put his hand over hers and then gently pushed it away. "Was this part of the week's agenda?" he asked. "I didn't see it on the schedule your mother sent me."

Piper smiled. "Not the written agenda," she answered. "But it was something I knew I'd do if I got a chance. Making love to you was always the best part of being up north. I remember the first time with you so clearly. You looked so scared!" She laughed, and the throaty sound of it thrilled him.

They had been so young when they'd first become lovers. Piper had initiated the relationship. She was a bit younger than Scott but more experienced.

"I'm just surprised we never got caught," she laughed.

"Did your mother have any idea what you were learning at that expensive private school?" Scott asked.

"It was progressive education at its best," chuckled Piper. "What Mother cared about was that I was being educated with kids from all the right families. In Manhattan it's important to start making connections early. Like lots of Dalton parents, she had no idea what happened after school or on weekends. She was buying me a ticket to the Ivy League. And it worked out."

"So what was I, a summer plaything?"

"So much more. You were the first boy I ever fell in love with. And yes, I had some experience before you, but you were the first person I had sex with that I really loved."

Many summer days, they snuck away from their parents, from their friends, and found a deserted beach where they drank wine and spent hours learning about each other.

"Your grandparents seemed oblivious," Scott said.

"Oblivious," Piper snorted. "They were oblivious to nothing. That first summer, our first summer together, Gram took me to town. We went to see one of her doctor friends. The woman gave me a physical and a prescription for the pill. And Gram was very matter-of-fact about it. It was like we'd gone to town for a new bathing suit. She asked me a week or two later if I was taking my pills, and that was it. The subject never came up again. And Grandfather didn't say anything, but I'm sure he knew. There were no secrets between those two. They were bohemian. They understood the ways of the world."

Scott lost himself in remembering those sun-drenched days, the smell of the lake on Piper's skin, the taste of it. Finally, he asked, "Are you sure you're marrying the right person?"

Piper sat up, and he couldn't see her face anymore. "What, instead of marrying you?" she said blithely.

"Well, I've always loved you," he said, grasping her bare hip. He tried but failed to keep the hope out of his voice. "We could work out a life together."

"Oh, Scott," she said and shook her long brown hair back. "It was a first love, a summer romance. But it was never a forever. You'd hate Manhattan, living in the city, working in an office." She looked back over her shoulder at him. "Great sex isn't enough to base a marriage on."

"You could live here."

"No, I couldn't. A few weeks in the summer is fantastic, and I've enjoyed seeing you again since you started working for my mother. It was almost like old times. But I'm a city kid. My work is in the city, my friends, my favorite restaurants, museums and concerts. Trevor is part of that world. We're a successful team."

"You talk about him like you play baseball together," Scott said. "Do you even love him?"

"Of course!" Piper said.

Scott folded his arms behind his head. "Then what are you doing here with me right now, just days before your wedding?" he asked smugly. "And why, every time you visit Gull Point, do we end up in bed?"

Piper rose from the bed, ignoring his questions. "In my memories of you, it's always summer," she said as she collected her clothing from the floor. "Whenever I think of you, I smile and remember the joy we've shared. Now we have one more good memory, right?" She sat on the edge of the bed and pulled on her panties. "How long have you been working for my mother now?" she asked.

"Seven years," he said.

"And how is that going? You never talk about it. Do you really want to do this as a career? After going to Harvard, and then Minnesota?"

Scott shrugged. "Your mother trusts me to do my job. She tells me what she wants in broad strokes—no micromanaging—and I make it happen. And I'm well paid. My rent is paid." He made a sweeping gesture with both hands, indicating the posh bedroom around them, the large windows that looked out over the woods and water.

"And she's never made a pass at you or required more…personal services?" Piper asked, turning and showing off her breasts just before she pulled on her bra.

"What?" Scott said, sitting upright in the bed.

"Oh, come on," Piper said. "I saw the way she looked at you this morning. She's always liked attractive younger men. And you, dear Scott, fit that description."

"No," he answered. "Nothing like that. There's always been a professional distance between us."

Piper raised her eyebrows and laughed. "Is that your final answer?"

"Do you spend a lot of time speculating about your mother's sex life?" asked Scott.

"No. But I am a long-term observer of her behavior. It's just one of her things."

"What about your dad, Piper? What's his story? I don't think you've ever mentioned him. Your mother certainly hasn't."

"You're wondering if I'm a bastard child?" she asked playfully. She turned away from him and wiggled into her jeans.

"I've talked to you about my parents and siblings over the years. You've talked about your grandparents and your mother. Never a word about your father."

Piper picked up her blouse and slid her arms into the sleeves. She sat down on the bed again as she buttoned it. "There's not a lot to tell," she said matter-of-factly, although the hunch of her shoulders suggested sadness or hurt. "My mother's story is that she met him—Wade Rosencrantz—in Paris, where they had the proverbial whirlwind romance. She was a graduate student in art history, and he was an itinerant foreign correspondent. She says they married in France, and he followed her back to New York. Mother settled into the family business. A few years later she got pregnant. After I was born, she said their relationship quickly soured. And at the first opportunity, my father headed off to cover some distant revolution or war. She divorced him a couple of years after that and took back her maiden name."

"Did you ever try to find him?" asked Scott.

"A few years ago, I found his byline on news articles from around the time of my birth and for maybe a decade or so after. He was always reporting from some exotic locale. Then his name disappears.

I found his picture on a Princeton alumni website. I contacted the alumni organization. They've had no contact with him since his graduation."

Piper lay back and rested her head on Scott's thigh, and he threaded his fingers through her hair.

"I spent so much time searching," she said. "I can tell you what I learned in one short paragraph: He was an only child. He was orphaned at an early age. Then he was reared by his grandmother, who died near the time he graduated from college. That's all I know. He just disappeared."

"I'm sorry, Piper" he said. "I really am." He bent to kiss the tip of her nose, and she gave him a sad little smile.

Then she stood, and her sorrow seemed to fall away.

"I've got to catch up with my grandfather. He says he has a special gift for me. He's making it sound very mysterious."

"When did he tell you that?" Scott asked.

"I called him last week to let him know when I'd be getting here, and he said, 'I have a surprise for you!'"

She imitated his wheezy voice, his German accent perfectly, and Scott laughed.

"How long has it been since you've seen him?" Scott asked.

"As you know, the last time I was here was Labor Day weekend last year. But we talk at least once a month on the phone, sometimes more often. I tried to teach him how to FaceTime," Piper laughed, "but it didn't work out. Why do you ask?"

"He seems to have gotten a lot frailer over the last few months, and his vision continues to deteriorate," Scott said. "I just wanted to warn you."

Piper frowned slightly. "OK, good to know." Then her normal cheerful expression returned. "I'll say hello to him for you. Cheers." She went to the bedroom door and pulled it open and then paused there, turning back toward Scott.

"We'll never have Paris," she said, "but we'll always have up north."

"And down the road you'll have three little kids."

"Yes, and a very attentive and discreet nanny to look after them," she responded with a playful smile.

Scott's smile faded as he watched her go. He listened to the sound of her shoes on the stairs and the door on the ground floor opening and closing.

11

P iper circled the cottage, making her way toward the back door. The building had once seemed almost as familiar to her as her own body, but now she noticed that there were areas where the decaying stucco had fallen away from the underlying lath and that the paint had peeled almost entirely from the window frames, which held murky panes of glass that hadn't been cleaned in decades. The gardens, once a neat conglomeration of patterns and colors, now had only a few hardy volunteers from the original carefully tended plots, the survivors struggling to compete with the encroaching native plants. When had the place become so run-down, and how had she not noticed it sooner?

She sank down on a stump on the side of the house and closed her eyes, letting the memories sweep over her. A maple tree had once grown here, and Gram and Grandfather had hung a swing from one of its thick low branches. She could hear her grandmother's voice calling her inside for breakfast, and she could smell the coffee, a burnt aroma that filled the kitchen every morning. Piper recalled the smoky sweetness of the special cup of coffee Gram would mix for her, the bitterness offset by heavy cream floating on the surface, topped with sugar and served demitasse.

And then there was the sound of laughter, her grandmother's a lilting soprano, her grandfather's a booming baritone. And the banter between the two, switching from English to German with some French here and there. Piper remembered trying to follow their conversations, grabbing at words and phrases but seldom achieving complete comprehension.

With a sense of foreboding, Piper climbed the few stairs to the kitchen door. She rapped on the window, waited for a couple of moments, then pushed her way into the dark interior.

"Grandfather?" she called loudly as she looked around the kitchen. Rather than strong coffee, the room reeked of decay.

Piper tried to hide her shock when her grandfather tottered into the kitchen from the studio area, leaning heavily on a cane.

"Oh, Grandfather," she said, wrapping her arms around him and noticing how much smaller he seemed since she had last seen him. "It's been too long." She held him close, trying to ignore the scent of mildew and tobacco that clung to his clothing.

"Oh, my girl, I have missed you so," Gerhard said in a thick German accent, his speech slow and halting. He squinted up at her from behind glasses that seemed as murky as the windows. "Your grandmother would be proud to see the magnificent woman you have become."

"I miss her," said Piper. "I was so lucky to have her in my life. And you, too, Grandfather."

"We were blessed, everyone who knew her. I still feel her presence here, in every spot that she loved. Here in the kitchen, out in the garden, along the trail in the woods we beat down in our younger years." He gave a wheezy little laugh. "That is why I remain. I want to hold on to her till I'm gone. There is nothing else for me now." He sighed and then gave her a little push toward the kitchen table. "I'll make coffee," he said. "A little brandy, too?"

"No, thank you, Grandfather, no brandy. But I will have coffee with you. And after we're done, I want to wash some dishes and clean the kitchen up a bit. Will you let me do that for you?" Her grandfather ignored her questions. "No dishes," he said. "You are the honored guest. I'll get to that later. There are things I must show you."

The afternoon sun was streaming through the tall windows on the back wall as Talmadge led Piper into the studio, the largest room in the cottage. Piper had always loved this room. And it still smelled the same, of paint, linseed oil, and turpentine. Piper breathed deeply as she walked among the easels, looking at the paintings of sky and water, a forest lit with dappled sunlight, some only rough sketches, others nearing completion. Her grandfather worked on the west side of the room now that the once panoramic view of the bay to the east was blocked by Piper's mother's mansion. She started to comment but decided against it. Her mother's irrational hatred for this man had damaged his career. She could have made him famous, but instead, she had him blacklisted by any gallery that wanted anything to do with Ingersolle Art.

"These are amazing. Your work is as strong as ever," Piper said.

"It is what I am. Take this away, and I am nothing. But not so good now. My eyes, the world dims."

"I would love to hang one of your paintings in my apartment. I have just the wall, it faces east toward the morning sun. If I can look at it every day, then you and Gram, your love, and this special place will always be with me."

"Anything you want, Piper. Upstairs, I have many more. In your bedroom, there are paintings leaning on the walls. You can have any of them or anything else in the house. But there is one thing you must take."

Gerhard took her arm and led her to the large central hallway that ran from the front door of the house to the back wall. A stairway along one wall of the hall led to a landing on the second floor. The space was capped with a clerestory rising above the rest of the roofline, and sunlight poured in through the windows and illuminated a lovely set of charcoal sketches of ballerinas that had hung in the hallway for as long as Piper could remember.

As a girl, Piper would mimic the poses of the dancers, but she was only able to hold her body in the correct position for a few seconds. One morning her grandmother had caught her in the act, and they both exploded in laughter as Piper fell out of one pose after another. Playing at being ballerinas became one of their special summer games, finally abandoned years later when her grandmother began to struggle with the tremors and stiffness of Parkinson's.

"This is what you need to see," her grandfather said, lifting his cane toward the place where a black and white photo hung, at the end of the line of ballerinas prints. He slowly crossed the room and unhooked the small framed photo from the wall, holding it so Piper could see it. It had always hung there, but she had never looked at it closely before.

"It is so faded now, a picture of the original pastel," her grandfather explained. "Old photos not so good. But you can see the five young dancers, each holding a different position." He handed the photo to Piper.

"Oh, yes, yes. How did I miss that? They're all here," she said as she carried the small, framed photograph from print to print. She looked from the photo to each of the five sketches. "The five dancers were all included in the final painting. Just exquisite."

"Degas liked dancers. That work, the original captured in that old photo, disappeared during WWII, stolen by the Nazis. The painting was never recovered and is thought to have been destroyed."

"Where did the sketches come from?" Piper asked.

Her grandfather continued to stare at the photo without speaking for a long moment. "I don't know exactly. My father was in the war, a soldier, only a corporal. He had been a student of art before the war. He was in a unit that transported and cataloged stolen art."

Piper felt a bolt of alarm. She had never realized that her grandfather's father had been part of the German army. Wasn't it funny, she mused wryly, that while her grandfather's German heritage was obvious, she had never considered its implications?

"I know he was in Hungary—that's where the Degas was stolen," her grandfather said, shaking his cane. "I wonder if the same people who owned it had these sketches.

"I found them after my father died," he continued. "They were tucked away in the attic. My mother was still alive then. She said she had never seen them before. I treasured them. I loved them so much that I never tried to find who has a right to them. I didn't have the courage to learn their story, because I feared then I would lose them.

"They are unsigned. There is no provenance. But the paper they're on, the paper is right for the period—that much I know," he said. "I hope that you will want them. Your grandmother loved them. They were my wedding gift to her. It would mean a lot to me to know that you have them. Maybe you will have a little girl one day that will dance like that."

Piper moved close to her grandfather and said softly, "If these are authentic, they could be worth millions."

"Without provenance, probably not. I've always felt guilty about having them. But so much time has passed. The original owners, their heirs, too, are all gone. Maybe it's all right now for you to take the sketches and enjoy them? But you must keep them private. And never mention them to your mother."

Piper hung the photo back on the wall. "This war with my mother, it wasn't about the cottage, was it, or even about Gram? It was about these sketches." Piper paused and inhaled deeply. *Mother wants them,* Piper thought. *She's probably always wanted them. These prints were part of her deal with Talmadge. She'll have no trouble creating a plausible provenance and finding a buyer. Cash would change hands, and the sketches would disappear into Russia, or Arabia, or China. Right now she's just waiting for Talmadge to die.* "Take them with you," pressed her grandfather. "They need to go with you."

Piper moved along the wall with her iPhone, capturing each print in situ.

"What are you doing?" her grandfather asked, and there was some impatience in his voice.

"I want to remember the drawings like this, on the wall in this lovely old cottage that has meant so much to me."

Her grandfather sighed wheezily. "You young people and your phones," he said.

12

Ray positioned his kayak near the water's edge, the bow pointing north and extending over the still surface of the lake. He looked toward the east. A delicate mauve band at the horizon was mirrored by the water, as was the gray sky above it. He checked the time, 6:17 a.m.

Sliding into the cockpit, he pushed the spray skirt into place, the thick layer of neoprene forming a watertight seal between his body and the boat. He sat for a few moments, stretching his arms above him, then turned on his marine radio and listened to the newest NOAA forecast—southwest winds five to ten knots. Waves one to two feet.

He switched the radio to channel sixteen, the frequency designated for safety, distress, and ship-to-ship calling.

Balancing the paddle across the spray deck, Ray pushed the kayak into the water with his hands. Then he slowly paddled away from the shore, over the submerged remains of pilings that had once supported a large dock during the eras of sail and later steam.

As he passed Sleeping Bear Point, he encountered the first gentle swells. He paused and considered paddling south along the dunes, a relaxing trip, then looked out toward South Manitou. The Manitou Islands were his favorite destination—he sought out quiet, empty spaces—and the moment he thought about going there, the static in his mind stilled.

By the time he reached the Manitou Passage, the waves had started to build. He paddled on toward the lighthouse on South Manitou, the structure gradually becoming taller as two hours passed. After landing on a sandy stretch of beach near the base of the lighthouse, he climbed out of his boat and stretched, walking off the stiffness in his limbs.

Sitting on the shore, looking back toward the mainland, Ray poured coffee from a thermos. The sun was now high over the distant ridgeline and the wind continued to strengthen. Finishing the coffee, he prepared for the return trip. Before launching, he listened again to the NOAA weather report. The forecast had changed. The wind had shifted, now from the north with increasing wind speeds and wave heights. Ray knew it would only get worse. There was nothing to do but head back to the mainland and hope for the best. Focusing on his destination, eight miles away, Ray pushed off from the shore and settled into a steady rhythm, left blade, right blade, body rotating with each paddle stroke.

As he had observed so many times during long open water crossings, early in the journey, the progress toward the destination was almost imperceptible. As the wind shifted from the west to the north, Ray adjusted his heading to compensate for the changing conditions.

He paddled parallel to the waves, moving forward in the troughs, sometimes bracing with the left-hand blade against the crest of incoming waves to keep the kayak from capsizing. Not long after leaving the lighthouse, he felt weary in a way that, before December, would have been unfamiliar to him. He began closing his eyes occasionally, only a few strokes at a time, trying to control his breathing and keep the fatigue from overwhelming him. The muscles in his arms and legs began to ache more with every stroke. And yet, the shore seemed just as far away as it had been thirty minutes before. He had a vision of climbing an endless sand dune. "Sisyphus," he muttered out loud.

And then, finally, he neared the foot of Sleeping Bear Point. Mustering the last of his energy, he paddled the few hundred yards to his landing point. Swinging the bow of the kayak into the wind, he surfed backward toward the beach, controlling his speed with his paddle before finally sliding onto the shore.

Releasing the spray skirt from the cockpit coaming, Ray pulled his legs out of the boat, one at a time, and crawled out onto the beach. Then he dragged the boat up beyond the pounding surf, collapsed onto the sand, and closed his eyes. The world quickly slipped away. When he opened his eyes again, it was because Simone, the terrier, was pawing at his arm. Sue was kneeling at his side, her eyes intense with fear.

"Are you okay?" she asked.

"Yes," he answered, "just winded."

"Elkins, I can't believe you were out there," she said, looking out at the rollers colliding with the shoreline. "I've been following the weather reports. I was worried when you didn't answer your cell. I knew where to find you, or at least your car. Why weren't you answering?"

"The battery was low. I left it in the car. I had my VHF radio and PLB. It was just a long slog."

"Did you forget that you were going to pick up Simone and take her to the vet?"

Ray stood and brushed at the sand clinging to his drysuit. Then he looked at the watch clipped with a carabiner to his PFD. "Sorry. I launched early. I thought I had allowed time."

"Not to worry. I took her. Shots are up to date. Can I help you carry your boat?"

"I'm okay. I just need to rest a bit."

"I'll toss Simone in my truck and come back and help you," she said, ignoring his comment.

After the kayak was secured to his car and the rest of his gear was stowed in the back, Sue said, "I'll follow you home."

Ray was too tired to protest.

Hours later, Ray woke as thunder shook his house. Simone, standing on the bed beside him, growled at the rumble. As he pulled the small dog down next to him, he became aware of noise outside his bedroom, the clatter of pots and pans—cooking sounds.

He found Sue in the kitchen. "Still here?" he asked.

"I was worried, so I stayed to keep an eye on you. I've been watching the weather. There have been some twisters on the Wisconsin side. Storm's coming across the lake."

"I'm OK. Any tornado warnings?"

"Not yet. Small craft advisories, severe thunderstorm warnings. It's all north of us but tracking south or south-ish. It may miss us completely."

"What's with the cooking?"

"I was hungry, so I started poking around the fridge. And then I had an epiphany. Don't groan, Elkins, I know you hate that word."

"And what new insight did you—?"

"That you cook because you have all this stuff in the fridge. You don't have any frozen entrees. You have no choice but to cook or starve."

"I could go out to eat, and, as you know, I sometimes do."

"Yeah, but you cook better than most restaurants, and you're picky."

"So, what are you making?"

"Lamb patties with a wine caper sauce, fresh roasted asparagus, basmati rice, and a green salad. I mean, meal preparation isn't that difficult if you have lots of interesting ingredients. You weren't saving the lamb for anything special?"

Ray nodded toward Simone.

"She can have lamb and rice. Now, if you would just get the table set, Elkins."

13

Jennifer Bidwell, filled with anticipation, crossed the narrow roadway that connected the Gull Point Peninsula to the mainland. She parked across the drive from the combination garage and maintenance building that housed Scott's second-floor apartment. Jennifer emerged from her car and stood for a long moment, scanning the area before she headed toward the door that opened to the stairway leading to his apartment. He had previously warned her that Ms. Ingersolle probably wouldn't like his dating an employee of the wedding planner. He suggested that she might even fire him.

After running up the stairs, she pushed the entry door open without knocking and burst into the apartment.

"Scott!" she called, but there was no answer. "Scott?" she called again as she walked from room to room. She stood for a long moment, imagining him appearing from the next room and pulling her into his arms. She just wanted to be close to him for a few minutes before they each had to go to work. Disappointed, Jennifer retraced her steps and walked out into the unseasonably hot afternoon and across the huge lawn, a carefully manicured carpet of green where the caterers were busy stocking the bar area and firing up the grills before the guests arrived.

Finally, Jennifer spotted him, clipboard in hand, chatting with the catering boss. Her heart pounded, as it did whenever she saw him or even thought about him. But she would try to be professional. After catching his eye, she walked down to the estate's private harbor, where a gleaming white yacht was anchored. She looked at the boat for a few minutes, blotting the sweat from her neck with a tissue and wondering who had the money to own such a thing, and then she tried to look busy by reading old messages on her phone.

After Scott joined her, they walked together along the shore, maintaining an appropriate professional distance.

"I stopped by your apartment, Mr. Nelson," Jennifer said, "hoping to catch you there."

"I'm so sorry I missed you, Ms. Bidwell," Scott said in a tone that made Jennifer blush.

"I assume the bride and her party have arrived, Mr. Nelson," Jennifer said, nodding toward the yacht.

"They docked shortly before you got here," he said. "Then Piper and her bridesmaids scampered up to the house to repair the ravages of some serious partying."

According to the evening's plan, the bride, the groom, and the wedding party would be making a grand entrance after the guests arrived. Piper and Trevor had collaborated on the guest list—old prep school classmates, college and law school friends, and professional and business colleagues—mostly people of their generation.

"Let me know when the last shuttle is empty and the people are headed down the hill," Scott said. "I'll alert the staff in the big house."

As they parted, they collided slightly in passing, a tantalizing, sensual dance, Scott's hand brushing against Jennifer's rear in a motion that he hoped no one else would notice.

Jennifer was still feeling the thrill of his touch as she reached her assigned position on the mansion's circular drive just as the first bus arrived. She moved toward the front door of the bus, a staff photo ID dangling from her neck on a lanyard. As the guests climbed out of the crowded vehicle, Jennifer caught the strong smell of alcohol and saw that many of them were already inebriated. *They must have started drinking early at the Manitou Shores Resort,* she thought.

"Hey, girly, I need a refill," demanded a red-faced young man as he draped an arm over her shoulder and passed her an empty champagne bottle.

Jennifer accepted the bottle and then ducked under his arm. "The food and bar are down there," she responded, pointing in the direction of a red canopy near the lake.

"Maybe I should stay here with you, honey," Red Face said, coming toward her again. "You look lonely."

A tall blonde woman moved in, giving the man a playful shove and Jennifer an apologetic look. "Benson, for better or worse, you're my date tonight," she said. "Stop hitting on the staff." She took him by the arm and pulled him in the direction of the beach, mouthing, "Sorry!" at Jennifer over her shoulder.

That bottle was the first of many containers handed to Jennifer or pitched in her direction with the arrival of each new load of partygoers. By the time the third shuttle arrived, Jennifer was sweating profusely in the heat and had commandeered a trash container and a supply of plastic garbage bags from the caterer.

So much for being the greeter, she thought as she collected bottles and cans.

Linda Wetherbee called between the third and fourth shuttles. "How are things going?" she asked.

"How are things going? I'd say chaotic, Linda," Jennifer said tartly. "The guests are mostly smashed when they arrive. This is worse than the Cooper wedding. Much worse. You remember what a fiasco that weekend turned out to be. Not to mention, it's hotter than blazes."

"Well, it might rain again tonight, if that makes you feel any better," Linda said. "Maybe it will cool things off a bit."

"I would hope so," Jennifer said, "although it didn't do any good last night." She sighed. "I guess I'll pray for rain."

"Have you met the bride yet?" Linda asked.

"No," Jennifer said. "I wouldn't recognize her. I'm hoping Scott will point her out sometime during the evening."

"I'm surprised Alice Ingersolle would put up with that kind of behavior on her property," Linda said. "Have you seen her yet?"

"No," Jennifer said. "Maybe she's on the huge yacht that's

parked in the harbor. I'll call you later, when the last guests have been rounded up and sent on their way."

"All right," Linda said. "And Jennifer? Thanks for all you do. I couldn't do it without you."

"That's why I get paid the big bucks!" Jennifer joked before ending the call. She really liked Linda, considered her a mentor, but she was going to have to talk to her about upping the bonus for this particular event.

There was another possible bonus she might be able to arrange on her own. After she had greeted the last arriving revelers and sent them toward the food and drink, she waited for a few minutes until they had merged into the crowd. Then she exchanged several texts with Scott and slowly meandered down the hill toward the spot where he'd said he would be waiting for her. She was appalled by what she saw along the way: Stumbling couples disappearing into the woods. Groups of guests smoking pot and sharing pills. Guests running toward the beach, shedding their clothing along the way. She had never seen anything like it—even during college, even during the drunkest football weekends. Certainly not while working for Simply Romantic. It was still daylight!

Suddenly, the stooped figure of a man crossed the lawn in front of her. It was Gerhard Talmadge, the bride's grandfather, accompanied by a young man Jennifer hadn't seen before. Mr. Talmadge must have recognized her, because he stopped, turned in her direction, and bowed politely before continuing on his zigzag course through the crowd. The gesture made Jennifer laugh.

When she reached the spot at the edge of the woods, Scott was already there—with a bottle of champagne and two plastic cups in hand. He poured, and they touched cups in a toast. Jennifer emptied hers in a few swallows.

"Go easy, girl," said Scott. "This stuff's a fast buzz."

"I'm so hot and thirsty." By that point the water bottle she always carried with her was empty.

"Go slower on this one," he said, refilling her cup.

"I just saw Gerhard Talmadge up on the lawn," she said, waving her hand in the direction she had come. "Who's the boy with him?"

"He's a nursing student who works as a home health aide," Scott responded, offering Jennifer more champagne. "Piper hired him to keep an eye on Gerhard during the party and to make sure he gets to the wedding all right. She was surprised by how much he's declined since she saw him last year."

"That was nice of her," Jennifer said, surprised. In her experience, rich people were not generally considerate of others, and the rich people at this wedding were especially awful. She checked the time on her phone. "It's almost time for the grand entrance," she said. "Let's move closer."

They walked down the slope toward the revelry. Music was blaring from the large tent, and they could see couples moving on the portable dance floor inside. The women were dripping with expensive jewelry that caught the light of the glitter ball. The men were all in perfect physical condition, and they danced with assurance, as though they'd had lessons. Some of the dance moves the couples on the floor were performing approximated the sex act in ways that mortified Jennifer, and she turned away.

"These people are different from us," she said to Scott.

"Yes," Scott agreed. "I know."

Then the music ceased, and the noise from the exuberant crowd fell away. The guests emerged from the tent, and all eyes followed the brilliant beam of a spotlight as it moved over the group and up the hill.

The lake-facing double doors at the center of the mansion opened, and two lines of lights appeared, illuminating the long winding pathway to the dock. Another kind of music rose from the speakers. It sounded familiar to Jennifer, like opera but with a techno beat.

Cheers and applause mixed with the music as the procession neared the crowd. Seven women, all striking, tall and lithe, dressed in identical costumes—short white skirts, sandals, and sleeveless tank tops—strode toward the beach.

"That's Piper in the lead," Scott said into Jennifer's ear.

The music started to build as seven beams of light, lined up in a row, became visible far out on the lake in the gloaming. The crowd moved toward the yacht basin. The music intensified as the crafts raced toward the shore, crescendoing with the roar of the Sea-Doos as they nosed onto the small sandy beach.

The groom and his groomsmen, in shorts and tight V-neck tees, leaped off the machines and splashed onto the beach, champagne bottles in hand, embracing Piper and the women in her bridal party. Then, together with all the celebrants, they moved toward the bars, the food, and the dance floor.

"What do you think?" Scott asked Jennifer.

"OMG, it's like Hollywood or Broadway. Did you dream this up?"

"No, no. I wish. A New York ad agency orchestrated the whole thing—lights, music, watercraft, costumes. It's amazing what you can accomplish with a little cash."

"Or a lot of cash," countered Jennifer.

"But you can't control the weather," he said, holding out his hand to catch the first few drops of rain as he looked skyward.

Jennifer pulled out her phone and opened a radar app. "Doesn't look like much, a few scattered showers." She passed the phone over to Scott.

"Yes," he said, peering at the screen. "Looks likes some thunderstorms west of us. Hopefully, the party will be over before they roll off the lake."

"We could disappear for a while. No one would miss us." Jennifer nodded in the direction of Scott's apartment.

"Tempting," Scott said, looking her up and down, "but what if something goes south? Given this crowd, before the evening is over, we'll probably have to rescue drunken skinny-dippers and find people who have gone missing in the woods."

"Well, then, we'd better get going," said Jennifer, holding out her cup. When Scott stepped in to fill it, she leaned toward him and said, "I want you now."

Ray and Sue were on their way back to the government center in the early evening when Ray, drawn by the rising wind and the roiling clouds, pulled off the highway onto a gravel side road that came to a dead end at the Lake Michigan shore. They sat in silence, watching the dense gray-green clouds march across the lake. Flashes of lightning illuminated the leading edge of the storm. The still relatively flat surface of the water reflected the distant lightning.

Then, in the blink of an eye, the sky turned black as the tempest rolled off the water and exploded in front of them, the wind colliding with and shaking their massive SUV like a toy. An almost solid sheet of rain crashed into the windshield. Sue reached out and grabbed Ray's arm as the stormed raged around them. Finally, the intense lightning and thunder moved past, but the downpour continued. Minutes ticked by. Slowly, the wind diminished, the deluge softened and thinned, and the intense darkness began to lift.

Sue said, "I've never..."

"Me, either," said Ray. "Nothing like this. Never."

"It's the stuff of horror movies," said Sue. "I thought we were going to have the windshield in our laps."

Sue loosened her grip on his arm. He looked over at her and caught her expression as she withdrew her hand and then looked away.

Sue stared at the radio and declared, "Methinks it's going to be a long evening."

The radio crackled as if on cue. "Central Dispatch to all units, Central to all units."

Sue reached out and turned up the volume.

"Leading edge of storm has crossed the western shoreline. NWS radar shows several microbursts along coast. Gusts estimated sixty to eighty mph or more."

The dispatcher's voice came again: "Central to all units, trees and power lines reported down. Proceed with care."

And seconds later, "Central to any available units. Medical emergency at Gull Point, 1411 Isthmus Road. Multiple casualties. Requesting assistance."

With the first sharp crash of thunder, Jennifer Bidwell was suddenly fully awake. Then she heard the wind. She reached across the bed. Scott was gone.

"Wham, bam, thank you, ma'am," she mumbled as she pulled on her clothes and checked the time: 9:10. How was this rain going to disrupt the schedule? Would this day never end?

She scrambled down the stairs and into the storm—a blast of wind and water that tried to blow her back into the stairwell. She was instantly soaked to the skin. Between the rolling peals of thunder, music still reverberated from the beach. She began to sprint toward the shore, splashing through quickly forming puddles and streams on the lawn. If any of the guests were still down there, they were asking to get struck by lightning. And there were still several groups of drunken guests down near the water, of course, dancing in the rain. Wiping the wet hair out of her eyes, Jennifer called to them to shelter inside the tent. Many of the dancers responded by laughing and then ignoring her, although some of them staggered up the lawn in the direction of her waving arms.

She looked around for Scott but didn't see him. She hoped he was rounding up anyone who had wandered into the woods. The wind began to howl like a freight train as Jennifer went inside the tent, and when she looked around, she saw that the shadowy faces of the guests were filled with panic. Some of the men were holding onto the numerous tent poles as if they could keep the tent from blowing away.

Through the clear plastic windows of the tent, through the rain, Jennifer saw lighted shapes that she realized were the windows of the mansion. As the storm intensified outside, she wondered what any of them were doing out here when they could be sheltering inside the house. Alice Ingersolle had given strict instructions that no one was to go inside, but Jennifer was about to make an executive decision.

She threaded her way quickly through the crowd inside the tent. "Go to the house!" she yelled over the music and the roar of the storm, motioning toward the mansion.

Then all was darkness. Thunder and the howling wind replaced the blaring music with a sound like jet engines.

Jennifer could hear herself screaming. She could see that the people around her were screaming, too, but the sound of their voices was lost in the maelstrom. And then the protective canopy of canvas vaulted upward and away, flying through the air and crashing to the ground near the beach, leaving them all exposed to the elements.

It took Jennifer several seconds to comprehend that the shelter was gone. There was sand in her eyes. Flashes of lightning revealed the faces of the dazed guests, some of them on the ground, some of them injured. Tables blew over and slid across the lawn, chairs rose on the wind. A tornado—it had to be a tornado. Jennifer bent and pulled a young woman to her feet, and then she saw someone running toward the woods, and panic overtook her, and she, too, began to run. In those moments, the darkness seemed impenetrable around her. She couldn't see the person who had run in front of her. Where was the house? Where was Scott? Suddenly she was flattened by the branches of a falling tree.

Jennifer was on her back in a shallow pool, where she lay stunned and motionless for several minutes. Then, with her hands and feet, she started to claw her way free, pushing away the foliage and smaller boughs. Using some of the sturdier limbs, she pulled herself to her feet, and then she worked her way out of the labyrinth of leaves and branches. As she stood there in the darkness, one shoulder throbbing with pain, the world came rushing back—the wind, the rain, the shouting, the anguished sobbing. And then the wind started to drop, and the cries of human misery increased.

In the version of the story she would tell people over the next few days, Jennifer followed the voices and shadowy forms of the walking wounded as they trudged away from the beach toward the flickering yellow light illuminating the windows of the mansion. Once inside the house, her awareness ebbing, she found an open spot on a wall to lean against, then slowly slipped to the floor.

14

As Sue keyed the microphone and responded to the dispatcher, Ray reversed out of the road end and retraced his route back to M22. Turning north, he raced toward Gull Point, siren on, lights flashing. Pulling off the highway, he followed the gravel road toward the estate. He slowed, then stopped behind the two emergency vehicles that stood idling near the narrow strip of land that connected the small peninsula to the surrounding terrain. Pulling on slickers, he and Sue joined four people looking at what used to be a roadway.

It took Ray a few seconds to comprehend the scene. The pounding surf propelled by the high winds had swept over the breakwater and washed away the sand and gravel that supported the macadam roadway, leaving a water-filled gap.

"Road's gone, Sheriff," said a boyish-looking redhead, his name, *J. Olson*, on the chest of his dark blue uniform shirt just under an EMT patch. "How deep do you think it is?"

"Not too," said Ray, peering at the tops of the submerged boulders that had once protected the roadway. "Can you wade across?" he asked.

"Sure," Olson answered after looking at his colleagues. "We'll gear up."

Ray turned to Sue. "Go to the township park and boat launch and coordinate the response from there. We'll need boats for an evacuation and then land transportation to the medical center. Request interagency support. You know what to do. Operationalize our disaster plan."

She nodded, then headed for the truck.

A few minutes later, Ray and four EMTs—two men and two

women, each carrying large crimson backpacks filled with medical supplies—splashed through the water, which was in a few places waist-deep. The first man across scrambled up the embankment and helped pull the others up to what remained of the road on the peninsula side.

From that point, Ray led the way toward the mansion, pointing out obstacles with the beam of his flashlight. They skirted several downed trees blocking their way. When they got to the circular drive on the side of the mansion, a scene of destruction opened before them. The storm had ripped towering trees from the earth. In a clearing near the shore, tables, chairs, and assorted litter lay scattered across the lawn and beach. The remains of a large tent, twisted and torn, were entangled in the branches of an uprooted tree. The mansion stood above the debris-covered grounds, curtains hanging outside of some of the empty window frames. Apart from a few glimmers of light, the whole area was shrouded by the encroaching nightfall.

People were gathered in small groups, standing or sitting on the ground, others clustered together near the mansion. Down toward the water, Ray could see the light from phones flickering.

Scott Nelson, the estate manager, sprinted in Ray's direction. "Where're the ambulances?" he demanded.

"Road's out. We're arranging boat transportation."

"The road, can it be fixed?"

"Not anytime soon. Injuries?" asked Ray.

"Cuts, broken bones. We're doing what we can with a first aid kit. Some of the injured are down on the beach. Others up at the house. There's a doctor up there."

"No backup power?" asked Ray.

"No."

The EMTs split up, one team going into the mansion, the other to the beach. Ray followed the team into the house. The interior was in shambles. Windows had been blown out, and shattered glass lay in a thick layer near the empty window frames. The EMTs joined the medical team that was already present—event guests who also happened to be doctors and nurses. They had set up the spacious kitchen and dining area as a field hospital. The more seriously injured lay on cushions the team had ransacked from the living room furniture.

Ray observed that most of the injuries were lacerations and fractures. Considering how many mature trees had been taken down by the storm, he considered this outcome a lucky one. He was standing in the kitchen observing the triage process when a young woman with long brown hair approached him. She was wearing a white skirt and a sleeveless white tank top, both of which were smeared with dirt and grass stains and blood. Her pale blue eyes shone with anxiety.

"Sheriff?" she said.

"Yes," Ray said, extending his hand. "Ray Elkins."

"I'm Piper Ingersolle," she said. "This is my mother's estate."

"Is she here, is she injured?"

"No, Mother left the area hours ago before the party started. Sheriff, I'm worried about my grandfather, Gerhard Talmadge. I haven't seen him since earlier this evening. He was with a young man, a healthcare aide named Nathan. I've checked his house—the cottage near the gate—but he's not there. Can you help me find him?"

"Of course," Ray said. "Did you check inside the house?"

"No," she said. "The doors were locked."

He asked her a few more questions, taking notes on a small pad, and then wrote down a description of her grandfather and his aide, along with her contact information. He would take a look around the property, he promised, and once the boats arrived to take the injured to the medical center, there would be more people available to help search for him.

"Thank you, Sheriff," Piper said. "I'll be here, helping, if you learn anything."

The county emergency coordinator set up on the beach, and Ray was there with her when the first department boat entered the harbor. Additional EMT teams scrambled from the boat onto the dock, and then a few of the most seriously injured were ferried across the bay to waiting ambulances. Among them, Ray ID'd the healthcare aide assigned to Gerhard Talmadge. The young man had been knocked unconscious by flying debris from the tent. Probable concussion. He was disoriented when Ray spoke to him, and he didn't have a reliable idea of when or where he had last seen Talmadge.

Soon the second department boat arrived. A National Park Service craft stood offshore waiting to dock, followed by a Coast Guard response boat.

Ray gathered three deputies, and the four of them moved from group to group with their Maglites but found no one matching the description of Gerhard Talmadge. Then they did a quick search of the property, knocking on Talmadge's cottage, and the sagging old garage set back in the woods behind it, calling Talmadge's name.

The woods that abutted the house and the outbuildings were thick and dark. When Ray shone his flashlight in among the trees, he saw that many of them had been uprooted, and some of them had become hung up against other trees in the process of falling.

"It won't be safe to search the woods in the dark," Ray said to his deputies. "We'll have to wait until sunrise." The problem was that it wouldn't be safe in the daylight either. Ray tried to call Piper, only to discover that his cell phone wasn't working. He found Piper on the beach with the last few people waiting to be evacuated. After explaining that there was little he could do before daylight, Ray assured her he would be in contact with her as soon he knew anything more about her grandfather.

Hours later, Ray and Sue stood near the beach, taking in the chaos wreaked by what had by then been categorized as a microburst. The area was now brightly illuminated by four banks of stark white LEDs mounted high on a portable light tower. Sue pulled Ray away from the din of the small diesel generator powering the lights and pointed to the information she had collected on an iPad.

"Everyone's been transported to the medical center, hotels, or local housing. I have a list of names, addresses, and phone numbers. The wedding party is intact. Most of them were inside during the storm. I've confirmed what Piper told you, Ms. Ingersolle and her guests were not onsite at the time of the storm. According to the owner of the catering company, the catering staff is accounted for. As for the guests, I can't say for sure. Scott Nelson says he never had a guest list, and he says the wedding planner—" she scrolled down on the iPad, "—Jennifer Bidwell, was injured and taken to the hospital by the second boat. I'll have someone on the other side see if they can catch up with her or check with Simply Romantic, where she works."

"No sign of Gerhard Talmadge," Ray said.

Sue shook her head soberly. She pointed up toward the mansion. "Who's left?"

"Scott Nelson and two private security guards," he answered. "They've swept the mansion and confirmed that it's empty. They also checked the immediate grounds surrounding the building. The deputies and I have searched the party area, checked along the beach, and done a cursory sweep of any outbuildings that were unlocked. Nelson said there were people dancing on the beach, swimming, and wandering off into the woods close to the time the storm hit." He looked toward the woods. "How many people might be in there, injured or dead?"

"Elkins," Sue said, "you know it's not safe to go in there now. And you've been in wet clothes for hours."

"Dry now," he responded with a weak smile.

"I need sleep, and so do you."

He nodded his agreement.

"The site is secure," Sue said. "The access road is blocked off. We'll organize a thorough search of the whole area first thing in the morning."

"Okay," he agreed and followed her to a waiting boat.

15

A few hours later, when the early morning sun was starting to burn off the low-hanging mist that enveloped the lake, Ray and Sue set up a temporary command center on the beach near the yacht basin and began to organize the search parties.

Standing on a picnic table, Ray addressed the crowd of law enforcement officers, emergency workers, and other volunteers, all dressed to ward off the seasonably appropriate morning chill. The storm had reset the weather to normal and left the lake smooth as a mirror.

"Thank you all for being here," he said. "And I appreciate the fact that some of you are back again with very little sleep. And thank you for your skillful work last night treating the injured and getting everyone evacuated. I talked with a hospital spokesperson a few minutes ago. Most of the injuries were minor. Only a few people remain hospitalized.

"At this point, we don't have an accurate count of who was here when the storm struck. We do have one report of a missing person: an elderly gentleman who lives on this estate, Gerhard Talmadge." Ray gave a description of Talmadge and what he was wearing. "We're going to search this little peninsula from one end to the other. One team will check the beach area and shallow water around the entire perimeter of the peninsula. A second team will search the inland area from the western shore back to the washed-out road at the eastern end, checking buildings, vehicles, and a large swath of the heavily wooded terrain. The mansion has already been checked, but as you do your sweep, check the grounds around that building and the nearby garage and maintenance building. There's an old cottage, with its own garage, and several other buildings scattered in the woods. Check the perimeters of all the buildings, any place a person might have sought refuge from the storm. Questions?"

"How about locked buildings?"

"Check the perimeters. If you think the interior of a building should be checked, let Detective Lawrence know. We'll look into the situation. Some of the buildings off in the woods look quite dilapidated. Please take care. This part of the search shouldn't take too long. When you reach the woods, the going will get tough. I had a quick hike through the area a few minutes ago. Lots of downed trees and others just waiting to fall. Please be very cautious.

"Detective Sue Lawrence will divide you into teams. Sergeant Rory Tate of our marine patrol will lead the shore search. Detective Lawrence and I will coordinate the land search."

As Tate lead his team toward the beach, Sue organized a search line. The initial search area covered only a few hundred yards from the lakeside end of the peninsula past the mansion, the outbuildings, and the adjacent lawns. When the line reached the twisted remains of the tent, the team members pulled back the fabric and found that no one had been trapped under the debris.

Then the searchers confronted the dense brush and rugged terrain. The straight-line wind had decimated the thick forest, snapping many of the tree trunks like twigs. Progress slowed to a snail's pace. The orderly line broke apart as people worked around the rubble, sometimes climbing over, under, or through the fallen timber, carefully skirting the precariously balanced trees that rested against some of their still-standing neighbors. In a few cases, two or more trees, their upper branches intertwined, leaned into each other like exhausted heavyweight boxers, desperately clinging to one another before their predestined final collapse.

Some of the trees—oak, maple, pine, and ash—were sheared off near the ground. Others pulled much of their elaborate root systems with them as they toppled earthward. A few snapped mid-trunk, leaving a pillar to mark their earthly existence.

Ray and Sue followed at a distance, trying to keep visual contact with the searchers.

When they were less than a hundred yards into the dense foliage, a woman called, "Over here!"

Ray saw a hand waving in the air. Everyone stopped, and the line collapsed toward the woman, an EMT, who was pointing toward a downed tree. "There's someone in there," she said.

Ray pushed back the foliage of a downed oak tree, and the woman helped him pull a branch out of the way, exposing the upper torso and head of a body that lay face down, pinned under the tree. The head was mostly bald, a fringe of gray hair showing. Ray went to his knees and peered through the foliage. The man's left arm was partially extended, as if reaching for something. A small hand, gnarled fingers pressed into the sand, was partially visible beyond the cuff of a white cotton shirt. The right arm disappeared under the body at the elbow.

Ruth, the EMT, moved in and reached around the man's neck. "He's gone, Sheriff. Cold. Probably dead for hours," she said. "Not a good way to die," she added, "out here, alone."

Ray nodded his agreement and backed out, allowing Sue to move in and view the body.

"Is it him?" Sue asked. "Gerhard Talmadge?"

"Most likely," Ray said. "We need the medical examiner and some firefighters with chain saws to cut him out."

"Yes. I'll get that organized and have Brett handle the rest of the search."

"I'll stay with the body," said Ray.

Sue gave him a searching look but said nothing.

As she headed for the dock, the search team began to move forward again. Their occasional chatter faded, replaced by bird calls and the sound of the wind moving through the trees overhead. In the dappled sunlight flowing down through what trees remained in the canopy, Ray sat on the trunk of another downed tree near the body. The man's position in death, his hand reaching out as though pleading for help, suggested to Ray the frailty, the vulnerability of the human form. It occurred to him that people built mansions like the one here at Gull Point in an attempt to compensate for the fragility of human physical existence. Then his thoughts flashed to the previous December and the searing pain as the bullet had entered his body, those moments before his consciousness slipped away.

He pushed that memory back, focusing again on the body a few feet away. Had the man been conscious after the tree hit him? Had he fought to pull himself free of the massive branch? Had he suffered? Had he lingered there in pain, or had everything just ended immediately, mercifully? If they had searched the woods last night and found him, would they have been able to save his life?

Ray stood and walked to a clearing near the water. The sight of a small sailboat moving out of the bay on the gentle winds calmed him. Turning north, the sloop-rigged craft slowly advanced into deeper water, and Ray returned to his vigil.

"Elkins, I was afraid I'd hear from you today," Dr. Robert Dyskin, the medical examiner, called as he tromped through the woods toward Ray, with Sue trailing behind. "What a storm. Whole new vocabulary. Microburst. Wind shear. You know, I live just up the road from here. Hell of a blow. Nothing like this, though." Dr. Dyskin made a sweeping gesture that took in all the downed trees. "We lost some branches. Not trees. How does this happen?"

Dr. Dyskin stopped and looked around, and his voice softened. "And then a beautiful morn. Lake is like a pancake. Climate change. A whole new world, Elkins. Our poor grandkids." Dyskin paused, then asked, "So what have we got here?"

Ray pulled back some branches, allowing Dr. Dyskin to see the body. The pathologist pulled on rubber gloves and knelt close to the old man's head. He reached under the tree, pushing his hand between the body and the branch that held it tight to the ground.

Dyskin stood and said, "Poor bastard. Wrong place, wrong time. Could have been any of us. Get these branches out of my way."

Ray waved in the four firefighters, each one wearing protective gear and carrying a chain saw. After they finished cutting back some of the branches, Dyskin moved in again and carefully palpated the man's head before moving to the shoulders, the left arm, the torso. Then he stood again and addressed the firefighters.

"Can you get the tree off the body without doing any further damage?"

"Sure," answered one of the men.

Dr. Dyskin, Ray, and Sue waited at a distance as the firefighters went to work cutting the upper reaches of the tree apart.

"Perfect, thank you, gentleman," said Dr. Dyskin, as he returned to inspect the rest of the body.

"Is there a wallet?" asked Ray.

"Not that I can find," Dr. Dyskin answered, brushing the wet sand off his knees. "Any idea who he is?"

"An elderly man who lived on the estate, Gerhard Talmadge," said Ray. "Any chance you knew him?"

Dyskin looked back at the body.

"Don't think so," Dyskin said. "I hate to tell you that we're going to have to send him downstate for a forensic autopsy."

Sue's brow furrowed in confusion. "The tree didn't kill him?"

"I think the postmortem will indeed show non-survivable traumatic injuries from the tree," Dr. Dyskin said to Sue. "But you no doubt observed me lingering over the skull. Did you see any branches near the head?"

"No," she said.

"The top of the skull is fractured, pushed in. I'm wondering if someone clubbed this guy. If he wasn't dead already, someone finished off the poor devil."

"What kind of weapon are we looking for?" asked Ray.

"Can't say yet. Something heavy."

"Broken branch?"

"Hard to say. I mean, it's impossible to visualize this jumble of branches coming down, but I don't think they could have hit the top of his head in a way that's consistent with a fractured skull. Something smooth and heavy—a croquet mallet, maybe, or some kind of tool."

"Tire iron?"

"We'll have a better idea after the autopsy."

16

"Is there any way we could have compromised a possible crime scene more?" asked Sue after Dr. Dyskin and the emergency workers had departed.

"This was unanticipated," Ray said. "We did what we could. No one left a pipe wrench or a hammer at the scene to tip us off that something untoward had happened. You took lots of pics every step of the way. And then we had heavy rain yesterday. Any footprints would have been obliterated. Let's get the body bagged and moved. You can do a final sweep, and then we'll work on getting a positive ID on this man."

"You okay, Elkins?" Sue asked.

Ray was shaken—by his time sitting with the body and by Dyskin's conclusions—and it took him a moment to speak. Finally, he said, "If Dyskin is correct and the man we're assuming is Talmadge was still alive, this was an execution. An elderly man trapped under a tree. What kind of person could have done this? What motive would have prompted this kind of cruelty?"

By midmorning, Sue had the body bag set on the lawn near the beach. Ray watched as Scott Nelson, looking worn, hovered above her as she unzipped the bag just far enough to make the face visible.

Scott looked briefly into the bag, then turned away. "Gerhard," he said. "Yes, that's Gerhard Talmadge. My neighbor, the man who lived in the old cottage."

"You're sure?" Sue pressed.

"Absolutely," he replied hoarsely, still looking away. "What happened to him?"

"We found his body under a fallen tree." Sue pointed into the woods.

"Oh my God, he was all alone out there and injured? Where was the nursing assistant Piper hired?"

"He was injured during the storm and lost consciousness," Sue said. "He was one of our first evacuees."

Scott rubbed both hands over his face. "That's terrible. I wish…"

Ray watched Scott closely. He was using the appropriate gestures, words, and phrases, but his tone was flat and without emotion.

"He probably died instantly," said Sue.

"Did you see Mr. Talmadge last evening?" asked Ray.

"No. I haven't seen him for maybe a week. But I've been crazy busy with the wedding arrangements."

Sue knelt and zipped the bag closed. She nodded to the two men who had been carrying the stretcher. "We're done," she said.

"So let me confirm this," Ray said to Scott. "You haven't seen Mr. Talmadge in recent days."

"True. But I haven't been following my usual routine. I usually have a walk around the property at least once during the day. That's when I sometimes see Gerhard. He smokes, not a lot, maybe two or three cigarettes a day, and he would usually stand just outside the garden gate to smoke. He'd leave the butts behind, and, on those days he wasn't there, I would dutifully pick them up—some old-fashioned brand without filters."

"Did you two talk?" Ray asked.

"Sure. I'd often stop and chat about the weather and ask how he was doing."

"Have you observed people visiting or staying with Mr. Talmadge?"

"Occasionally people visit Gerhard. I think he's selling his paintings." Scott looked confused. "If his death was caused when the tree fell on him—an accident of nature—why all the questions?"

"Routine," answered Ray offhandedly. "I'm making a list of who to inform of Mr. Talmadge's death. Do you have contact information for his next of kin?" He watched Scott Nelson carefully.

"Of course," Scott said, pulling his cell phone from his pocket. "Piper Ingersolle's cell number is—"

"I have her contact information, Mr. Nelson. I spoke to her last night," Ray said. "But I will need Alice Ingersolle's number."

Scott hesitated. "I try not to bother her," he said. "She'll want me to take care of it."

Ray exhaled sharply. "Look, someone is dead, a person who lives on her property—a person who is related to her by marriage. This is official business, and I will be contacting her directly." Ray handed Scott a small notepad and pen and waited as Scott wrote down the number.

"Anything else, Sheriff?" Scott asked wearily, handing back the pad. "I've got a mountain of work to do if I'm going to get this place up and running again. Speaking of which, is there a way I can catch a ride on one of your boats? I need to get somewhere that has cell service."

"We can make that happen," said Ray. "Can you be down at the dock in ten minutes?"

As Ray and Sue watched Scott Nelson cross the lawn toward the mansion, Ray said, "Would you call Piper Ingersolle…better yet, run over to the Manitou Shores Resort and do a death notification. And just say it appears he was killed by a falling tree."

"Of course," Sue said.

"Also, see if you can get the autopsy expedited."

"Yes," she said. "And I'll get a search warrant for the Talmadge property."

"Get one drafted for the whole area, just in case—houses, outbuildings, vehicles, this whole little peninsula. And you should probably list them. In addition to the mansion and garage maintenance area and the Talmadge cottage and garage, there're some other outbuildings off in the woods. Then get everything you can on Talmadge. We need to know if anyone might have had a motive to kill him."

17

Linda Wetherbee stood next to the passenger door of her Lexus as Jennifer Bidwell was rolled out of the medical center in a wheelchair. Linda held the car door open as an orderly assisted Jennifer into the car and attached her seatbelt, carefully avoiding the sling supporting her injured arm.

"Are you okay?" Linda asked before starting the engine.

"I've got a torn ligament in my shoulder," Jennifer said in a tight voice. "Time will tell if I need surgery. And I'm totally exhausted. Linda, I was so frightened during the storm. And then everything took so long. Waiting for help, waiting for the boat and the ambulance and the triage doctor. I wasn't a high priority. I was breathing, I wasn't bleeding, and I didn't have chest pains."

"You poor thing! Why didn't you call me immediately? I would have been waiting for you at the hospital."

Jennifer looked over at her boss. She was surprised by what appeared to be genuine concern on Linda's part. Why was she always surprised when someone seemed to care about her?

"There was no cell service out there afterward," Jennifer explained, "not until we got to town. I probably wouldn't have bothered you, anyway. It was too late. There was nothing you could have done."

"I could have listened," Linda said firmly. "Now tell me what happened. We had the storm down here, you know, thunder and lightning, but nothing like the damage I saw on the news this morning. A microburst—that's what the meteorologist called it. The last I heard from you, the guests were behaving badly right off the shuttles, and you were hoping a little rain might cool things down."

Jennifer laughed abruptly at the irony of that wish. She couldn't keep the disgust out of her voice as she described how the guests had behaved. "Is it that they're rich?" she asked. "They can do whatever they want without consequences?"

Linda sighed. "I don't know. That's probably part of it. What about Scott Nelson? Did he try to help you keep things under control?"

"I think he was mostly worried about safety—people drowning or overdosing on drugs," Jennifer said, "things that could ruin the whole event and embarrass his boss. But some things you just can't control. It was total chaos."

She turned her head away from Linda, toward the window, and Linda got the sense she was fighting back tears.

"It's not your fault, dear," Linda said. She reached out and patted Jennifer's good hand. "You did the best you could with a situation that was terrible in multiple ways." Linda stopped short of saying that she regretted sending Jennifer on the job. This job was tough, and she thought Jennifer was tough enough to recover from even this experience and go on to plan another wedding.

Jennifer struggled to respond. While she appreciated Linda's supportive attitude, she wanted to be as straightforward as she could without divulging too much about her relationship with Scott Nelson or the fact that she was in his bed for part of the evening when she was supposed to be working.

"But I didn't do everything right, Linda," she said, looking into her mentor's eyes. "I was standing on the hill above the tent and the food area just fuming about it all, when Scott came and found me with a bottle of champagne. We drank a couple of glasses and commiserated about how badly things were going, and then I remember Scott saying I was drinking too fast. It was so hot, and I was parched. He walked me down toward the beach, to where they were grilling the steaks and brats, and made sure I ate something. Then one of the caterers needed help with something, and he left. As soon as I ate something, I didn't feel so tipsy. I'm really sorry, Linda. I hope you know it's not like me to drink on the job. But the stress—"

"I know," Linda said. "Nobody's perfect, Jen. Just tell me it won't happen again, and I'll believe you."

Jennifer breathed a sigh of relief. "I swear it won't happen again."

"Were you there, down by the beach, when the storm hit?" Linda asked.

"Yes," Jennifer said. She described the solid wall of rain, the deafening sound of the wind. "I was so scared, Linda. I thought I was going to die. I was just running. And then I was flat on my back, and all the branches were on top of me.

"And suddenly it was quiet—weirdly quiet. The music had stopped. I don't know how much time passed, but I started to hear people, shouting and crying and sobbing. All these people in a dark, unfamiliar place. I was completely disoriented."

"How terrifying!" Linda said. "What did you do?"

"I was able to push the branches aside and get up. I worked my way over to where I saw lights, phone lights. I saw lights in the mansion, candles, and then I was inside. I guess I followed the crowd toward the lights. I was running on instinct."

She described the evacuation and the transportation of the wounded to the medical center.

"Was Scott Nelson hurt? Have you talked to him?" Linda asked.

"I don't think he's hurt," Jennifer said. "I saw him helping people into the house for first aid, but I didn't get a chance to talk to him. I tried to call him just before you got here, but it went to voicemail. Maybe the cell service is still down at Gull Point."

Linda started the car. "Well, we need to get you to your apartment," she said. "You need a shower, a meal, and then sleep." She pulled away from the curb. "Until I know you're all right and able to take care of yourself, I plan on keeping a watchful eye on you."

"But the wedding," Jennifer said, panicked. "What's happening with the wedding?"

"Remember that line in all of our contracts, it's part of the standard boilerplate: 'In the event of acts of God, we and our contractors are protected from responsibility for goods and services that we are unable to provide.' In all my years in the business, I've never had to use that clause. Today, I'm delighted it's there."

"But shouldn't we be doing something, looking at—?"

"Jennifer, you need a shower, food, and sleep. I have my cell phone on. It's up to Alice Ingersolle to contact us."

18

After walking with Sue to a waiting boat, Ray followed the path on the left side of the mansion to the road that ran past Gerhard Talmadge's cottage. Now in the daylight, he was surprised to see that unlike the mansion that stood a few dozen yards in front of it, the cottage had no broken windows. He wondered if the mansion had taken the brunt of the powerful microburst, protecting the old building in its lee.

He had checked both the front door and the kitchen door the previous night, after Piper Ingersolle had reported her grandfather missing. Now he went up to the front of the house again. If a key were hidden somewhere, where would it be? He checked under the doormat and then ran his fingers across the flat surface at the top of the door frame. Other than the grime that had collected over the decades, nothing. He looked around and under the legs of a small bench that stood near the front door. Finally, he checked under two flowerpots, and then ran his fingers through the dry soil at the top of the plantless containers. As he exited the porch, Ray stood for a long moment and looked at the crushed stone walkway. That path disappeared into the grass a few yards beyond. Its right of way to the shore was now blocked by Alice Ingersolle's monolithic structure.

He walked a few yards down the path and stopped in a patch of sunshine and studied the incongruous collection of materials and architectural styles that had been combined in the creation of one of the largest summer homes in the county. He attempted and failed to find any aspect of the house aesthetically appealing, and he wondered if it brought its owner any pleasure other than the bitter satisfaction of blocking Gerhard Talmadge's view. Was it possible that for some people that kind of pleasure was the only one worth pursuing?

"Sheriff," came a familiar voice.

Ray turned quickly, startled by the unexpected intrusion on his musings.

"I'm sorry," said Scott Nelson. "I didn't mean to surprise you."

"I thought you had gotten on the boat," Ray said.

"I need your help," Scott said in a quivering voice. "Someone stole some artwork from Ms. Ingersolle's gallery." Scott's soiled cotton T-shirt was now soaked with perspiration near the neck and under the arms. He seemed much more upset about the missing artwork than about viewing Talmadge's body a short while before.

"Tell me what happened," Ray said.

"Let me show you," Scott said, motioning for Ray to come with him. "It was a set of sketches—they're probably irreplaceable." He rushed toward the entrance of Alice Ingersolle's mansion with Ray in tow. Along the way, Scott explained, "I was going to head over on the boat, but when I got back to the house, I ran into Sal Abato, head of Ms. Ingersolle's security team, and we decided to go through the place and assess the damage from the storm and make a priority list of needed repairs. That's when we found the doors of Ms. Ingersolle's art gallery had been forced open. Sal checked the place after everyone had been evacuated last night. He's sure that the doors were locked. And now they're open, and the sketches that were hanging in the gallery are gone."

"How many people are on Ms. Ingersolle's security team?" Ray asked.

"Just two here at Gull Point. Sal and Helio Lopez. They travel with Ms. Ingersolle."

"And they were both here last night during the festivities?"

"Yes," Scott said.

"Where's Mr. Abato now?"

"He was headed to his office. He said something about a loss protocol he needed to initiate."

"Didn't you get any alerts from the security service when the doors were forced open?"

"When we lost power in the storm, the system must have gone down." Scott paused for a moment at the lakeside entrance to the mansion. "As soon as my cell starts working again, I'm sure I'll get an automated message saying the security system is down."

"A place like this, no backup generator?" said Ray.

"We were waiting for the utility company to run a gas line for the new generator. It should have been in place by now."

Ray gave Nelson a probing look. "So after we finished our evacuation last night, there were only the three of you left, you and two security men employed by Ms. Ingersolle."

"Well, yes, us, and whomever you had assigned here overnight. We didn't see your people. I assume they stayed on the beach. But, Sheriff, there could've been other people—people who didn't get on the boats for less-than-honest reasons."

Ray nodded in agreement. "Were you up all night?"

"No, I went back to my apartment around 2:00. That was after Sal and Helio had done a final sweep of the mansion and given me the all clear. The place was a mess, but they assured me they had checked all the secured areas—Ms. Ingersolle's personal quarters and the gallery area. Everything was exactly as it should be. Sheriff, Sal is the real deal, former Special Forces, a former New York cop. He's been directing the security at her New York gallery for years. The man's a total pro.

"Let me show you the gallery." Scott led the way up a broad winding staircase to the third floor and stopped in front of a set of double doors, which were ajar. Without touching either one, Ray looked at the damage—pry marks near the center, wood ripped from each door, the hardware torn loose.

Then he entered the room and slowly scanned its contents. The morning light streamed through the windows on the lake side onto backless couches in an oyster linen that were spaced along the center of the room. The hooks on the white walls were empty, and damaged frames and torn matting materials were scattered around on the wooden floor. There were four sets of French doors leading to a balcony that ran along the front of the house, and one pair of doors was wide open. Ray walked out onto the balcony and noted both the stunning view of the lake and the low eaves that would make it easy to climb over the roof from one of the several other balconies that were features of the house.

"Under what circumstances would this door to this balcony have been left unlocked?" he asked Scott, coming back into the gallery.

"Never, unless there's a function going on in this room. The doors to the balcony are always locked. And there are cameras and motion sensors in this room." Nelson pointed toward some of the hardware attached to the ceiling. "This wall, the one directly across from the windows, was covered with a stunning collection of sketches. They're gone, every one of them."

"You said they were valuable?"

"I assume so. Ms. Ingersolle said that she had assembled a collection of sketches from the early 1900s. From that group, these prints were selected for a private sale, by invitation only. She does this a few times during the summer each year. They're events for a select clientele."

"What's special about them, this clientele?" asked Ray.

Nelson looked away, toward the lake. Then he made eye contact again. "As she explained it to me, these people have unlimited budgets, and they are only interested in museum-quality works. They demand complete confidentiality, including private viewings, and often bring their own experts. They come by private jets, stay a day or two, make their decisions, and then leave."

"The prospective customers are housed here?"

"Absolutely. In addition to Ms. Ingersolle's suite, there are six executive suites at the far end of the mansion. Ms. Ingersolle brings her own chef and kitchen staff and a security detail. She insists that everything is perfect for her guests."

"And if they buy something, do they take it with them, or do they have it shipped?" asked Ray.

"I don't know the details, Sheriff. My job description doesn't include anything on the art side."

"We will need an inventory of the missing items immediately. I want the house closed off. I'll assign officers to secure the exterior of the building. No one comes in without my permission. Please take me to see Sal Abato."

"He's probably in the kitchen," said Scott, leading the way.

19

"Sal," said Nelson, "Sheriff Elkins is here."

"Sheriff," the man stood and extended a hand. He was wiry, about Ray's height, perhaps a bit taller, wearing jeans, a black Patagonia T-shirt, and running shoes. His shaved head and arms were deeply tanned, tattoos on each muscular arm disappearing beneath his short sleeves. His grip was firm, his voice deep.

"Sal Abato, pleased to meet you. Coffee? I just perked it. Not too bad." The three men, now holding mugs, settled on stools near a long, stainless steel counter that ran beneath a bank of windows.

"You've seen the gallery?" asked Abato, gravel-voiced with a rich New York accent.

"Yes," said Ray.

"Last night, after the place had been evacuated, we did another walk-through. It had to be after midnight. We were convinced that everyone was gone," Sal explained. "That room, the gallery, and all of the private areas in the mansion were locked." He shook his head. "Last night, for the first time since this place was built, we needed the kind of security system we have in the city."

"You and your assistant, the two of you checked all the doors?"

"Yeah, me and Helio—Helio Lopez. I check. He double checks. We use a paper checklist on a clipboard, fill it out in pencil. No phone or iPad stuff. My kids say I'm a 'pencil man.' Of course, they don't mean it as a compliment."

"Give me a chronology of what happened last night," said Ray. "Start with the storm. Where were you before, during, and after? Did you have any responsibilities other than protecting the art?"

"Usually, we're only here for a few days at a time. I get to ride in Ms. Ingersolle's private jet. And the food is great—she brings her own chef. And I usually have time to get some fishing in. A good break from summer in the city.

"She's got a special showing scheduled next week, but she also wanted me here for the wedding, to help keep a lid on things, so we planned for two weeks this time. The wife, she's not happy with me being gone for two weeks. We got teenagers, you know."

Ray could see that Sal was losing track of his question.

"Ms. Ingersolle thought Helio should come along this time, too," Sal said. "We figured I could use the help with the wedding, and the guy's hardly ever been out of the city." He stopped and looked at Ray for a beat.

"And what exactly were you doing before, during, and after the storm?" Ray asked again.

"Yeah, okay. Well, beforehand, Helio and me met with Scott to talk about the layout of each stage of the festivities and where the problem spots might be."

"What kinds of problems were you anticipating?" asked Ray.

"Drunks, Sheriff," said Sal. "Weddings are the same everywhere. When you give people free booze…they tend to overindulge. We took turns circulating, Helio and me, one of us at the house, making sure no one unauthorized went inside, while the other mixed with the crowd. As it turned out, the storm hit before things got too out of hand."

"Then what happened?"

"Helio got caught down by the tent. Truth be told, when it started to rain, I came up here and stood there in the doorway having a cigarette. I've never seen anything like it.... The wind and rain came right off the lake and ran over us like a truck, you know, like getting smacked by a big wave when you're wading in the ocean."

"And then afterward?" Ray asked. "What did you see?"

"After the storm, people started coming up to the house, and of course we let them all in. We got candles going; I found some flashlights. Me and Helio are both ex-military, so we know how to bandage cuts and splint fractures. And it turned out that, in this kind of crowd, there were a few doctors and nurses, so we did what we could to help them. There was a big first aid kit in the kitchen. When the emergency workers arrived, we were all happy to turn things over to them. And then you guys organized the evacuation. We helped get people down to the dock. After everyone was gone— everyone we know of, anyway—Helio and me broomed glass and filled garbage bags and then did an inspection, inside and out."

"What time was that?" asked Ray. "When did you start cleaning up?"

Sal considered the question. "I'd say it was 2:00 a.m. by that point, more or less."

"You must have been exhausted," Ray said.

Sal shrugged. "We had a job to do. Once everything was cleaned up, we did the final walkthrough, checking Ms. Ingersolle's apartment first—she brings lots of jewelry. Then we checked the doors on the gallery. They were locked."

"Did you go into the gallery and check the doors opening onto the balcony?"

"No, no need to if the other doors are locked, which they were. Then we checked the rest of the house, bathrooms, halls, garages, kitchen. Didn't see no one. We closed things up as good as we could. With the glass out in some of the windows and sliding doors, well, it wasn't perfect, but…"

"Then you went to bed?" Ray asked.

"We took two-hour shifts," Sal said, "mostly in a chair near the busted-out glass near the pool and some of the time walking around to stay awake."

"You didn't see anyone during the night?"

"Nah, no people up here."

"Same for Helio?"

"Yeah, except he was kinda freaked. Too dark, too quiet for a city boy."

"When did you discover the break-in?"

"This morning we did another walk around, which is what I

usually do when I'm here. As soon as I saw the door busted open and looked in and saw the chaos, I said to Helio not to mess with anything. Get the cops. This is their problem."

"Have you ever had a situation like this since you've worked for Ms. Ingersolle?" Ray asked.

"Never, not here or in the city. And I've been with Ms. Ingersolle lots of years."

"How much info do you think we'll get from the security cameras?"

"Well, truth be told, not much. The system is primitive, Sheriff." He looked askance at the body camera clipped to the front of Ray's jacket. "Ms. Ingersolle is not keeping up with the times like your department is doing with the body cams. The stuff here is seven years old, and that's a long stretch when you're talking about technology. A lot has changed in the past seven years. In the Manhattan store, we upgrade every couple of years or whenever the tech improves in a way that makes the property more secure. I've been harping at Ms. Ingersolle to upgrade the stuff here, but I just couldn't get her ear. Scott knows. He and I have talked about it. Right, Scott?"

Scott nodded. "The system depends on electricity, landlines, and a cable connection. We were starting the upgrade this year with a generator that used natural gas. That should have been operational. It wasn't. "Ms. Ingersolle seems to think this remote location provides most of the security we need—unlike the New York gallery—and that when there is some valuable art in the gallery here, Sal and I can keep an eye on it. Her thinking is that the place is isolated, and no one knows what happens here."

"Someone knew," said Ray, giving Sal a long look, knowing that Sal would know he, Helio, and Scott would be prime suspects.

Sal asked Ray, "How can we help?"

"I'm going to have my deputies cordon off the house," Ray said. "Sal, are you staying in the house?"

Sal nodded.

"We will cordon the gallery area and the hallway and stairs leading to the crime scene. It might be a while before we can get the scene processed. No one, including you three, is to enter the area. Also, I'll need images of the missing art…"

Sal shifted uncomfortably on his stool. "They're cataloged in a database on our main company computer. Usually I can access that on my phone or from my laptop, but we're not doing usually this morning."

"But you did see the artwork in this gallery. Right?"

"Sheriff, I'm constantly surrounded by paintings and stuff, but truth be told, this art stuff, it's not my thing."

"Any impressions at all," Ray pressed. "Landscapes, people…?

"No, no, they were sketches, mostly black lines. Maybe one had some color. They were people. I think."

"How did they arrive here for the showing?" Ray asked.

"They were packaged at our New York gallery. We have people that do that. Me and Helio, we brought them on the jet," Sal said. "How were they packaged?"

"Individual cardboard boxes. Our people really know how to do it."

"Did you hang the prints in the gallery."

"No, Ms. Ingersolle did that yesterday morning. Some woman from the boat helped her. After they were done, we secured the gallery and the hallways."

"The people who snatched these prints cut them out of their frames. Can you speculate on how they would have gotten them out of here?"

"At the gallery, our shipping and receiving department gets unframed prints rolled up in cardboard tubes. If someone planned this out, that's probably what they'd use."

"How do you think Ms. Ingersolle will take the news that these prints are missing?" asked Ray.

"Let's just say it's not going to be a fun day," Sal said. "She doesn't like her world messed with." He looked pointedly at Scott Nelson. "Right?" he asked.

Scott, who had been chewing on his lip nervously throughout the conversation, nodded.

Ray closed the pad he had been using to take notes and put it and his pen away. As he rose from his stool, he said to Sal, "One more thing. Gerhard Talmadge, you know him?"

Sal, who had been about to stand, sank back down. "The old guy, yeah, what about him?"

"Have you seen him around?"

"Not this trip. But usually I see him when we're here. He's German, but he speaks Italian pretty good, maybe better than English. We've had some good conversations, on the sly."

"Why on the sly?"

"My boss, she's not his biggest fan."

"So you didn't see him last night?"

"No. Did he get through the storm okay?"

"We found his body under a downed tree this morning."

"Dead?"

"Yes, dead. The only known casualty of the storm."

Sal shook his head. "Dying alone, that sucks. Nice man. I liked talking to him. Anything else, Sheriff?"

"Do either of you have any questions for me?" Ray asked, looking from Sal to Scott.

"No," Sal said and shook Ray's hand again.

Scott Nelson shook his head. "You'll keep us posted on what you learn?" he asked Ray.

"Of course," Ray said. "And one more thing, Scott. Can you get me a key to the Talmadge cottage?"

"Sorry, Sheriff. I've never had a key to that cottage."

"Maybe you know where one was hidden?"

"Can't help you with that, either."

Once outside, Ray used his radio to contact central dispatch. He read off the cell number Nelson had provided for Ms. Ingersolle. His parting words were, "If you get this woman on the phone, tell her I want to meet with her ASAP. Message her, too. Police business, urgent."

20

When Sue returned to Gull Point, Ray met her at the dock. She was carrying two toolbox-like evidence collection kits and a brown paper bag that Ray hoped might contain lunch.

"How did Piper Ingersolle take the news of her grandfather's death?" he asked, taking one of the evidence kits from Sue's hand.

"She was really broken up about it," Sue said, her mouth turning down at the corners. "She asked if he was in any pain before he died, and I didn't know what to say. I caught up with her at the Manitou Shores like you suggested."

Sue continued. "I didn't say anything directly about the head injury, but I did let her know that her grandfather's death is still under investigation. She seemed confused, but she let it go when I promised to be in touch."

As they walked from the beach toward Gerhard Talmadge's cottage, Ray told Sue about the stolen artwork.

"Elkins, we're totally out of our league on that one," she said. "We don't have the time and resources."

"We'll do our best with what we have," Ray said. "You can process the scene and then ask your friends at the Bureau for guidance."

As they neared the Talmadge cottage, he changed the subject. "The two entry doors are locked tight, and I couldn't find a key. I want to check the cellar door." He looked over at Sue. "Did we get the search warrant?"

"We're good. I have the copies," she said, stopping to pull them out of a shirt pocket. "You might want to keep this with you in case someone demands to see it, even though that's highly unlikely."

"How about the autopsy?" asked Ray.

"Talmadge's body is still in transit to Kalamazoo."

Ray stood for a long moment. "I was thinking," he said.

"I noticed."

"That blow to the head, pre- or postmortem injury? In the first case, we're dealing with a murder, and we've got to start searching for motives. In the second case, we're looking at the abuse of a corpse, and…"

"Motives again," said Sue. "Who was still angry enough to give this old man one more whack, whether he was dead or alive? We're looking at a transient cast of characters, some of whom may be long gone. Had Talmadge harmed one of these people in some way? Was this harm real or imagined? Was it motivated by a recent event or something that happened decades ago and is now difficult or impossible to uncover? Do you think what happened to Talmadge is connected to the burglary?"

"I don't know," Ray said. "It's certainly possible. Let's look around back of the cottage. These old places often have a basement entrance. Scott dragged me away before I had a chance to check that."

As they started to circle the building made of stacked limestone, Sue said, "What a beautifully constructed old place. When do you think it was built?"

"Hard to say. Maybe the 1920s or 1930s. It looks like a Cotswold cottage. Did you ever see the one in Greenfield Village?"

"I was there with my sixth-grade class, but all I remember is that everything there was really old."

"I'd guess sometime in the '20s, definitely before WWII." He stopped and gestured toward the stones held together with mortar. "The masonry construction, that's really unusual up here. The honey-colored limestone, it's unique. I wonder where it was quarried. It's not local. Maybe not even domestic. Someone spent serious money on this place."

Sue looked over at the new house. "And then someone else came along and spent serious money to cut off the view from this house."

"Yes," said Ray. "And if this ends up looking like murder, we need to start with Alice Ingersolle."

"Here's what I'm looking for," he said. He bent and carefully lifted the right panel and then the left panel of the slanted cellar doors set in their own stone foundation abutting the house. A damp, musty smell rose out of the stairwell. "You probably didn't have one of those growing up in Livonia."

"Elkins."

"My grandmother had one in her old farmhouse. Real spooky. She used to tease me by saying if I wasn't good, she was going to lock me down there."

"You never told me your grandmother was so mean."

"I think she knew it gave me a thrill," Ray said, flashing a brief grin that gave Sue a glimpse of the boy he had been. "They're the perfect hangout for insects, rodents, and snakes. You never know what you'll find. Sometimes I would open one of the cellar doors just to see what critters were hanging out there."

"Go for it. I'll stay here and cover you," said Sue with a wry smile. She rested a hand on her sidearm.

They looked down the cellar steps and saw that at the bottom a dingy, weathered door in the basement wall stood ajar. The window in the upper half of the door was broken near the center. Some pieces of glass remained stuck along the sides of the frame. Ray descended the steps.

"New damage or something that's been there for a while?" asked Sue.

"No idea," Ray said.

"The owner of the house is dead under suspicious circumstances," Sue said, "so I think we have to treat it as a possible crime scene."

"I agree," Ray said, climbing out of the cellar.

Sue handed him the paper bag. "Here's a grilled tofu on whole wheat and a tall green tea, no sugar," she said.

"What about you?" Ray asked.

"You know me," Sue said, "I couldn't wait, so I ate on the boat.

While you're eating, I'll start checking for fingerprints on and around the door. I'll look for shoe prints, too."

"Bet you've never done a casting in mouse droppings before," he said.

"Elkins, just eat. Then put on a Tyvek suit. There's a headlamp for you, too."

Twenty minutes later, after Ray had enjoyed his sandwich and pulled on the protective suit, Sue climbed up the stairs.

"Anything?" he asked.

"I got a few partials," she answered, returning materials to one of the toolboxes. "They might be more than forty years old, or maybe we got lucky. The ones on the interior door handle, the position of the prints, they're sort of consistent with reaching in from outside the door. Not great prints, but maybe enough."

"The shoe prints, anything worth casting?" asked Ray, pointing down the stairs to the concrete slab near the door.

"No. I was hoping there'd be a lovely shoe print, perhaps an Air Jordan, but there wasn't much of anything, just a layer of sand."

"The A-J print," said Ray, chuckling. "Funny, the same thing crossed my mind."

"Just think, earlier this spring we didn't know Gull Point existed. And now the place has become our home away from home." Sue gestured toward the basement. "It's really foul in there." She opened the second evidence kit and took out two dust masks and handed Ray one. They put them on, and Sue motioned for him to follow her back down the steps.

"Watch your step, Elkins," she said. "You could be swept away by an avalanche."

They stood together just inside the basement door. There was a narrow path through a pile of collapsing cardboard boxes and other junk to the staircase leading up to the main floor of the house.

"Why do old people do this?" Sue asked.

"And not-so-old people, too," said Ray.

"Yeah, but mostly old. You got a theory?"

Ray gave her a disingenuously innocent look.

"Usually, you have a theory or at least a few lines from a Victorian poet or perhaps some of the wit and wisdom of Jim Harrison that will shed light on the whole situation. And then there's an appropriate line from *Moby Dick.*"

Ray did his best to look pensive. Then he said, "OPP. Other people's problem."

"What are you talking about?"

"Well, eventually, everyone has to accept that immortality is not a likely outcome. So they start rationing time. And when you accept the fact that there's only so much time left, cleaning the basement or emptying the garage, it's going to be someone else's problem, probably the kids. It's the price they pay for their inheritance. And if you don't like your kids, it's sort of a revenge forward. Getting even by leaving a pile of junk for them to clean up."

"Revenge forward. Did you just make that up?"

"Yes. It's good, isn't it?"

"In this case, who's getting revenged forward? I'll add that to the list of things we probably need to know about Talmadge. Let's get going."

Ray followed Sue's lead through the labyrinth of decaying detritus to the foot of the interior staircase. She paused there to take some photos. The flash from her camera revealed bits of the basement a few milliseconds at a time—long discarded remnants of several lives decaying in a dark and damp cellar.

They ascended the stairs and scanned the clean and well-ordered kitchen.

"If someone did break in," Ray said, "they didn't trash the place. At least not this room."

"Damn," said Sue, starting to fish in her Tyvek suit for a vibrating phone.

Ray listened and tried to guess at what was being said on the other end of the conversation as he looked into the next room, one filled with light from the large windows on the north-and south-facing walls. Paintings of various sizes and shapes covered the other walls, and more paintings sat on the floor, leaning against the walls, stacked three and four deep. Numerous easels, holding large canvases in various stages of creation, took up most of the floor space. The only furniture in the room was a small couch off to one side, its heavy purple upholstery faded in places that caught the sun.

Ray studied the paintings in progress, large landscapes and seascapes. All of them looked familiar, they reflected the land and water of northern Michigan. Some of the canvases were little more than sketches. Others appeared to be completed or close to it. And then there were a few where the images were just beginning to emerge. Now with the death of their creator, they were permanently frozen in a gestational state.

Ray heard Sue thanking the caller and, turning in her direction, his eyes met hers just as she rang off.

"Yes," she said, "we're looking at a murder. Preliminary findings, but enough to go on. Talmadge's injuries from the falling tree were extensive and life-threatening, but they didn't kill him. Someone probably finished him off."

"Probably?"

"Best guess, best science, but not 100 percent. There are too many variables."

"So full employment for expert witnesses at trial," said Ray.

"You're right about that. This is what we're working with. The deceased received a blow that crushed his skull. Nothing was imbedded in the skin, so the object used was relatively clean. But there is the possibility the murder weapon might have ended up with skin, hair, and traces of blood on it."

"If the traces weren't washed away by the rain," said Ray. "Any suggestions as to the type of weapon?"

"Bat, croquet mallet, something like that. What should we do now?"

Sue walked into the large room and moved to Ray's side. "Oh my," she uttered. "This is amazing, just amazing. Look at this work, Elkins."

"Subtle, emotive. A palette of mostly earth tones. Each one explores similar terrain."

"Yes, but it's not so much about the terrain. It's about light, or what's revealed by light. And maybe it's about truth or at least truth for the painter. Maybe different truths. Can you see what I'm getting at?"

When Ray didn't respond immediately, she said, "You're more of a word guy. This is a different way to experience the world. Now look at the painting on that easel." She pointed toward the only easel facing west, the view now obliterated by the mansion.

Ray moved to the front of the canvas, which at first appeared to be blank. The longer he stood, the more he became aware of the texture laid down on the canvas, a careful, subtle design in a shade of off-white. Ray reached out and touched its three-dimensional surface.

"So the message here?" he asked, looking at Sue.

"We can only guess. No light, no work. No light, no truth. I think this was clearly staged to tell a story. I would guess that it's probably been in place since shortly after the mansion went up. If Ms. Ingersolle had come up dead instead of Talmadge, we'd have a prime suspect."

She turned back toward the other paintings. "I love the smells when someone is working with oils. They're earthy, sensual. My painting classes in college…thinking about the life of a painter, it was a dream. And look at this table—a couple of palettes, brushes, tubes of paint, many missing their caps. A bit of a mess, but you get the feeling that the artist was in the midst of the creative process, the cleaning up would come later." Sue looked around the studio and toward the next room. "Oh, Ray, there's so much here. I'll need light, as in electricity, and some background on this man, and someone with the kind of knowledge that's way beyond my undergraduate studio art degree."

"Understood," said Ray. "How does this sound: We'll have this place secured and guarded and come back later when we have a generator and adequate lighting. To keep people away until we're finished, we'll make the whole peninsula a crime scene. In the meantime, we'll start the interviewing process. First on our list: Alice Ingersolle."

21

"This couldn't have been done quietly," said Sue, looking at the damage to the twin doors of the gallery in the mansion. "And why bother using force? I mean, you can open this kind of lock silently with a credit card or a butter knife."

"My thoughts exactly," said Ray.

"Pry bar?" she said, looking at the damage to the doors.

"Yes," he said. "You can see the depression made by the chisel end. The hardware is residential grade. This is not the kind of lock you'd use if you were concerned about security."

"Maybe using this space for business purposes wasn't part of her original plan?" said Sue.

"Makes sense," he agreed. He stood and waited as Sue checked for prints and photographed the damage.

"Well?" he asked.

"Everything was carefully wiped. The perp could have at least left the pry bar behind with a few partials."

After they entered the room, Sue stood near the center for several moments, her eyes carefully sweeping the interior space. "Nice light, especially at this time of day. This is the light that Gerhard Talmadge was deprived of."

"Don't forget, Ms. Ingersolle has a story, too."

"I don't know, Elkins. Spending fifteen or twenty mill to wall off someone you're pissed at." Sue paused. "Okay, sorry. I'm just worn out and grumpy. Let's get started checking the frames. It shouldn't take long."

After they had finished the last one, Ray asked, "What do you think?"

Sue gave him a playful smile. "I think we've got the prints of the person who hung these, the person who placed the matted prints in the frames, probably some prints from the person who packed them for shipping, and none from the person who cut prints from the frames. They were wearing gloves. But we'll check, just to be sure."

"Would you dust the balcony doors, just on the off chance." He stood and watched Sue work.

"Nothing," she said, after dusting the door handles on the French doors.

"Come out onto the balcony," said Ray.

"Great view," she said, standing for a long moment to take in the view of Lake Michigan as he wandered down to the far end of the balcony.

"Come down here. I want you to see something."

She joined him and looked around. "You want me to tell you how easy it would be to use the roof to get in and out of here."

"Yes, exactly, easy. Easy access across the roof to some of the smaller balconies and windows. So why would someone break in in such a crude way? What do they call it when people set up their houses to show? You know, the real estate term?"

"Staging," Sue answered.

"Yes, that's the perfect term. Tearing into the entry doors was a bit over the top. A strong guy could have popped those locks with a good pull. No need for a crowbar."

"And what if the art was removed from the mattings long before this break-in, or maybe the sketches were never here the first place? It's like someone has created a narrative and then left all the clues to make it appear plausible."

Ray dropped onto one of the backless linen couches. "It's really lovely here."

"Come on, Elkins. We need to get you some coffee."

"Can't we just ring a bell?"

"No, Elkins, the butler's got the weekend off."

22

"Circuitous route, Elkins. I'll never know this county as well as you."

"You won't, not ever," he said, "because you didn't spend your teen years exploring all the back roads."

"Aren't we giving Alice Ingersolle preferential treatment? I mean crossing a county line and all."

"On a death notice, no. And she's the first person we need to talk to."

Ray and Sue had learned that the yacht was anchored in the bay near the marina in the next county. They had been advised to call when they arrived, and a tender would pick them up at the fueling area. They still weren't sure who the ship belonged to.

They rolled down the last big hill, the harbor town opening before them. He circled a bit before finding a parking spot near the marina. The small resort village was flooded with holiday visitors on the long weekend. Ray made the call to the boat as they walked toward the marina.

A young woman in khaki shorts and a white polo was securing a rigid-hulled Zodiac as they approached. The name embossed on the right side of her polo was Daria. Looking up, she asked, "You are the sheriff?"

Ray nodded. Had the uniform given him away? He couldn't discern the woman's accent, but it sounded vaguely eastern European. After Daria checked their ID cards, she helped them board the small craft. Sue was seated in the stern to the left of the steering wheel. Ray was in a bow seat, looking back toward the stern.

Daria untied the boat and climbed aboard. "Where's home?" Ray asked.

"Moldova," she answered.

"Are most of the crew from eastern Europe?" Ray asked, and Daria inclined her head to indicate the affirmative.

She started the engine and motored a few hundred yards to a large yacht anchored close to the opposite shore, stopping at a small platform attached to a stairway leading up to the ship's deck. From her seat, Daria attached a stern line, then jumped onto the platform and secured the bow line. She extended a hand to steady each of her passengers as they scrambled off the Zodiac, first Sue and then Ray. As he climbed the stairs to the deck, Ray noticed the name of the ship on the aft end, *Hermes II*. The home port, Grand Cayman, was painted just below in smaller letters.

A second woman in a matching costume, *Sophia* embossed on her shirt, was standing at the top of the stairway. Ray wondered if everyone on the ship wore a label. Other than a somewhat halting, "Hallo," Sophia used hand gestures rather than language to guide them to a table on the aft deck where a small woman waited for them.

It was one of those moments, and there had been many of them over the years since Sue had joined the department, when Ray wished he could communicate with her telepathically. Here he was, standing on the biggest yacht he had ever seen in northern Michigan waters, obviously an oceangoing vessel, with a foreign crew and a home port that was a known tax haven. He was curious about Sue's take on their surroundings.

They sat down across from the petite woman, who was dressed in a sleeveless navy-blue silk dress and high-heeled sandals, her medium-length blond hair perfectly coiffed, her makeup flawless. Ray thought she had to be in her sixties, but she had a trim figure and hardly a wrinkle on her face. She did not greet them or introduce herself.

"Please, sit," Sophia said. She seemed nervous. "Coffee?" she asked as they sat down, and when Ray and Sue each said yes, she went to a counter behind Ms. Ingersolle, poured two cups of coffee, brought them to the table, and then placed a silver tray with sugar and cream within easy reach.

Ray, irritated with Alice Ingersolle's rudeness, took a sip of his coffee before speaking. It was good coffee, of course. He was certain Ms. Ingersolle only had the best of everything. Sue followed his lead, and the only sound for several long moments was the loud clinking of their cups as they set them down in their saucers.

"I assume you're Alice Ingersolle?" Ray finally said.

"I am. And I assume you are the local sheriff," Ingersolle countered.

"Yes, and this is Detective Sergeant Sue Lawrence," Ray said. "I'm afraid I have bad news. A body was found on your property under an uprooted tree this morning. Scott Nelson identified the decedent as Gerhard Talmadge."

Alice Ingersolle displayed no emotion. Ray thought that perhaps Piper Ingersolle had shared the news with her already. But when she spoke again, her tone was dismissive, suggesting that, as far as she was concerned, the interview was over. "I understand. If there's nothing else, Sheriff, I have a wedding to try to pull together."

In the chair next to his, Ray felt Sue's minute twitch.

"We are here for more than just a death notification," Ray said evenly. "Based on early autopsy findings, it appears that Mr. Talmadge may have been the victim of foul play."

"I'm not following," Ingersolle said, her pale blue eyes sharp, her voice tinged with irritation. "A tree fell on him, right?"

"That's correct," said Sue. "Mr. Talmadge was trapped under some branches of a large tree. I was with the search team that found the victim and with the medical examiner who assessed the body."

She turned slightly toward Sue, and Ray studied the thick gold hoop earring that peeked out from her hair. The only lines on her face, at the corners of her mouth, suggested habitual bad humor. The taut muscles in her tanned arms and calves suggested vigorous exercise of some sort. Tennis?

"We believe that he was trapped by the tree as it fell," Sue said.

"But our medical examiner wants a forensic autopsy before he rules on the cause of death."

"This is tragic, I'm sure. And I know you have to fill in all bureaucratic boxes, but what does this have to do with me?"

"The man was your stepfather, correct?"

"One of the few mistakes my mother ever made."

"The incident took place on your property, and we are obligated to ask, what was your relationship with your stepfather?"

"Relationship," she repeated, making a popping sound at the end of the word. She gave Sue a bitter smile. "There was no relationship. I did my best to tolerate the man while my mother was alive. He came into her life long after I had left home. My mother didn't deal well with widowhood. She was lonely. People said Gerhard was charming. Whatever attraction he held for my mother, well, he kept it hidden from me. He was an opportunist, plain and simple."

As she was talking, Ray was listening with one ear as he scrutinized his surroundings and looked through the glass into what he thought must be the main salon, a large open space where he glimpsed gleaming metal and leather-covered furnishings. The walls and ceiling were white. The floor was covered with wide pieces of reddish-brown teak separated by narrow, contrasting strips of lighter wood. The chic interior was flawless. No water glass, or magazine, or book, or any other object that suggested human habitation interrupted the sleek spartan space.

"You were at odds with Mr. Talmadge?" asked Ray, bringing his gaze back to their host. Her blue eyes widened slightly, as though she was startled by his question.

"'At odds,' that's a peculiar way to phrase it. But, yes. I didn't think he was particularly good to my mother, especially during her final years. He was focused on his art and left her care to others. And then, after she died, well, I don't know how to explain it."

Ms. Ingersolle looked away, past the boat and toward the horizon where the blue sky met the blue-green water. Then she looked back at Ray, momentarily dropping her imperious pose and leaning in his direction.

"Sheriff, Detective, I thought he was a real bastard. He lived off my mother for decades, and his presence came between us. And after she died, he tried to steal the property, my property—land that had been in my mother's family since shortly after the Civil War."

"I imagine you had wills and trusts."

"All of the above. But my mother's cognitive abilities were slipping in her last few years. After her death, there was only a handwritten document with some suspicious witnesses. He was the sole inheritor of the property at Gull Point. Fortunately, I had better lawyers and the funds for an extended legal fight. It all ended with a compromise of sorts. He was allowed to occupy the old cottage until his death. At that time, that property, the old cottage, would revert to me or my heirs."

"The property and the contents of the house?" asked Sue.

"Correct. It can't be much. Gerhard came with nothing. I'm sure he ran through most or all of my mother's money over the years."

"We've been told he was still painting and selling his work," said Ray.

"I wouldn't know. My gallery doesn't represent that kind of work." Her tone said that Gerhard Talmadge's paintings were little more than paint-by-numbers. "I would never have shown his work. I'm sure his paintings sold in the local galleries. People want to take a little bit of up north back to Chicago, or Grand Rapids, or Fort Wayne. There's always a market for that bourgeois kind of work."

"Do you know anyone who might have wanted to harm your stepfather?" asked Ray.

"Sheriff, you're not listening. I haven't talked to him in years. And now that he's gone, family heritage be damned, I'm going to have that cottage flattened and hauled away. I'm going to remove anything that might remind me of that SOB."

"Your daughter," said Sue, "was she in contact with Mr. Talmadge?"

"She and her grandmother had an extraordinarily close relationship. My mother's death was traumatic for Piper. After Mother was gone—she died when Piper was maybe sixteen—I sent Piper up to Lake Winnipesaukee for summer camp. I shielded her from my legal battles with Gerhard. And by the time that mess was settled, Piper was an adult with her own life. We've had a 'don't ask, don't tell' policy where Gerhard is concerned."

"Where were you last evening during and after the storm?" asked Ray.

"I was here, on the *Hermes*. And we were in this harbor. Anchored. The captain had been watching the storm move down the lake all afternoon. He wanted a protected mooring. We left my dock at about six o'clock. The party was just getting started. In truth, it looked like they were going to trash the place. I didn't want to see it."

"And was anyone here with you?" Sue asked.

"Scott Nelson," Ms. Ingersolle said. "We were going over wedding details. He got off the ship just before we departed."

"Anyone else?" Ray asked, looking up from his notepad.

"The captain and the crew," Ms. Ingersolle said.

"Do you know if Gerhard Talmadge had any other relatives, people that we should inform of his death?" Ray asked.

"I think I've made it abundantly clear that to me he is just someone my desperately lonely mother dragged home from one of her European holidays."

"We also have to inform you of a robbery at your estate," said Ray, watching for her reaction.

"Robbery? What are you talking about?"

Ray described what Scott Nelson had shown him in the gallery.

Ms. Ingersolle's lips tightened in anger. She gripped the edge of the table and pulled herself forward. "When? How could this have happened?"

"Sometime during the night. Mr. Abato discovered it this morning."

"What exactly was taken?"

"Artwork, prints I believe," said Sue. She described the scene of the crime and shared the fact that no fingerprints were found on the balcony door.

"Where were Sal and Helio when this was happening?" Ms. Ingersolle asked.

"They were reportedly on the premises, providing security and later first aid and then, because many of the windows on the main floor were shattered by the storm, they were keeping an eye on the place in two-hour shifts," Sue said blandly.

"Useless idiots," Ms. Ingersolle said under her breath. She silently mouthed an obscenity.

"We will need written descriptions and, preferably, digital images of the stolen works as part of our investigation," Ray said. "Given the nature of the crime, all the evidence we gather will be passed on to the FBI."

"Sal Abato can provide that to you. Everything is cataloged in a database."

"Yes, Mr. Abato said he would do that as soon as power was back on," Ray said. "But understand that until we have that information, we can't begin our investigation in earnest."

"Fine," Alice Ingersolle said tersely. "I'll print out the images and the descriptions here and have them sent to your facility." She lifted her hand, and Sophia approached from where she and Daria had been standing off to the side. Seemingly unbidden, she took a notepad and a pen from the pocket of the narrow waitress's apron she was wearing and handed them to her boss. Alice Ingersolle scribbled some details onto the pad and handed it and the pen back to Sophia, who then disappeared around the corner.

"Do you have any idea when the electricity and cell service will be restored?" Ms. Ingersolle asked.

"Out to Gull Point, it could be several days for the cell service and probably longer for the electricity. I assume your lines were buried under the roadway that was washed out."

"Great," she hissed. She stood. "Now if there is nothing else, my attention must be with the affairs of the living."

She cocked her head at Daria, who escorted them to the gangway and back onto the Zodiac.

After they docked at the marina and Daria had secured the little boat, Ray asked, "The *Hermes*, does it belong to Ms. Ingersolle?"

"Oh, no, she is rich woman but not that kind of rich. The *Hermes*, it belong to Roman Adamovich, he is one of Ms. Ingersolle's friends. They do business."

"And where is Mr. Adamovich from?"

"Russia."

"Is he on the boat, too?" asked Sue.

"Oh, no. He flies in tonight for wedding." She looked at Sue with her dark almond-shaped eyes. "Will there be wedding?"

"We don't know," answered Sue.

"Ms. Ingersolle, she wants something, she make it happen," said Daria.

23

They walked along the crowded sidewalks back to their parking space in silence, dodging parents pushing strollers, dogs held on short leads, and shoppers with arms filled with packages.

Ray opened all the windows to allow the heat to escape from the vehicle, then started the engine. He pulled onto the main thoroughfare in the three-block-long business district, stopping at each intersection to permit the clusters of pedestrians to cross the road.

"What are you thinking?" asked Sue.

"Lake trout, smoked or fresh?"

"Elkins."

"While we're here, we might as well get some fresh fish for dinner. My brain doesn't work well when I'm skipping meals or eating junk."

"I vote for fresh," she responded.

"That was quite a show, wasn't it," he said, "and right here in River City, so to speak." He pulled into the lot at the side of the fish store. "I'll be back in a minute."

When he finally returned, Sue said, "I thought you said a minute?"

"Place was jammed. That's the last decent fillet. But it's salmon, not trout. I know you're disappointed."

Once Ray had pulled back onto the highway, Sue said, "My mind is reeling. There's just too much to process. The crew, the *Hermes II*, the flag of Grand Cayman. The whole scene. And then there's the enormously wealthy Russian, Roman Adamovich, whoever he is. And what does he do to be able to afford a boat like that? It's all too much. I'm struggling to wrap my brain around the whole thing. Where do we ever begin?"

"We pick up the dog from the sitter," Ray said. "I make a nice meal. We walk Simone at the big lake. You know how she loves Otter Creek. Then I suggest an early night. I want to read, capture some of today's strange events in my journal, and let my brain chew on it while I'm sleeping. We'll get an early start tomorrow and figure out our next steps. How does that sound?"

"Elkins, I'm so beat I don't know if I can do this. Maybe you should just drop me off at home."

"I've already got the fish."

"Okay, but I might just need to crash after dinner. Can I use your guest room?"

Jennifer Bidwell sat in the recliner in her apartment—her shoulder and arm supported by pillows, her discomfort blunted by Vicodin—listening to Linda Wetherbee's end of a phone conversation.

"If you talked with your daughter, you probably know more than I do."

Jennifer watched as Linda paced back and forth in front of the doorway to the small kitchen.

"I understand, I understand," Linda responded to something Alice Ingersolle had said. "And no, I've never had anything happen like this before. Never. Unfortunately, this is a big holiday weekend. All the best wedding venues were booked a year or two ago. As I said from the beginning, I could only accommodate your daughter's wedding because we were using your property."

Linda chewed on a knuckle and listened intently. Then she said, "I'm sorry. I can't rent what's not available."

Linda briefly held the phone above her head, looked at Jennifer with sheer exasperation in her eyes, then brought it back to her ear. "There is one possibility," she said. "If you like, I can check with the National Park Service. At this point, the weather looks good for

Monday. I know this isn't what you planned, but beach weddings can be extraordinary."

She pulled the phone away from her ear again. Jennifer could hear bits of the other side of the conversation.

"At this point, it's all I can offer," Linda said firmly but kindly. "Pulling things together in less than twenty-four hours will still be a challenge."

Linda listened again, for a long time. Finally, she said, "The only option I can think of is food trucks, maybe two or three. They are all the rage now, and the guests can find places to sit on the shore. I have to say, it's one of the most beautiful spots on the planet."

There was another long silence as she listened. Then, finally, "Alice, this is all I can offer. I can try to get you a beautiful spot for the wedding and interesting food and wine. It will be a spectacular wedding. If you want to go with this option, let me know within the next hour, and I'll get started. And Alice, this is not covered by our contract. I'll be billing you cost plus for this."

Linda ended the call and came to sit on the sofa near Jennifer, who looked out from the cloudlike embrace of the Vicodin and saw Linda as a benevolent, magical being superior to most humans. The doctors had confirmed that Jennifer had suffered a torn ligament, which might heal on its own or might need surgery. Linda, upon hearing this news and the probable weeks of physical therapy it would require, had vowed to cover any medical expenses that weren't covered by the business's liability policy, and she had insisted that Jennifer take at least the rest of the week off, with pay, of course. Jennifer felt that, going forward, she would do anything for Linda.

"Do you think you can pull this off?" Jennifer asked.

"With luck," Linda said. "We can pull in some favors from the food truck people—we've thrown a lot of business their way. On the last day of a long weekend, I'm sure we can find an available beach, and the weather forecast is okay."

"And if she doesn't call you in an hour?"

"We've fulfilled our contractual obligations and we've been paid. Did we deposit that check?" She winked at Jennifer.

"We did."

"Now, how are you doing? Is it time for another painkiller yet? Do you want me to rent another movie?"

"I'm okay," Jennifer said. "I'm going to try to skip the next painkiller for now. The doctor said I could try ibuprofen. I want to help you see this Ingersolle wedding through. We're only talking about a day."

"How was the salmon?" asked Ray.

"It was perfect. Wasn't it, Simone?" said Sue pulling the Cairn terrier into her arms. "And we've made it through a whole meal without talking shop. Although given how quiet you are, I think you're someplace else."

"I was thinking about a word, one that I've seen in print many times, but I've probably never used it."

"And today's word is?" Sue lifted the pitch of her voice like a game show host.

"Imperious."

"I think of royalty. I assume you're referring to the Ingersolle woman."

"Everything was so strange, from the moment Daria picked us up at the dock, almost like being on another planet. We certainly weren't in Kansas, anymore, Dorothy." Ray pulled out his phone and awkwardly keyed in the word on a phone app, his fingers too big for the tiny keyboard. "According to this dictionary, imperious means 'a: befitting or characteristic of one of eminent rank or attainments' and 'b: marked by arrogant assurance.'"

Sue thought about it and then said, "Makes perfect sense. A king or queen, they don't have to introduce themselves to lesser beings they've consented to give an audience to, even if they're on the afterdeck of a yacht rather than in the throne room. And those two women, Daria and...?"

"Sophia."

"Courtesans?" said Sue.

"Perhaps not." Ray typed the word into the dictionary and passed the phone to Sue.

"Oh," she responded, blushing a bit.

"More like ladies-in-waiting or personal assistants," said Ray.

"Anyway, they were taking in everything. I was watching them. They were alert to Ingersolle's words, her tone, her every gesture. I've never seen anything quite like that before. Who commands or deserves that kind of attention?"

"A person who can improve your life in unbelievable ways, on a whim, if you're willing to pay the price," answered Ray.

24

Early Sunday morning Sue settled into her usual place at the center of the conference table, coffee mug to her right, laptop open in front of her. Her eyes moved over the large new whiteboard that covered one wall of the room, an addition that had been part of redecorating after the fire the previous December.

"Elkins, I know I did specify a bigger board than the one that was here, but I was surprised when I saw this jumbo specimen. At the time, I wondered if we'd ever need that much space. Now I don't think it's big enough, not for this case."

"Let's start with search warrants," Ray said, arranging a stack of pages from a legal pad covered with his untidy scrawl, thick lines from one of his fountain pens.

"Like I told you, all homes and outbuildings on Gull Point Peninsula are approved," Sue said. "Also, warrants for any phones and computers that Talmadge might have had."

"Did you see any?" he asked.

"No, just hoping."

"Vehicles," said Ray. "I saw at least two stranded there after the road washed out."

"I'll have those added."

"We will also need to get access to any surveillance video. Nelson says the equipment is all out of date, but it's better than nothing. Maybe we'll get lucky."

"How far back?" she asked.

"At least a week, possibly two. I'd like to have the seven days leading up to the incident. A week's worth would give us a sense of the normal flow of activity on the peninsula. The security company is out-of-state. Scott Nelson can give you the contact information.

The real challenge is going to be trying to find a way to process all this digital material."

"I've been thinking about that," Sue said. "Why don't we pull Barbara Sinclair off road patrol and let her work on that task? She's excellent at detail work. Initially, I'll work with her on identifying the central cast of characters."

Sue circled the conference table, moved to the whiteboard, and started a list of names:

Gerhard Talmadge
Scott Nelson
Alice Ingersolle
Piper Ingersolle

"The two security guys?"

"Yes," said Ray. "Sal Abato and Helio Lopez."

Sue added their names. "Anyone else?"

"Ask Sinclair to look for people who were on-site a lot in the days just before the big event. You know, like electricians, lawn people, wedding planners, caterers, etc., anyone who might be suspicious or who might have noticed anything usual. Special focus on Gerhard Talmadge and anyone who might have been visiting his house."

"I'm sure she will extend our list of people to interview. Okay, if I authorize overtime?"

"Absolutely, whatever she needs."

"Let's do Nelson first," said Sue.

"Then security guys next, and how about Piper Ingersolle?"

"Yes," said Ray. "She doesn't share her mother's rancor toward Talmadge, but I wonder if she shares the same world view."

"That was delicately put," said Sue. "I suppose we'll find out. But before we do any of these interviews, I want to process the Talmadge cottage. Maybe we should interview Piper Ingersolle there. I want her to go through the interior with us, to tell us if there is anything obviously missing. When do you think they will have electricity back on?"

"A week or more," said Ray.

"We'll need a remote area lighting system. I'll bring one over with me," said Sue. "Let me get started processing the interior. We should also ask Scott Nelson if anything else on Ingersolle's property has been disturbed or gone missing."

"I'm not sure how much of what he tells us is true," said Ray. "I think what comes out of his mouth is carefully curated for his audience."

"I've had that feeling from the beginning. That night he made me dinner, I felt like I was getting felt up in a touchless kind of way. You know what I'm saying."

"A mixed metaphor?"

It wasn't difficult for Sue to persuade Ray to stop at the Last Chance for a quick lunch on their way to catch a boat for Gull Point.

Just after their food was served—a burger for Sue and a salad for Ray—Ray said, "Stu Baker just walked in."

"Good old Stu," Sue said, with little enthusiasm in her voice. Stu was a renowned painter, famous not just in Cedar County but in national art circles. Sue had in the past observed that, as a big fish in a little pond, Stu assumed everyone in town would be riveted by his rambling stories, which she admittedly found tiresome.

"Do you think he might have known Gerhard Talmadge?" Ray asked now.

Sue's eyes lit up. "Yes," she said. "What are you waiting for? Invite him over."

Ray stood and waved Stu over, and the older man greeted them enthusiastically and settled in the chair to Ray's right.

"What's happening with your gallery?" Ray asked, referring to the arson that had destroyed Stu's art studio the previous December. "Did you ever get things sorted out with the insurance company?"

"Sorted, yes, after a fashion," Stu said, leaning his tall, thin frame into the table. "I got jacked around a lot at first. Finally, the company wrote the building off, and I had to settle for cash. I'm in the process of moving down the road to the old school. Shared space. I think it will be okay."

Ray nodded. "I wonder if you've heard about what happened out at Gull Point on Friday night."

Stu's brow furrowed. "I don't think so. Should I have heard something? Sorry, my memory's not what it used to be."

Ray nodded. "Gerhard Talmadge was killed. We're actually investigating his death."

Stu frowned deeply. "That's terrible," he said. "I haven't seen Gerhard in years. I didn't even realize he was still in the area. Do you know if he was still working? Have you seen his paintings?"

"Yes," Ray said.

Sue nodded. "They're stunning. Did you run in the same circles at any point?"

"We were never friends," Stu said. "When I was coming up, I thought of him more as a rival. I've always envied his skill with oils, and I never understood why he wasn't better known. The art world is nothing if not fickle and unpredictable."

"Would you be willing to tell us what you remember about him and his family?" Sue asked, pulling a small pad and a pen from her pocket.

"Of course," Stu said. His face took on a stricken look, as if the fact of Talmadge's death was just reaching his conscious mind.

"Do you need a moment, Mr. Baker?" Sue asked. "Can we get you a beer?"

"I'd appreciate that," Stu said, leaning his elbows on the table and holding his head in his hands.

Sue summoned their waitress, who brought Stu a pint of a local IPA.

"I'll bring your cheeseburger, Stu," the waitress said.

"Thanks, Dot," Stu said. When the waitress left, Stu said, "I never order here. I just catch Dot's eye when I come in."

Stu drank from the pint. "I'm sorry, what was the question again?"

Ray and Sue exchanged a look. Stu had been an important source of background information on the Patozak/Osmann case, and they had noticed then that he had been exhibiting signs of memory loss, perhaps even the beginning signs of dementia.

"Gerhard Talmadge and the Ingersolle family?" Ray prompted gently.

"Right," Stu said. "The Ingersolles and their old family cottage, what a place. I mean it wasn't the Ingersolle cottage back in the day. It was Irene's family name. I can't remember any more what that was. But Henry, his people were gallery people big time. Not like us locals. I mean high end. New York. International connections. Old masters and modern art. Irene and Henry Ingersolle started summering at the cottage at Gull Point after her parents passed. Then he died and a short time later Irene married Gerhard. He was younger than she was, maybe by a decade, and I think the marriage was a scandal in the family. The rumor was that he was after Irene's money."

"Did you see any evidence of that, Stu?" Ray asked.

Stu shook his head. "Not at all. They graced us with their presence—and their sponsorship—at several local shows over the years, and they were totally in love. They ended up retiring up here. As I remember it, Irene's daughter had taken over the gallery business by then. Gerhard's work was incredible—big moody landscapes. Too expensive for this market, even for most of the summer people. I remember his work selling out east, maybe even abroad, but it never took off the way I'd expected it to."

"Anything else you remember about him? Did he have any enemies in the area?" asked Ray.

"There was a crazy rumor—"

Stu's narrative was interrupted as Dot set a cheeseburger in front of him. "Thank you, Dot," Stu said. He became absorbed with putting ketchup on his burger and taking a large first bite.

"The crazy rumor?" Ray pressed.

Stu looked perplexed.

"You said there was a crazy rumor about Gerhard."

"Oh, yeah," Stu said, but then he took another bite of his burger, and Ray and Sue had to wait again for him to chew and swallow.

In his peripheral vision Ray could see Sue, and he could tell she wanted to roll her eyes. Of course, she was too professional to do so.

Finally Stu said, "Local artists up here usually make a pretty good living during the tourist season, summer into fall, but in the winter, resources are scarce, and people get hungry. I don't know if there's any truth to it, but the story is that some of them did sketches for Gerhard to make some cash."

"I'm not following," Ray said.

"Sketches," Stu said. "You know, van Gogh, Degas, maybe Picasso, names you'd recognize if you had Art 101. They weren't exact copies, more 'in the style of.' Nothing signed. No provenance."

"Sketches Gerhard could sell as if they were the real thing?" Sue asked.

Stu nodded. "He would have them use old paper, or at least old-looking paper, stuff he brought in. To scam middling art collectors. The story was that he would sell them to art gallery curators, and then a clever gallery salesperson could hint that the sketches might be more than they were."

"More than they were?" Sue said. "They weren't anything. They weren't old and they weren't sketches by van Gogh or Picasso. That sounds like fraud."

"Wait, wait," Stu said. "No one ever said they were the real thing. There was just the suggestion—just the sizzle, not the steak. No crime there—really just a joke. The sketches were original... fakes. Something nice to frame and hang on the wall. Money for the artist, the gallery, and the middleman, and a novelty for the art collector, something to show off to company. There was no big money in it. Gerhard could get two, three thousand bucks for each one, at the most. Enough to get a starving artist through the winter, anyway."

"And you're saying Gerhard Talmadge was the ringleader for this scam?" Sue asked. "Who did he sell the sketches to?"

"I don't know," Stu said. "I just heard about it. Something to talk about over a few beers. Someone told me he'd give the artists printed sketches to work from and any necessary materials. He didn't take them all, but he'd pay cash for the ones he accepted. I heard he always paid with crisp hundred-dollar bills, but who knows if that's true."

"Did you ever hear anything else about Talmadge?" Ray asked. He waited as Stu washed down the last bite of his burger with a swallow of beer.

"Yeah, one more thing. Remember Roxie? What was her last name?" Baker looked toward the ceiling as he did a memory search. "Roxie, she did installation art, giant cobwebs made of rope strung between trees. Tall redhead. She was kind of crazy. Stalked ex-lovers. Did bizarre shit. Got in trouble with the law. I heard she moved south somewhere."

"Never on my radar," answered Ray. "She must have been before my time."

"Well, anyway. I was smoking with Roxie one night. You know, the stuff that's legal now. She got to talking about Talmadge and how he had some valuable paintings stashed in that big old house. But she also said he had a good security system to keep anyone from getting the idea that they could come in and take them."

"What do you mean by 'valuable paintings'?" Sue asked.

Stu shrugged. "Now that I think about it, I'm not sure what she meant. I'm sure she was just making it up that he had smuggled paintings over from Europe."

"Well, if it was true," said Sue, "how would Roxie have known?"

"She said she…aah…well…" Stu lowered his eyes, embarrassed. "She always bragged about who she had shagged. At the time, it was a good story." He shook his head. "I'm sorry to hear Gerhard's gone."

Ray and Sue shared a charged look across the table as Stu finished his beer.

Then the older man stood. "Thanks for the beer," he said. "And Sheriff, I only had one. I'll walk a straight line to the gents', and a straight line out of here. Good seeing you two." He shook Ray's hand, bowed to Sue, and disappeared into the lunch crowd.

25

Ray commandeered a wheelbarrow from Gerhard Talmadge's garage and used it to transport the remote lighting system from the beach to the cottage. A more thorough search of the cellar revealed little more than a pile of old suitcases bearing Gerhard and Irene Talmadge's names and stickers from European destinations.

On the main floor of the house, Ray waited for Sue as she photographed each room, taking care not to disturb anything as they went. In the kitchen, they noticed the scarcity of food and concluded that Talmadge must have eaten out at least some of the time.

"We need to talk to people in local restaurants. Talmadge had to be a regular somewhere," Ray said.

"Yes, I'll add that to the list. We'll need a recent picture of Talmadge," said Sue as she scribbled on a small notepad.

They checked the drawers and cupboards in the kitchen. One of the drawers was crammed with mail. "What do you have?" asked Ray, watching Sue flip through the envelopes.

"Bills, bank statements, and the usual assortment of junk stuff."

"Bag it on the way out. We need to know about the financial side of this man's life. He's probably got financial stuff somewhere else in the house. You know, check books, brokerage statements. We need to grab that, too, when we find it."

Then they moved into the large studio.

After Sue had photographed Talmadge's studio they walked through a set of double doors into a long hall that ran from the front entrance to the back wall. A faded and threadbare oriental carpet ran almost the length of the hall. The walls were light yellow.

Five picture hooks were evenly spaced along one wall. Rectangles in a darker shade indicated where the framed material had previously hung. They walked down the hallway at a museum pace, absorbing what wasn't there.

Not touching the surface, Sue ran her finger around one of the rectangles. "Five frames, all the same size, pieces of art or photos. Did they suddenly go missing or were they removed years ago?"

"I was wondering the same thing," said Ray.

The three doors on the opposing wall of the hallway stood open. Moving toward the front door of the cottage, they looked around each room. Two bedrooms, one larger than the other, were separated by a bath.

"So this was Talmadge's bedroom," said Sue as she peeked into a closet in the larger bedroom that was filled with men's clothes. She inspected the neatly made bed. Turning to Ray, she said, "Still no sign that whoever broke in was searching for something."

After Ray and Sue checked the smaller bedroom and the bath, they moved to the second story, where they found three bedrooms, all smaller than those on the first floor. Each one was filled with unframed paintings, leaning against the walls in stacks of three or four or more. Furniture—beds and dressers and chairs—were pushed against one of the walls. They found a few articles of clothing and a jumble of hangers in the closets of each of the rooms.

"These all look like Talmadge's work. He must have been incredibly productive," said Sue as she leafed through one stack of paintings. "But they're different from the ones downstairs, his newest work."

"How so?" asked Ray, coming to her side.

"These landscapes are much more realistic. They're about objects—ridges, forests, buildings. The paintings in his studio, the ones on easels, were more about light. Nothing was clearly defined."

"I see what you're getting at," said Ray. "Do you think he was taking his art in a new direction?"

"I don't know. Possible."

"He was eighty years old. Maybe he had cataracts," said Ray.

They entered a large bathroom, complete with a clawfoot tub, pedestal sink, and tiny white octagonal tiles on the floor. "This has got to be 1920s plumbing, perhaps earlier. Look at the heavy faucet and valves. You can probably date the cottage by the plumbing."

"Yeah, I've never seen anything like this stuff," Sue said, looking around appreciatively. "These little tiles are cool." Turning her attention to Ray, she said, "So what have we learned, other than that, for an elderly man living alone, Talmadge was a pretty good housekeeper?" She let the question hang as she walked out of the bath and moved to a sitting area near the stairwell at the front of the house. The view from the windows was blocked by the solid back wall of the neighboring mansion.

Sue dropped into a rattan chair and looked at Ray. "Nothing out of place, nothing rifled."

They were used to seeing places pulled apart, the contents of drawers dumped onto floors, bookcases emptied, cupboards rifled, furniture slashed and broken.

"What's going on? I mean, it looks like a break-in, the window and all."

"Yes, but we can't say for sure when that happened. Talmadge might have locked himself out. He might have smashed a window to get in and never gotten around to getting it fixed."

"Possible, Elkins, but my gut says no. I think we should run with the idea that there was probably a break-in and that it took place after his death. And if we accept that possibility, then we have to consider the rumors Stu Baker heard about Talmadge. What if the perp walked in, grabbed what they wanted, and left?"

"Let me muddy the waters even more," said Ray. "What if they broke in and discovered what they were after was already gone?"

26

Ray jotted down the plate number of a dark green Subaru Forester sitting on a paved parking area directly across the drive from the garage. A pine grove partially hid the building from the main house.

The garage, a brick and stucco structure, was constructed of the same materials used in the main building. Four double garage doors and a steel entry door faced away from the mansion, toward the access road and the woods beyond.

Ray was checking the doors of the vehicle as Scott Nelson approached. They were all locked.

"Anything I can help you with, Sheriff?" asked Nelson.

"This car, do you know the owner?"

Scott squinted at the vehicle. "It might be Jennifer Bidwell's."

"And she is…?"

"She works for Simply Romantic, the wedding planner. They're doing the local arrangements for Piper's wedding. I've been meeting with her for the last few weeks, checking and rechecking all the details." He smiled sheepishly. "Now I understand why people elope."

"Ms. Bidwell, was she here Friday night?"

"Yes, she was. Simply Romantic was taking care of the local transportation, and Jennifer was greeting busses, keeping count or something, and directing guests to the food and music."

"Was she injured during the storm?" asked Ray.

"Yes, one of the walking wounded." Scott tapped his right shoulder with his left hand. "She had some kind of shoulder injury. I don't know how serious it was. I need to reach out to her." Ray regarded Scott for a long beat, then asked, "The cleanup, how's that going?"

"Nowhere. Nothing's going to happen till after Tuesday. I should be grateful that the cell service is back up, but I'm not."

"How's that?" asked Ray.

"You won't believe this. I just had a call from Ms. Ingersolle, and she wants me to get a temporary bridge in place, bring in emergency generators or have the utility string new lines, get necessary repairs made to her house—today. She has this wild fantasy that I can make that all happen, so she can still have the wedding here tomorrow.

"I literally had to cover the phone because I was laughing out loud. I told her it isn't going to happen today, tomorrow, or even next week. Maybe in a month, if we're lucky, but definitely not this weekend. I said, 'Fall weddings can be lovely.' Boy, did that not go over well." Nelson stared out at the lake, then back at Ray, a steely expression in his eyes. "My tenure here may be coming to an end. She seems in the mood to shoot the messenger."

"She can hardly hold you responsible for—"

"That's just the point, Sheriff, she thinks you can make anything happen if you throw enough money at it. When an employee can't do the impossible, they get sacked. I saw it happen when this place was under construction. I've been lucky. I've never been in the line of fire before."

"Well, I'm sorry to hear it," Ray said. "While I have you here, may I ask you a question?"

"Sure," Scott said.

"You mentioned that you hadn't seen Gerhard Talmadge around in recent days."

"Right."

"Sometimes people remember things after I've talked with them the first time. A day or two later, I'll get a call, 'Hey, Sheriff, remember when I said….' I'm sure you've had that experience."

"I have, yeah, but in this case, I just hadn't seen Talmadge around. That doesn't mean he wasn't around. But I didn't see him around the grounds or taking walks in the woods as he sometimes likes to do."

"I understand," said Ray. "The yacht, the *Hermes II*, have you been on the boat?"

"Once, just briefly. Ms. Ingersolle called me over to check on some details concerning the wedding, things that don't really matter anymore. She's a compulsive micromanager when it comes to this wedding."

"When was that?"

"Friday night, just before the party started. She planned to spend the night cruising on the boat. She didn't want to be around for the party."

"Why?"

"She likes order and quiet. She didn't want to see her place getting trashed. She told me the party was Piper's idea."

"Has that yacht ever been here before?"

"Never. Other boats, yes, but not that monster. It arrived around noon on Friday and left around 6:00 p.m. I guess it belongs to one of her friends or business associates. He was coming to the wedding and Ms. Ingersolle's special art event next week."

"These special art events, what can you tell me about them?"

"With Ms. Ingersolle, it's all about the need to know. My job is to keep the estate running, lawns cut, everything in repair. I don't need to know anything about her art business. Nothing is shared with me by her or her other employees.

"When she and her guests are here," Nelson continued, "we're to be invisible as much as possible. If they need a driver, it's usually Sal. All the artwork—the unpacking, installing, removing, and repacking—is looked after by someone from her New York staff."

"So you never saw the artwork that was stolen?"

"No, just the empty frames on the floor in the gallery. And I was there at Sal's invitation. If I happen to see any of the guests at one of these affairs, it's usually from afar. It's all rather mysterious."

"I can imagine you speculate a bit."

Scott looked slightly abashed. "Oh, yeah. I've read too many books and seen too many movies. I've created a James Bond scenario. Ms. Ingersolle and her guests work for SPECTRE. They're on a campaign to steal all the art from the greatest museums in the world and redistribute it to the oligarchs in Russia, China, the Gulf, and maybe Texas, too."

"What's their motive?" asked Ray.

"They're nouveau social Darwinists. They've decided that since they are the richest people on the planet, they must be the most highly evolved. Ergo, they should be surrounded by the greatest works of art, since they can appreciate the art so much more than lesser beings."

"Are these SPECTRE people trying to corner the market on all the great literature, too? I guess that would be first editions and antique manuscripts."

"No, reading isn't their thing. Reading is passé. They like visual art, vintage Ferraris, Strads—not that they can play them. They want things you can show off. Books are all about ideas. How do you show off an idea?"

Ray started to reply, then shifted gears.

"The security office—is that only used when Sal is here?"

"Essentially."

"Do you have access to the office?"

"Sheriff, I have access to everything. It's necessary for my job."

"So you would have a key to the gallery?"

"Yes, but the house is essentially off-limits when Ms. Ingersolle is in residence. I'm not to enter the main building unless summoned."

"And does that happen?" Ray pressed.

Scott thought about it. "I can remember her calling me once, and then I was only in the kitchen. I needed to bring in a refrigeration guy to repair the big walk-in."

"Sal, where is he now?"

"Last I saw him, he was sulking on the patio near the kitchen with Helio. Ms. Ingersolle really tore into him, too. He was messing with his laptop, trying to use his cell phone as a hub. Maybe he was trying to update his résumé."

27

Ray found Sal Abato on the patio, holding a cigarette in one hand and a steaming mug of coffee in the other. His eyes narrowed slightly as Ray approached, perhaps against the rising smoke from his cigarette.

"Why didn't you tell me about Gerhard Talmadge?" he asked in an accusatorial tone, cocking his head.

"I did," Ray responded.

"You didn't say anything about the cause of death being suspicious."

"Death notices first, that's probably SOP everywhere, including New York, right, Mr. Abato? I take it you talked to your boss this morning."

"Yeah, the damn phones are working again. Ms. Ingersolle, she tore me a new one over the missing paintings, only then did she mention the suspicious death."

"People have different priorities," said Ray.

"Yeah, priorities. That's a rather innocuous way of talking about it," said Sal before pausing to take a long drag on his cigarette. "How's the investigating going?" he asked, exhaling spurts of smoke with his question.

"It's going," said Ray.

"I know what that means," Sal said. "Been there, done that. I was a detective before I retired from the NYPD. What you're saying is that you don't got nothing yet."

Ray nodded.

"You probably did your share of homicides, but I don't guess you've ever investigated an art theft."

"True," answered Ray. "We've sent a formal request to the

Bureau for assistance. We'll depend on their expertise. At this point, all we can do is process the scene and keep it secure."

"Yeah, and you've done that. I've seen your people lurking about."

"Right. Maybe you could help by sharing some of your expertise on art crime," said Ray.

Sal took another deep pull from the cigarette, then exhaled as he crushed the butt under a shoe, picking up the remains and dropping them into his now empty coffee cup.

"I can't really say I know a lot about art theft," he said, "but I know a lot about building security. I do my best to try to protect Ingersolle's business. I try to be proactive."

"How so?"

Sal glanced out at the lake, which was glittering blue in the sunlight, then looked back to Ray. "Smash-and-grab, for example. Back in the day when we were having a show for a painter, we'd have samples of their work in one of our front windows before and during the show. Then it came to my attention that several European galleries were being hit by smash-and-grab robberies." Abato lit another cigarette.

"So what changes did you make?" pressed Ray.

"We didn't change a thing. At least it didn't look like we changed anything, other than putting cameras around and making them real obvious. The big change was the pieces of art on display. Instead of the real stuff, we substituted high-quality copies, framed just like all the pieces in the show."

"Where did you get that idea?" Ray asked.

"Well, I don't mean to brag, but it was something I thought up," Sal said.

"Anyone smash and grab?" Ray asked.

"Just once. Word spreads fast in the criminal community. Articles in the *Daily News* and the *Times* didn't hurt, either." Abato smiled. "The trick, Sheriff, is to guess what the bad boys will try next."

"Do you have a background in art?" asked Ray.

"One course at City College. You know, a humanities requirement for graduation. Some old broad waiting for retirement showed us washed out slides from European museums she had taken over the years. She had a reputation for passing everyone who attended her lectures and failing those who didn't. The woman took roll at the start of every class. I was there every time, front row center."

"So how did you get the job with Ms. Ingersolle?"

"After I left the force in 1998, I got a gig with an insurance company, loss prevention. Something my wife's sister's husband made happen. You know how that goes—family welfare. Help a cop to a better life.

"Ms. Ingersolle, she was insured with the company. I did a study of her business after they had a couple of high-end pieces go missing. By that time, my company was ready to cancel her coverage. I got to tell you Sheriff, the advice I gave Ms. Ingersolle wasn't rocket science. I mean, their idea of security at the gallery wasn't much more than locking the front door at night. I started by recommending that they install an up-to-date alarm system and a CCTV. And then I hooked her up with an HR consulting firm to get background checks on all her current employees. When you hire felons, you can expect a lot of in-house shrinkage. I also suggested that she have the same firm do background checks on all prospective employees. I laid out everything she needed to do. Put things in rank order—you know one, two, three—in an action plan. She thought I was some kind of genius. She immediately tried to hire me. I put her off for a bit, thinking I should be loyal to my company. But, hey, when she offered more than twice my salary…"

"So if Ms. Ingersolle took all of your suggestions for her New York gallery, why are things so lax up here?"

"You tell me, Sheriff. She treats Gull Point like another planet. That and these special sales just started a few years ago, one or two a year. And she seemed to think that as long as she brought me along, everything would be cool. And it was, until Friday night."

"These special events, what can you tell me about them?"

"She's never told me anything, but I'm sure the people she invites come from a carefully vetted pool of customers. And by vetted, I mean big bucks. From what I've observed, they're mostly foreign. You don't hear much English. Ms. Ingersolle, I can't guess how many languages she speaks, some of the staff, too. The customers, they're mostly men. And they don't come alone. They have an entourage of advisors in tow."

"How about the art? I imagine it's expensive."

"It's not like the gallery and not like any art auction I've ever seen. There are no prices. No catalog. No bidding. From what I've observed, the transactions are all handled through hushed negotiations and handshakes. And no one is writing checks. It's all wire transfers. I don't quite understand that world, other than it's how rich people move money, probably without having to pay taxes."

"But you must have some idea how much the pieces go for?" Ray pressed.

"Look, Sheriff, these people, they all come in their own private jets. I usually do the airport transportation. Ms. Ingersolle's guests, they are treated like royalty. Her personal chef does all the meals. The wine and spirits are first class. I may not have learned much about art working here, but I've learned a lot from her sommelier, Michel."

Ray wouldn't have been surprised if Sal had winked at him, but instead he lit another cigarette. Ray wondered if he was, like Scott Nelson, worried about losing his job.

"What I'm trying to tell you," Sal said on a stream of smoke, "is no expense is spared. And I think millions of dollars changes hands at these events. Guys like you and me, we don't know how to think about that kind of money. Not that I want it, you know what I mean. I got a good life. But these people live on a different planet."

"So, Mr. Abato, how is it that you and your assistant didn't hear the perps breaking into the gallery?" Ray asked. "They would have made quite a bit of noise tearing that door apart. And then they tore the frames apart and left at a time when no one else was around besides you and your assistant—I've forgotten his name?"

"Helio Lopez. And, Sheriff, please call me Sal. That's what I go by."

"All right, Sal. I'm confused about how this could have happened without your noticing."

"Well, truth be told, I've been thinking about that a lot. I went up and looked at that door. It didn't take much to pop that lock. Maybe a big screwdriver. And if they were careful, it wouldn't make too much noise. Helio and me, we were at the other end of the house or outside. And there was still some wind noise as I remember it."

"Yes, but how about the perps coming and going? There wasn't anyone around but you two guys."

"Yeah, Sheriff, there's that. But Scott Nelson was around, too. What I think happened was this: A couple of people came in with the crowd to case the place for a burglary. They must have been planning on doing it before the showing next week, right? These are people who know about the showing and know the value of the art—they did their homework. I mean, to the average crook, there's a lot to grab around here that looks more valuable than some stuff hanging on the wall. But put that aside for a minute. Low and behold, the mother of all storms hits. The perps recognize it as the perfect opportunity to take advantage of the confusion, and they hide out in the house waiting for an opportunity to do the deed. Or maybe they even did it right after the storm. There were all kinds of people in and out of the house, lots of noise and confusion. People screaming and crying. Of course, I wasn't in a place to see much of anything. As you know, other than a little core where we had some candles going, the house was totally dark. Helio and me had flashlights, but we were focused on helping people, not on protecting the art."

"How about the tools used?"

"Sheriff, near as I could tell, only one tool. If they didn't bring it with them, there's a whole wall of maintenance tools in the garage. These kinds of people are resourceful."

"Did you check the tools in the garage?" Ray asked.

"How did you know?" Sal asked with the glimmer of a smile. He shook his head. "There wasn't nothing missing."

"Where would the perps have gotten information about the show?" Ray said.

"I thought about that, too. It had to start with someone at the gallery in New York. Maybe someone who just has loose lips in the wrong company or someone working with the people who did the deed. Then there's Scott, and you got us, too."

"You and Helio? You said you had kids. A little college money, if you can find a buyer on the black market. Or maybe Helio is trying to buy an apartment in the city."

"Bingo on both of those. But we're still here. And we are well paid for the work we do. My kids got a solid college fund."

"Okay, I'll give you two a pass for the sake of conversation. Getting off the peninsula would have been an unforeseen problem."

"Not really," Sal said. "If they hit the gallery right after the storm, they could have just been part of the evacuation. Cool, right, they do a burglary and the cops send them safely on their way. If they arrived after the storm, they could have paddled over in a canoe. And I walked over and took a look at the access road. Hell, you can wade across. I'd get wet for a few million. And they might have had accomplices, someone with a boat to drop them off and pick them up."

"All great possibilities," Ray said as Sal lit yet another cigarette and turned to blow the smoke away from Ray. "On the other hand, they might have been here all along. I'm back to the inside job. They might have been waiting for the opportunity. They knew where to find a crowbar. They had the luxury of time to break into the gallery and steal the prints. And lots of time to stash them. Come back for the goods when things cool down. Maybe wait till the road is back in so they don't have to get their feet wet." Ray held Sal's gaze. He could see him struggle against the impulse to offer an excuse.

Finally, Sal sighed and said, "It doesn't look good, does it? We're either the crooks or we're total fuckups as security guys. And if we are the crooks, we're total fools to think we can pull the wool over the eyes of some backwoods sheriff."

Ray let the silence hang.

"Sal," said Ray, "I'd like to take a look at the security system cabinet in your office."

Sal crushed out his cigarette and added the butt to the others in his coffee mug. Then he led the way to the security office.

"Hope you got a flashlight, Sheriff," said Sal, pointing to a gray metal cabinet mounted in the wall.

Ray used the flashlight on his phone. He looked at the steel panel that featured an array of switches and ports that held various USB drives. He asked, "These USB drives, they're the backup?"

"Yes. They overwrite every seventy-two hours. If the system was working, there's probably video up to the time the power failed."

"I'd like the USB flash drives," said Ray.

"Do you have a search warrant this time?" Sal asked.

"Yes. It covers all electronic data," he answered, making no attempt to fish for the document. One by one, he removed the flash drives from the panel and dropped them into his pocket.

As they left the office and walked down the hallway, Ray, who was behind Sal, said, "Don't go anywhere, Sal."

"No problem, Sheriff. I plan to do some fishing."

"One more thing," Ray said. "Where is Mr. Lopez? I have yet to see him. I'm starting to think you have an imaginary friend."

"He did the graveyard shift last night. I haven't seen him since he woke me at seven. I imagine he's still sleeping. Do you want me to get him?"

Ray passed Sal his business card. "Please call me as soon as he's awake. I want to talk to him."

28

As soon as he returned to the office, Ray delivered the flash drives from the Gull Point security system to Sue, who was looking forward to, with Barbara Sinclair's help, building a rogues' gallery and a timeline of where in the video each of the key players appeared. "You need to figure out where each camera was mounted. Maybe make a diagram, so Barbara can get the lay of the land."

Ray summarized his conversation with Sal and then said, "I'd like to get this written down."

"Have you checked your messages?" Sue asked.

"Oh, yes, the messages." Ray turned back toward Sue. "What did I miss?"

"Three things: First, more autopsy results. Talmadge had steak, French fries, coleslaw, and beer in his stomach. The food had been ingested an hour or two before his death."

Ray took in the information. "Sounds like the menu being served down at the beach."

"So do you think he and his healthcare aide went down and stood in line with the rest of the guests?" Sue asked.

"That would work. The healthcare aide has a concussion, but maybe he remembers these details from before the storm hit. Or maybe someone saw them watching the party and brought them food and beer. It might have been Scott; he doesn't seem to share his employer's animus for Talmadge. And then there's Sal, who told me he liked talking to Talmadge. And then there are the good old random acts of kindness."

"Maybe we can find the answer on the video," Sue said.

"What's the second message?"

"The weapon, heavy, probably iron or steel, crudely rectangular, approximately three inches across. Here's the drawing he sent. It doesn't show up very well on the screen," she said, passing her iPad to Ray so he could see it. "Anything more?" asked Ray.

She reached out for the iPad, then flipped to Dyskin's message. "'An old hand sledge made of mild steel. The face was about two inches by two inches at the time of manufacture. Now a bit larger, distorted by years of pounding. If you want to see what to look for, come by. I've got one in my garage. You'll probably find one in every garage or barn in the county that predates WWII. The damage to the skull was modest, but enough to dispatch the victim if he wasn't already dead.'"

She looked at Ray. "Does that make any sense to you?"

"Absolutely. A big, heavy hammer with a handle about a foot long. It is the go-to tool when you really need to pound something."

"Like a head?"

"Well, usually it's used when you need a lot of force, to flatten something or drive a stake into the ground. The hammer is heavy and clumsy, not something you'd carry about with you." Ray paused momentarily as he shifted gears. "This was a crime of opportunity. The killer found Talmadge trapped under the branches, maybe Talmadge was shouting for help, but he could have been dead already." Ray paused and put himself in the scene for a few seconds. Flashing back to his memory of the storm, he could hear wind and rain and almost sense the man's fear and pain.

"Given the hammer, Dyskin is suggesting the assailant could have really crushed the skull," Ray said. "I think this person wanted to make sure Talmadge was dead, but they were trying not to be too obvious about it. Maybe they hoped we'd assume all the trauma to the body was caused by the falling tree. Did Dyskin offer an opinion on whether the injury to the head was antemortem or postmortem?"

"He did," answered Sue. "I called him after I got his email. He believes the final report will be inconclusive on the ante or post question. Then he said that it's his best judgment that we should proceed as if Talmadge was murdered and see what we discover in the process."

"Done," Ray said. "And the third message?"

"We need a press release."

"Okay, how about, 'A fatality at Gull Point that appears connected to damage caused by the storm. The death is still under investigation. Updates forthcoming...yada, yada, yada.'"

"Got it," said Sue. "If there's nothing else, I'll write the press release and get Barbara Sinclair started on reviewing these videos."

"And I'll organize a search for the possible murder weapon," Ray said.

"I imagine you'll do the in-water search, Elkins? You're good at hanging upside down in your kayak."

"I'll defer to our younger deputies wearing all the appropriate gear. You know, the stuff that looks good on social media."

"Optics," said Sue. "It's all about optics."

"Yes, and let's head back there for a bit. I want another walk around."

Linda Wetherbee's phone rang. She picked it up off Jennifer Bidwell's coffee table and looked at the screen. She touched the screen then brought the phone to her ear. "Hello, Ms. Ingersolle," she said.

She listened for a long moment, rolling her eyes at Jennifer, then responded, "We have everything in place as per our conversation. I personally went over to the park offices and walked the permit through the process. We're good to go. And the contracts with the food trucks are in place, too."

She listened again for quite some time. Finally, Linda said, "I can't help you with that. Everything is in place and will be onsite at eleven o'clock. And I like your thinking. We'll make either option work. See you tomorrow." Linda ended the call.

"What was that all about?" asked Jennifer.

"It seems that Alice Ingersolle and her daughter, Piper, have had a real falling out. As far as Piper is concerned, having a wedding immediately after her grandfather's death is unthinkable. Alice said she reminded Piper that Talmadge is only her step-grandfather. So the wedding ceremony is up in the air. Alice's closing words, 'In disputes with my daughter, I usually prevail.'"

"Oh my God," exclaimed Jennifer. "What a bitch."

Linda laughed. "Something like that," she said. "Alice said that regardless of the outcome, she is going to have a beach party for her friends and relatives. If Piper decides to tie the knot, everything is in place. If not, Alice hopes a great party will help dull the memory of an absolutely horrible weekend."

"And what's this about a grandfather?"

"The man who was found dead. That's Piper's grandfather. Well, not by blood. He was Alice's mother's second husband. But Piper doesn't think it's appropriate to have a wedding before they get the poor man in the ground."

29

Trevor Thornley lay on the hotel bed, listening to one side of a phone call between Piper, his fiancée, and her mother, Alice Ingersolle. He turned off the muted television when the conversation turned from an exchange of pleasantries to a hostile confrontation, and he rose from the bed and hovered near his bride-to-be when Piper held the phone in front of her mouth and shouted a volley of recriminations at it. She ended the exchange by hurling the device at a nearby couch. Then she collapsed onto the couch in tears. As Trevor moved in to comfort her, she fended him off with a stiff arm to the chest.

"Bitch, bitch, bitch!" she shouted, rising and turning a tight circle and then marching out onto the hotel room's small balcony, then returning and throwing herself onto the bed.

Trevor was unsure what to say or do. Finally, he started, "Is there…?"

He jumped back as Piper rolled off the bed and stood. "It's all about guilt with her, how I owe her everything, with no consideration of the fact that Grandfather Gerhard is dead and that he was probably murdered."

Trevor's hands rose as if to defend himself from the word. "Murdered? I don't understand."

"Who the hell does? Every time I hear that syrupy sweet voice, I know I'm about to be violated by a stream of lies."

Trevor took a step closer to her and opened his arms. Piper moved in, beating on his chest with fists clenched, her hands striking more to release frustration than to hurt. Finally, she sagged into him, and he wrapped his arms around her and held her close.

"What did she mean about your grandfather being murdered?" Trevor asked, his lips moving against her hair.

"It might just be another one of her lies. I have to reach out to the detective who came to tell me he was dead. I have her card here somewhere," Piper said, sniffling. "Who would want to hurt him?"

"I don't know, but that's horrible," Trevor said.

"Mother wants us to go forward with the wedding tomorrow. Her people found a new venue. I love that—'her people.'" Piper laughed bitterly. "We're all in the service of the queen. If we don't go through with the ceremony, she'll just have a party for her friends. We're welcome to invite ours."

She began to sob against his shoulder. "How did we get here?" she asked. "It's like a nightmare."

"Honestly, I don't know," Trevor said.

Piper heard something in his voice that stopped her crying instantly. She stepped back and looked into his face, which bore a stricken expression. "What do you mean you don't know?" she asked, wiping the tears from her face with both hands.

Trevor sat down heavily on the couch. "None of this was my idea. It was something I thought you wanted, but as the date got closer and neither one of us seemed at all excited about the wedding, I started to wonder if you even want to marry me. Tell me if I'm wrong, Piper, but you and I didn't plan this wedding because we were eager to get married. Your mother planned this wedding because she wanted us to get married."

Piper's mouth fell open in surprise.

"I mean," Trevor continued, "everything has been good between us. I'm not sure how our being married will make anything better."

"But you never said anything," she countered, "and we've been engaged for four months." She crossed her arms over her torso, feeling hurt.

"Everyone else was getting married, and it just seemed like something we should do at our age."

For the past couple of years, it seemed that they had spent at least one weekend a month going to weddings—friends from childhood, college, and law school. Getting married seemed contagious. "So yeah, when you brought it up," Trevor continued, "I was okay with the idea. But I never imagined something like this. It's—I'm sorry, but it's like a damned circus."

"When you thought of getting married, you know, when we first got engaged," Piper asked quietly, "what did you think it would be like?"

"I don't know," he said. "Maybe a fall weekend in Vermont, one of those little towns, an outdoor ceremony. Just immediate family and close friends. A nice dinner afterward."

Piper felt a wave of shame wash over her. Trevor was a good person, and she had not taken their relationship seriously or even considered his opinions or his feelings regarding their wedding. "Why didn't you say anything about what you wanted?" she asked.

"I don't know," he said, his shoulders hunching. "I guess I was afraid I'd hurt your feelings." He took a deep breath. "And, honestly, I was afraid to disagree with your mother. I've seen her make other people's lives a living hell."

"How did this happen?" Piper said, more to herself than to Trevor. "I shouldn't blame Mother completely. I was in on it, too. I let it happen."

"I let it happen, too, Piper," Trevor said, "so I have to share the blame."

"I admit, I've been feeling ambivalent, too," said Piper. "But then Friday night, before the storm, I got caught up in the excitement. I thought everything would be okay. I felt real joy. I thought you did, too."

"I did!" Trevor said. "Watching you walk down to the beach looking so stunning. I was living the dream. But then that world vanished," he continued, "and suddenly we were in a horror film. I don't even know how to talk about it. I've never been so frightened. I thought I was going to die. And then I lost you in the darkness, the rain, the wind. For lots of minutes I was afraid you might be dead."

Trevor stopped and wiped away a tear. "It's like we invited all these people to a weekend in hell. And now this, your grandfather, dead. Murdered."

Piper covered her face with her hands. "I don't even know what to do next. I'd understand if you and your family wanted to get out of here as soon as possible." She paused for a beat, then asked, "What should we do about the wedding?" Trevor hesitated, and Piper had her answer.

"It's okay," she said. "We'll talk about it when we get home."

"Yes," he agreed. "We need to have the conversations we've been too busy to have. Or maybe they're the conversations we weren't brave enough to have. Friday night, we could have died. The fact that we survived, it's like we have a chance to reset our lives. For years I've been following a script: go to college, law school, meet the girl of my dreams, get a job in a prestigious firm, start to make decent money. I was checking off all the boxes. But is this the life I really want? I love you, Piper. But I hate New York. Being a lawyer, doing corporate law, the work bores me. Do I want to do something for the next forty years that I don't enjoy in a place I don't want to be?"

"So you're not happy?"

"It's not you, Piper. It's me. After what's just happened, I feel I'm somehow different. I have to imagine what other lives I might live. And I want you to do the same—if you want to. Once we've done that, we can see if our lives still fit together."

30

Ray walked Sue to the beach and watched her board a department boat. He was talking with the head of his marine division, Brett Carty, when their attention was drawn to a private craft, a small runabout, moving into the protected water. The sole occupant, a young woman with long brown hair, sprang out onto the dock, attached bow and stern lines, and did a quick scan of the area before marching in their direction. Ray recognized the woman as Piper Ingersolle. She recognized him, too, and walked purposefully toward him. He saw as she approached that her hair was in disarray from the high-speed boat ride. Her body was tense, her eyes puffy and her nose red.

"Sheriff Elkins," she said. Then she closed her eyes and brought a closed fist to her lips. She held the pose for a long moment, took a deep breath, and opened her eyes again. "Is it true what my mother told me—that my grandfather was murdered?" she blurted before bursting into tears.

"Why don't we sit for a bit," urged Ray. He guided her to a nearby picnic table and handed her a packet of tissues before settling on the opposite side. "We're still investigating the circumstances of your grandfather's death," he said, "but they are suspicious."

"I don't understand," Piper said through quivering lips. "I thought he was killed by the falling tree—and my mother wouldn't tell me anything more. Who would want to kill him?"

"We're not sure," Ray said.

"She fucking *enjoyed* telling me that he was murdered," Piper said, her voice rising with indignation.

Ray remained silent. He thought about his conversation with

Ms. Ingersolle. He wondered about the public face he had seen and the private face, the one that Piper had grown up with.

"So I called her back and told her the wedding was off—but I wasn't that polite. I can't even believe she thinks I would get married under these circumstances. Trevor totally gets it. I let her badger me into it in the first place. That's never going to happen again. Never."

She went quiet and looked at Ray as if realizing for the first time that he was there across the table from her. He noticed how different she was from her mother. She wore simple clothes—shorts, a T-shirt, and worn running shoes—and her face was devoid of makeup.

"I'm sorry," she said. "You probably think you're dealing with a crazy woman. I've just been holding all of this in. Will you tell me what you know about how he died?"

Ray described the massive internal injuries mentioned in the autopsy report, then told her about the skull fracture, the injury that couldn't easily be attributed to the falling tree.

After, Piper sat quietly and wept. Finally, she looked up at him again. "Was he in any pain?"

"I can't answer that question. With the massive internal injuries inflicted when the tree fell on him, he probably lost consciousness instantaneously. I hope that was the case." Then he asked, "You said you last saw him on Friday night, before the storm?"

"Yes, I saw him with the healthcare aide, Nathan, and made sure they had gotten something to eat." She told Ray that she had called the health service and hired Nathan on Wednesday, after seeing how frail her grandfather had become. "I arrived late Tuesday and spent much of Wednesday and most of Thursday with him. His house needed cleaning, and he wanted my help with a couple of tasks. I think more than anything, he wanted my company. I'm so glad to have had that time with him."

"And when did your mother arrive?"

"Friday, late morning. On her friend's yacht."

"Have you met this friend?" Ray asked.

Piper shook her head.

"And your mother left before the party started?"

"Yes. As far as I know she didn't get off the boat, at least not while it was here. We had to queue up for an audience with her. I know that sounds catty, but it's true."

"Who else saw her on Friday?"

"Scott Nelson and Sal Abato."

"Didn't she have relatives or friends coming in for the wedding?"

"Her friends were coming mostly on Saturday. As to relatives, we're sort of the end of the line for the Ingersolles. I never had cousins or aunts and uncles like most kids. The Friday party was ours, Trevor's and mine. Sunday was supposed to be her big production."

"Do you know if your grandfather had any enemies?"

Piper shook her head. "I can't imagine he did. He was a sweet old man. And that was true all through the years I knew him. He was kind and caring. And he was a jokester, too. There was always laughter and joy at their cottage."

"We've looked through his house," Ray explained. "We found a broken window in the basement door. I don't know if that occurred before or after his death. The house didn't appear to have been ransacked. Since you were in there before his death, would you do a walkthrough with me and tell me if anything has been disturbed or is missing?"

"Yes, any way I can help."

As they approached Gerhard Talmadge's cottage, Piper said, "Now that's he's gone, I'm sure my mother will bring this place down, as she's threatened to do so many times. I don't understand her thinking. This place is just magical. I've always loved it."

"Magical is the right word," said Ray. "There's nothing else quite like it in the region. Scott Nelson said you spent summers here when you were younger."

"Oh, Scotty," Piper responded. "We spent some golden summers together. We had a whole gang of friends, and we sailed and hiked and biked and lay in the sun. Back then, I had two lives, my city life—which was all about school and organized activities like music and tennis lessons—and my up north life, where Gram and Grandfather provided me with an easel and paints, concerts and farmers markets, and it was all so casual. Every morning at breakfast, they'd ask how I wanted to spend the day, and they'd help make it happen. And if I just wanted to wander around on my own or read a book, I could do that. As I got older, they expected me to show up for supper, but that was it. And if I wanted to bring five other kids with me, that was fine, too. I was so lucky to have that kind of freedom in this magical place. Gram and Grandfather knew how to deal with a kid. I'm sorry, I'm babbling, but it was so remarkable."

"How many summers?" asked Ray.

"Hmm," said Piper, "I think Mother parked me here the summer after I started school. Sadly, my summers up here ended with my grandmother's death."

"How old were you then?" asked Ray.

"I was sixteen, in high school. That fall, I was a sophomore."

"And you didn't return…?"

"No. After the funeral, my mother went to war with my grandfather about the property. I was so heartbroken—I couldn't imagine being here without Gram. I guess I didn't think of what it must have been like for him, here alone, fighting the dragon that is my mother. I just didn't have the strength to get in the middle of it."

"You were still a child," Ray said. "So you spent your summers elsewhere from then on?"

Piper nodded. "The next year I went to camp at Lake Winnipesaukee." She grimaced. "It was horrible. So the next year, I got a summer internship at a law firm in New York. And that was the end of my childhood. I'm being dramatic, of course, but that is what it felt like. I wrote to Grandfather, and we talked on the phone, but I didn't come back until the summer after Mother built that monstrosity." Piper gestured toward the back of the mansion looming over the much smaller cottage. "Just for a few days or a week at a time, not for the season. I wouldn't stay here in the cottage—my mother would have freaked out—but I did spend time with Grandfather. We'd drive over to Sleeping Bear, have lunch at Art's and dinner at the Last Chance, go to concerts at Interlochen, pick up smoked fish in Leland and have a picnic."

"But when you saw him this time?"

"He seemed so much older, and it happened so quickly. His vision has been deteriorating—he had macular degeneration—but I could see in his more recent paintings that it had gotten really bad. The paintings are okay. There's still form and color, but everything is out of focus. They're more poetic, metaphoric, pointillistic. Let's go into the house, and I'll show you."

Once Piper and Ray were in the kitchen, their hands covered by rubber gloves, Piper looked around and said, "Dishes."

Ray gave her a questioning look.

"The kitchen was a mess. I should have arranged for a housekeeper years ago. On Thursday, over my grandfather's protests, I washed all the dishes and cleaned the counters and the floor. He was still able to vacuum."

She moved to the sink. "These must be Friday's dishes, coffee cups. He seemed to be living on coffee and cookies."

"What did you two do on Wednesday?"

"I'll show you," she said, walking into the studio. Stopping in front of a large partially completed painting, she said, "This was exactly what I was talking about. Everything is rather fuzzy. Now look at these over here." She guided Ray to the back wall of the studio. "This is mostly old work."

Ray walked among the easels, stopping and carefully looking at the older paintings. "I see what you mean. You're sure he wasn't experimenting with a new technique?"

"No. When he showed me that new painting," she pointed, "he was lamenting what he had lost. But he said if he stopped painting, he might as well lie down and die. He seemed depressed and lonely. And in a way, that's perhaps why he was so fixated on giving me a series of photos of Gram and me."

Ray gave Piper an inquiring look.

"Let me show you," she said, leading him out of the studio and into the main hallway. She gestured toward the empty walls. "As you can see, all that's left now are picture hangers. When I used to spend the summers here, every year Grandfather took lots of pictures of

Gram and me. And sometime during the winter, they would select what they thought was the best picture of the two of us, have it framed, and put it on the wall. When I arrived the next summer, there it would be. And I just loved walking past the photos, lingering and studying them. I could see how I was growing and changing year to year, but I could also see or feel—it's hard to explain, the one constant—my grandmother's love."

"And where are the photos now?"

"This is what Grandfather was so focused on when I first saw him on Wednesday. He wanted me to have the photos, and he wanted them out of the house before my wedding. Maybe he felt that he wouldn't live much longer"—her voice thickened with emotion—"and he was thinking of my mother's threat to have this place flattened and hauled away less than twenty-four hours after his death. So we took them down, took them out of their frames, packaged them up, and shipped them to my law office in New York—the mail there is much more secure there than at our apartment. He actually made me drive him to the FedEx store to make sure I shipped them right away."

"What happened to the frames?"

"I put them in the dumpster next to the garage behind the mansion. I didn't think Grandfather would ever get around to cleaning up the mess.

"These photos, Sheriff, they connect me to the two people who were very important to me as I was growing up, especially Gram. Having those pictures hanging in my apartment will be like having her with me every day. She's part of me, and it's more than genetics. She was my adult role model as I was growing up, the person I wanted to be—still want to be. She taught me about kindness, compassion, empathy. And I think honesty, too." Piper paused for a long moment, brought her right hand to her lips, and briefly nibbled at her index finger. Moving her hand away from her face, she continued, "I'm not sure how well I've lived up to the standards she modeled."

Ray let her words settle. Then he looked toward the first-floor bedrooms. "How much of the house were you in on Wednesday and Thursday?"

"The whole place, every room. I even looked in most of the closets like I used to do when I was a kid. I guess Grandfather's sense of impending doom was contagious. I wanted to cement all the memories just in case I never got a chance to come back here again."

"Have you noticed so far that anything is out of place, disturbed, or missing?"

"No," Piper said.

Ray asked her to check the first-floor bedrooms and bath, then he followed her up the stairs as she checked the three bedrooms on the second story.

"Everything seems just the same as when I was here on Thursday," Piper said as she and Ray lingered near the top of the stairs.

"You're sure nothing looks disturbed or is missing?" pressed Ray.

"Of course, I didn't look through all of the paintings up here, so I can't be sure that none of them are missing," said Piper, "but everything looks the same to me."

"You and your grandfather personally took the photos to the FedEx office, the main office in town?" asked Ray.

"Yes, Grandfather insisted on it."

"Did you use your grandfather's car?"

"No, I'm not sure it even starts. He hasn't been driving for a while. I borrowed a Toyota pickup from Scott. It's one of the vehicles that's kept here."

"So how was your grandfather getting groceries, going to doctor appointments?"

"Since he mostly stopped driving, probably Scott."

"Scott didn't mention that," said Ray.

"No, he wouldn't," said Piper. "Scott wouldn't advertise that he was helping Grandfather. He'd be putting his employment at risk."

"Any side trips when you were in town with your grandfather?" asked Ray.

"We stopped at his lawyer's office. Grandfather said it was important for me to meet her. One more way he seemed to know…"

"Did you go into the attorney's office with him?"

"Yes," Piper said. "He'd already had the papers drawn up to give me power of attorney over his affairs. He also told me that I was the sole heir to his estate."

"Was that new information?" asked Ray.

"Not totally," Piper answered. "About a year ago, he gave me medical power of attorney. That's when he was diagnosed with macular degeneration. He said he wanted me to make decisions as necessary. He tried to talk about the estate then, but I wasn't ready for the conversation. This time, he had the lawyer explain to me that I would inherit the contents of the cottage including all of Grandfather's paintings."

"So the estate is worth approximately…?"

"It's hard for me to give you an answer. Other that the paintings, his assets are very limited, some savings and maybe a brokerage account. I know he continues to sell art. Maybe a hundred thousand. I'm just guessing."

Ray turned toward Piper. "Any chance you'll end up in court trying to save this house?"

Piper turned away and started down the stairs. "I don't know," she said. "That possibility is just beginning to seep in. I need to find someone to look through the earlier litigation. It's not a happy prospect. But first, I need to organize a funeral. I know my grandfather wanted his ashes here, where he spent the happiest years of his life."

"I understand," said Ray. "Is there any chance you have easy access to a photo of your grandfather?"

"There's one in their bedroom," she said, "the two of them standing near the lake. I'm guessing that was the last photo of them together before she died. It's old, but his face is very recognizable. He was a very handsome man, and charming, too. I can see how he swept Gram off her feet."

31

As Ray crossed the lawn toward a waiting boat, he replayed his conversation with Piper Ingersolle. He wanted to get his impressions down on paper as quickly as possible.

Several loud shouts drew his attention toward the mansion. Turning, he saw Sal Abato waving at him. Ray stopped and waited as Sal descended the hill. He was accompanied by a second man, younger, taller, and stockier than Sal.

"Sheriff, glad I caught you before you left. This is Helio Lopez. You said you wanted to talk to him."

"Yes," said Ray, looking at the younger man. "Mr. Lopez." he said, extending his hand, which the younger man accepted in a strangely limp grip.

"Helio," Sal said, "tell the sheriff anything he wants to know, capisce?"

Ray suggested they sit at the picnic table near the beach, and as they settled in, Ray set his phone in the middle of the table. "I'm going to record this," he explained.

"Is this an interrogation or something?" asked Lopez, sneering at Ray.

"Hardly," said Ray in a friendly tone. "We're trying to sort out what happened here. Having recordings helps us keep all of the accounts accurate. You okay with that?"

"Go ahead, fire away," Lopez said, his tone less than enthusiastic.

"When did you arrive at Gull Point, Mr. Lopez?" Ray asked, taking in the young man's thick sandy hair and green eyes. Where Sal Abato looked New York Italian, Ray had trouble finding a category for Helio Lopez. He had a last name that suggested Latin-American heritage, but his appearance said something else altogether.

"Me and Sal, we got here Wednesday."

"And what time did you get to this location?"

"Three, maybe a little later. In time to do a little fishing."

"Have you been here before?"

"Once, last summer, late August, for about a week. I was supposed to get the lay of the land. Sal wanted me trained so I could take over this assignment from time to time."

"You don't sound too enthusiastic," commented Ray.

"I'm not. It messes with my life. I'd rather be in the city."

"What are your duties here compared to your duties in New York?"

"In the city, my duties are obvious. Most of the time, I'm on the gallery floor. We have one or more security people on the floor from open to close. Then part of the time I'm monitoring the CCTV. There's me, plus two more full-time people and a few part-time people who come in for major events."

"And your job description when you're up here?"

Helio shook his head. "That's the problem. There isn't one. I need to be available at all times in case something happens. This weekend we were told to keep people away from the mansion during Friday's party, guests and contractors alike. Same for the wedding day. Everything the guests needed—food, drinks, music, johns— was on the beach. And you know how that went down."

"What was your assignment after the wedding festivities?"

"Ms. Ingersolle's private sale?" asked Lopez.

"Yes."

"Like I think I said, we were to be around if needed, whatever that means." His irritation was apparent in his voice.

"You must have some specific responsibilities," said Ray.

"Yeah, we do. We secure the peninsula, which means we keep the gate closed. One of us has to stay in or near the office in case someone calls wanting it opened. We take turns carting people to and from the airport. That kind of stuff," he said, yawning and flexing his muscular arms.

"And what's your background?"

"Military police for four years."

"How did you get this job?"

"I was moonlighting as a personal trainer at a high-end health club. Ms. Ingersolle was one of my clients. She asked me to apply—without mentioning all the hoops I'd have to jump through."

"What were the hoops?" Ray asked.

"Oh, hell, I think the background check included talking to my kindergarten teacher. If I had stolen a candy bar as a kid, I wouldn't have gotten the job."

"Was it worth it?" Ray asked. "Has it been a good place to work?"

Helio shrugged. "It's a job. Salary's okay, people are all right."

"Are you interested in art?"

"Not really. I like some of it, but the way these rich people talk about it makes no sense to me. But maybe they don't know what they're talking about either, you know? I think they need to surround themselves with stuff that costs a bundle. You know, maybe as a way of showing off."

As Helio spoke, Ray noticed something like a Southern drawl in the way the man prolonged his vowels. "Your accent. Where did you grow up?"

"Mostly on the west coast and in Texas," he said. "We were a military family. My mom married my stepdad when I was a baby."

"The man found dead after the storm, Gerhard Talmadge, did you know him?"

"Know him, no, not really. Sal introduced me last year. I've seen him around a few times."

"Since you arrived this year?"

"I don't think so."

"Have you ever been to his cottage?"

"No. Sal pointed it out. But I've never been in there. Maybe Sal has. They're friends, I think. Were friends, I should say."

"The night of the party, did you see Mr. Talmadge before the storm hit?"

"I don't remember seeing him. There were so many people here, though."

"What were you doing during the party?" asked Ray.

"We were posted up at the house to keep people away. The wedding party had special badges. No one else got in till the storm hit. After the storm we opened doors on the lower level near the pool and let people come in. They might have come in anyways with all the broken glass. We were just making it safe. Then we did what we could to help till you people started showing up. After everyone was evacuated, we did what we could to secure the place, considering some of the windows were broken."

"When you secured the building, did you check the doors on the gallery?"

"Absolutely."

"When was that?"

"Midnight or after, I wasn't paying attention to the time."

"And after that?"

"We took turns guarding the entry to the building. Everything was locked up except the one area where the glass had been blown out."

"Did you see or hear anyone during the night?"

"After everyone else left, things went kinda quiet. I was mostly trying to stay awake."

"Think you might have dropped off occasionally?"

"It's possible. I was doing my best, but I caught myself a few times."

"How about food during the evening, did you guys get something to eat?"

"Sal made several trips down to the grills and brought back food."

"I hear they had some good beer, too."

"Wouldn't know about the beer, Sheriff. We were on duty. But the steaks were fantastic."

"I want to recheck something," Ray said thoughtfully. "From the time the evacuation was completed until daylight, you didn't see anyone moving around the area?"

"No, not near the house. I could hear people talking down here near the water and occasionally the sound of a boat motor. But it was dead up there."

"So, Mr. Lopez, when do you think the break-in at the gallery took place?"

Helio thought about it awhile. Finally, he said, "It had to be sometime between midnight and six a.m." He glared at Ray.

Ray didn't take Helio Lopez's crossed arms and narrowed eyes personally. He knew Helio was just feeling guilty and insecure about having failed at the one thing he had been charged with doing: keeping his employer's property safe and secure.

"Next, you're going to be asking why we didn't hear or see anything." said Helio. "And then you're going to want to know how someone got in and got out. Sheriff, our heads weren't into that likelihood. Our first responsibility was to keep the partiers from flowing into the building and tearing the place up. And then after the storm hit, like I said, we were doing our best to help the injured. By the time everyone had been evacuated, we were falling-down exhausted. The possibility that something would be stolen didn't cross my mind. You know what I'm saying?"

"Yes," Ray responded. "How long do you expect to be here?"

"We were originally scheduled to be here for two weeks. I think everything is up in the air right now, so I'm really not sure."

Ray passed Lopez a card. "Don't leave town without checking with me. We'll probably need to talk with you again."

32

"How was your trip?" asked Sue after Ray had scrambled out onto the makeshift dock in the township park.

"You mean my watery detour around the Isthmus of Gull, or more correctly past the missing Isthmus of Gull."

"Something like that. How are you?" Sue asked as they walked toward the parking lot. She already knew from the slump of his shoulders that he was tired and from his empty stare that he was already off somewhere in his own world.

"Exhausted," he said, yawning and stretching his arms. "Overwhelmed. I don't seem to have the energy I used to have."

"Not surprising. You're still recovering, Elkins. And I don't know if it will make you feel better or worse, but I also feel overwhelmed by this case."

"How are we ever going to sort this out?" he asked.

"I don't know, Elkins. We just have to keep moving forward."

He nodded. "Where's Simone?"

"She's already in the truck. I just picked her up from Doggie Daycare."

"I need to sit at a keyboard and get some of these thoughts down," said Ray. They got into the vehicle, and Simone jumped onto his lap. While petting her, he said, "How about dropping me at the office? You and Simone have a quiet evening. Do some yoga. Get some extra sleep. I can get one of the road patrol people to run me home later tonight."

Sue paused before starting the engine. "Elkins, you know how that will end up. You'll work until you fall asleep at the keyboard."

"What's the problem with that?"

"You'll wake up with a face covered with indentations like your pillow was stuffed with Chiclets."

"So?"

"How about this, Elkins? I'll order takeout, a pizza from the Last Chance—Kalamata olives, artichoke hearts, lots of feta cheese, just a hint of sauce, on a sesame crust. We'll have a fast dinner at your place. Then I'll take Simone for her evening stroll, and you can pound away on your notebook for as long as you like. What's causing this sudden need to get everything on paper?"

"Piper Ingersolle."

"You got a chance to talk to Piper?"

"I'll tell you about it after you order the pizza."

Jennifer Bidwell—wine glass and an open bottle of Vouvray on the kitchen table in front of her, left arm in a sling—held her phone in her right hand and stared intently at the screen. "Pick up, dammit," she hissed. Finally, when she heard the call go to voicemail, she ended it with an angry jab of her thumb.

She dropped the phone on the table and then reached for it again moments later when the phone started vibrating and emitting a tinny ringtone. "Scott," she said, switching to speakerphone.

"Hey, Babes, been thinking about you."

WTF Scott, she thought, taking a moment to consider how to respond. "You got my messages," she said.

"Oh, Babes, I'm so sorry. The cell service just came back up. I mean, not just, but when it did, I was immediately tied up with Ingersolle. She chewed my ass, like the storm was my fault. And then the phone just kept ringing. But I've been thinking about you. Looking over at your car, worrying. I saw you get on the boat, and I was hoping you were okay."

"Are you going to ask me about my injuries?"

"Of course! That's the first thing I want to know. The way you were holding your arm, I was afraid to give you a hug. And then all the people around, I was trying to help everyone. I tried to catch up with you again before you were evacuated. I searched for you down at the dock. I must have missed you somehow. Sorry. So how are you?"

"The doctor said I have a torn ligament in my shoulder. It might heal on its own or I might need surgery. It's wait and see. Are you okay, Scott?"

"Yeah, a few cuts and bruises. Nothing major. I don't know how I got off so easy. What a nightmare. I wish I could have just looked after you."

"That nice old man, Mr. Talmadge, it said on the news he was killed."

"Sad, so sad."

"I took him a plate of food," said Jennifer.

"You did?"

"Yes. He and his helper were at the end of the food line, which ran way back almost into the woods, so I asked them what they wanted and went and got it for them so they could sit down and eat. I thought that was the least I could do for an old man who's almost blind."

"You are so kind, Jennifer."

"Where was he found?" she asked.

"Somehow he had wandered into the woods by himself. Most of the big trees in that area were torn out by their roots, and one of them fell on him. The police found his body Saturday morning when they searched the area."

"Do you think he suffered?"

"I hope not."

"The poor man. I'm sure it was terrifying. I thought that I was going to die, too…" she trailed off, waiting for Scott to comfort her.

Should I tell him? thought Jennifer as she waited for Scott to say something more.

"Sorry about your car," he said after a long silence.

"Is it damaged? Did a tree fall on it?"

"No, nothing like that. It's just that you won't be able to get it anytime soon. The road is washed out at the narrows. I don't know how long it will take to fix it."

Another silence followed, then Scott said, "Listen, Babes, I gotta go. There are a million things on my plate." She heard him take a deep breath, and then he said, "Glad you're okay. I'll call you later today or tomorrow."

Jennifer tossed the phone on the table a second time.

"Piper confirmed our observation that it doesn't appear that anything in the house was disturbed or taken," Ray said as Sue pulled into the parking lot at the Last Chance. "As you said, she appeared to be sincerely distressed about her grandfather's death. And she seems to have none of her mother's abrasive qualities."

"Elkins, you sound rather taken with this young woman. It reminds me of that crunchy granola woman a few years back that you found so charming."

"Who are you talking about?"

"The one that turned out to be a stone-cold killer."

Ray waited a few beats and then said, "Oh, yeah, that one. She did have some negative traits, didn't she?"

"But other than being a bit homicidal," Sue continued, "she was artsy, petite, athletic, and a budding poet. It's a good thing I'm around to keep you grounded."

Ray gave her a look, then asked, "Do you want me to go in and get the pizza?"

"I'll get the food. You stay with Simone. She hasn't seen you all day."

"Wait," said Ray when she was halfway out of the truck. He fished the color photo from his pocket and passed it in her direction. "Here's a picture of Gerhard Talmadge with his wife. See if Talmadge looks familiar to the people working inside."

"Bingo," Sue said when she returned to the truck a few minutes later, setting the pizza in the back and sliding into the driver's seat.

"Bingo what?" asked Ray.

"The three people working the takeout window, two women and a man, they all know Gerhard Talmadge. They said he used to come in by himself. But in recent months, he always came in with someone named Scott Nelson. They said they didn't think Talmadge was driving anymore. One of the women, the one working the counter, graduated from high school with Scott."

"That's interesting," said Ray. "I wonder what else Scott's been less than honest about? We need to bring him in and do a formal interview."

"Yes," agreed Sue. "I'll get that set up for tomorrow, if possible."

"What about the search team looking for a weapon?"

"Today they did a grid search in the area where Talmadge's body was found. Nothing. With all the downed trees, they did the best they could. Tomorrow they'll move into the water, starting at the beach directly out from where Talmadge's body was found. They'll begin close and work the shoreline, some people walking the shallows, others working the area at and just beyond the drop-off. I don't think the weapon could have been pitched much farther that."

"Agreed," Ray answered. "How about the FBI and art theft?"

"Holiday weekend, Ray. I've gotten zero response to my emails and phone calls. Did you get anything from Alice Ingersolle or Sal?"

"Nada," he answered. "The video, does Barbara Sinclair have anything yet?"

"There's a mountain of video. When last we spoke a few hours ago, she hadn't put much together."

"Let's get her on the phone right now," said Ray. "We've been face-to-face with most of these people. Given that we're starting to know the cast of characters, maybe we can see something that she might miss."

Sue pulled over to the shoulder, but instead of pulling out her phone, she tossed Ray Simone's leash and got out of the car.

Ray looked at her quizzically as she opened the back door and took out the pizza.

"There's a picnic table right there," she said, nodding in the direction of the table next to the water. "I'm starving, and I'm going to eat pizza while it's still hot. Then I'll make the call."

33

Barbara Sinclair, the newest full-time member of the Cedar County Sheriff's Department, was sitting at the central desk in the department's technology area. An array of screens along the wall showed various scenes from the Gull Point security cameras.

Officer Sinclair pointed to different screens as she talked.

"The screen in the center shows the activity from the camera Sue identified as being mounted on the garage. I've edited the video down to just the periods of activity. You can see the time and date stamp at the bottom of the screen. This video begins on Friday morning shortly before 8:00 a.m. and ends around 9:30 or 9:40 p.m. Toward the end, the power must have been intermittent for a period before finally failing completely. The end times are consistent across all the feeds.

Is the person you see here the one you identified as Scott Nelson?"

"That's correct," Sue responded.

"I'll just jump from one segment to the next. In these early segments, it's just Scott coming back and forth. Now this one," she said, "introduces a couple of new characters." She stopped the video on the frame where they could clearly see the three faces.

"That's Sal Abato and Helio Lopez," said Ray.

Barbara Sinclair used her list of names to add Sal and Helio to her notes specific to this digital recording.

"The elusive Helio," said Sue. "He's quite attractive."

"This isn't a screen test," said Ray. "Anything interesting on the audio?"

"Not here," said Sinclair. "Later, there's some chatter that seems to relate to security arrangements for the evening. I've set up a database that will tie all of this information together. You'll be able to quickly review the stored material. When the audio is clear enough, I'll make text files, too."

"Anything especially interesting from this camera?" asked Ray.

"Nothing really out of the ordinary for a party," Barbara said. "Scott Nelson comes and goes, a van arrives with—going by the way they're dressed—food service workers. Later, the shuttle busses come and go. The most interesting thing is here, at 4:01. As you can see, a dark green Subaru Forester parks directly across the drive from the camera. A young woman emerges, crosses the drive, and enters the garage. Several minutes later, she exits. What's in the garage?"

"Scott Nelson's living quarters, on the second floor," said Ray.

"Can either of you identify the woman? Did he say whether he has a girlfriend?"

"Let me check my notes," Ray said.

"I think I saw her during the evacuation," said Sue. "If I'm right, she was among the injured."

"Her name is Jennifer Bidwell," said Ray. "Scott Nelson told me she's the owner of the Subaru. She works for the wedding planner. He said they had met quite often to work out details for the event."

"Lots of little details," Barbara said in a mildly mocking tone. "Here are some of the highlights."

Two people enter the frame from the left and move in the direction of the camera. Barbara paused the video and said, "Old cameras, old technology. The video goes from low-res to almost no-res as it gets dark. But it's good enough to identify the people and perhaps speculate on what's happening."

She started the video rolling forward again. Two figures moved toward the camera, a man and a woman. They stopped. The man poured champagne into a cup and then poured some into the woman's cup. She giggled and lifted the cup to her lips, taking several long sips. Then they disappeared into the building. The segment was punctuated at the end by the sound of a door slamming.

"About how much time passes before they reappear?" asked Sue.

"That's the interesting part," said Barbara. "It's about twenty-three minutes and change. Now watch this."

A figure emerged from the building and walked away, a man.

"Scott," said Sue.

"That's funny," Ray said. "In my previous conversation with Scott Nelson she was one of the contractors he was working with. Nothing more."

"Okay, now in the next segment, which is stamped 8:35 p.m., you'll see Sal Abato and Helio Lopez come into view." She started the video. "You'll notice each has a champagne bottle. They were kind enough to stand near the camera for a bit and shoot the breeze."

They never would have thought to stay out of the camera's purview, Ray thought, *because they never expected anyone to watch the security footage. No one would ever have discovered that they were drinking on the job, if not for the burglary.*

"By their gestures and laughter, it appears that a lot of guy talk is going on," Barbara continued. "Unfortunately, by this point the wind has picked up. The wind blowing across the microphone makes most of their conversation indistinct. You can see something's going on with the weather, the trees in the background are starting to move around, but there's no lightning or the sound of thunder yet."

Sal and Helio clutched their champagne bottles. They laughed wildly. Sal lit a cigarette. Then they moved away from the camera.

"Okay, there's no action here for about fifteen minutes. Then the woman you identified as Jennifer Bidwell exits the building." Barbara clicked her remote, and the video began again. "What's interesting here is how the weather has changed. It's raining hard. See how Bidwell goes to the left, presumably toward the beach."

Jennifer Bidwell stopped at one point and looked back toward the garage and then disappeared from view as lightning flashed and thunder cracked.

"Now I'll jump forward about fifteen or twenty minutes. Notice how rapidly the weather has deteriorated."

The video flickered in front of them, the sound of thunder intense, the flashes of lightning brilliant. And then everything went blurry as a wall of rain marched across the screen.

"From this point forward, no one enters the area near this the camera, and eventually, the recording stops. As I mentioned earlier, based on the time stamps on this camera and the others, I can give you an accurate reading on when the power went down."

"The other cameras, what do you have?" asked Ray.

"I have two views of the beach, one from near the water looking up toward the mansion and a second one that provides a wide-angle beach view looking toward the lake. The second one especially provides a good view of the party. The area is very well lit."

"How about the other flash drives?" asked Ray.

"Only those three drives have any data. The others are blank."

Ray gave Sinclair a long look.

"I don't know, sir. Either the equipment wasn't working, or it had been turned off. Once power has been restored, I can go over and check it out. Then I can give you a good answer."

"How long will it take you to work through the rest of the video?" Ray asked.

"It depends on how you want me to approach this task. I can use facial recognition software on the images from those two cameras. If I'm just looking for Nelson, Abato, Lopez, and Bidwell, I can do that rather quickly. Along the way, you'll probably see people you want to add."

"Please include this man," said Ray, passing the photo of Gerhard Talmadge and his wife. "Just the man in that photo," he added. "It's an old photo. Will that make a difference?"

Barbara looked at the photo. "I'll extract the man's face and blow it up. His features are very distinct. There shouldn't be a problem."

"Could we have this by, let's say, 8:00 tomorrow morning without you having to stay up all night?" asked Ray.

"No problem. This will only take a few more hours."

They stood, and when they did, Barbara Sinclair, once a college basketball player and WNBA hopeful, towered over Ray and Sue.

"Thank you," said Ray. "Your expertise is really making a difference in this case."

"I love this stuff," she responded. "My brain is buzzing."

34

Ray woke up to the sound of the espresso machine and the aroma of coffee. He pulled on a bathrobe and wandered into the kitchen.

"I wondered how long you were going to sleep. I stayed quiet as long as I could. But after seven, I thought it would be okay to make some noise," said Sue.

"What time did I fall asleep?"

"I took Simone for a walk. When we came back, you were propped up in your bed, laptop next to you, sound asleep."

He gave her an abashed looked. "I was typing and then dreaming. I'd force myself to wake up, and then everything would fade away again."

"You managed to upload some of your interview notes."

"Were they okay?

"I think you're going to want to do some revising."

"That bad?"

"Not bad, in a stream of semi-consciousness, dreamlike kind of way."

"How far did I get?"

"All the way to Piper and the photos with grandma and the trip to FedEx with Gerhard Talmadge. Despite your 'just the facts, ma'am' approach, you really seem to like Piper."

Ray did like her. "She's, ah, how do I explain—?"

"Attractive?"

"Well, there's that. But that's not why I like her. She seems real. Like, she told me she cleaned up her grandfather's kitchen. Acts of kindness and a sincerity say a lot about a person."

"Especially when that person is an attractive woman…"

"Don't go there, Sue. She's young enough to be my daughter. Besides, she seems very wholesome."

"Hmm. Don't tell me we have to go through a list of your past wholesomes again. Ready for your coffee?"

"Yes."

"Cappuccino?"

"Yes, with two shots of espresso. What did Barbara Sinclair get done last night?"

"Elkins, I almost got you up at 6:00 a.m. when I saw the first clips she's isolated from that mass of data. Unbelievable."

"Show me."

"Coffee first, then the clips."

Sue made the cappuccino and set it in front of Ray. Then she pulled a stool up next to his and opened her computer. "First, we have Scott Nelson. Lots of clips of him from the two cameras near the beach, some with Jennifer Bidwell. The clips with Bidwell, the body language, the facial expressions suggest they were in a romantic relationship. There are also a few with Scott and Piper.

The bridal party must have made a grand entrance at some point. In the first clip, Piper's wearing a ribbon diagonally across her chest that says 'Bride.' She must have shed the ribbon immediately after that. She was not wearing it in any of the other clips. The clip of her with Scott...you've got to see it."

The clip showed Piper, who had already shed her ribbon, standing with Scott, their forms visible in the shadows outside the brightly lit tent. Piper was talking, leaning in close to be heard. Then she was listening to Scott and laughing, the sound of it lost in the loud music coming from the tent. Then Scott reached toward her, and she dodged away and feigned a slapping motion. She turned and began to walk away. Scott reached toward her again, at which point Piper turned back in his direction once more before finally moving back inside the tent.

"Is that the way one greets an old childhood friend?"

"It's rather intense," said Ray.

"I wonder what the groom was doing at that moment?"

"We haven't identified him yet. But going back to Scott, he's constantly passing the cameras. Most of the time, he seems to be busy doing the kinds of things he should be doing. You'll see him directing people, helping the caterers, that kind of stuff."

"This is all interesting, but it doesn't seem relevant."

"Just wait, the clips are arranged chronologically, and the most fascinating clips are close to the end. First, look at this series."

Ray saw Helio Lopez at the bar, where he procured two bottles of champagne.

"And here he is again," said Sue, starting another clip that showed him back at the bar forty minutes later, leaving with two more bottles.

"This time he doesn't wait for the bartender," Sue said. "He just goes around and grabs them. We don't know if they shared their bubbly, but it looks like he and Sal had at least six bottles in their possession over the course of the evening."

"If they drank it all, that's a lot of champagne. Makes you wonder about their job performance later in the evening," said Ray. "Or maybe Helio was doing his best to get his boss drunk or vice versa. Their accounts of the evening are pretty fishy."

"The last few pieces of video are especially interesting. These are very blurry, because it's getting dark." Sue pointed. "Look in this area of the screen. See the face?"

"Yes."

The camera, positioned on a light tower near the waterfront, provided a wide-angle view of the beach area and the grassy slope running up toward the mansion. On the slope, just at the edge of the crowd near the grill and the food tables, Ray spotted Gerhard Talmadge's unmistakable face. He was standing with the young man, Nathan, whom Ray had met and questioned at the hospital. Jennifer Bidwell approached them, and they had a brief conversation. A few minutes later, she returned with two plates of food. She left and returned again with two beverages. She stayed with Talmadge and his helper for a few minutes more, then she disappeared out of frame, moving toward the woods.

"Now, the last clip," Sue said.

Ray squinted at the screen. "This is almost too fuzzy."

"Just keep looking. Same area. Talmadge is still there."

"Looks like he's getting a hug."

"Wait till she turns. The frame freezes at that point."

"Is that Piper?" asked Ray.

"That's Sinclair's best guess. What do you think?"

"I can't really tell, but that's consistent with what she told me."

"Well, whoever it is, the woman looks quite wholesome," Sue teased. "Where do we start?"

"How about Jennifer Bidwell?" said Ray.

"My choice exactly. She's an outsider, but she can probably give us some useful background information about how things operate at Gull Point."

"We'll invite her to come in first. Then Helio and Sal. Tell Officer Sinclair that I want to use some video clips when we're questioning them. Also, have her run background checks on the three of them."

"Anything else?"

"The mail we found in Talmadge's kitchen. Did you have a chance to look at it?"

"Nothing much in most of it, electric bill, phone, etc. But the bank statements, I only have the last three months. Talmadge was running out of money. And in each of those months, he was withdrawing $1000 in cash. I wonder what that was all about?"

"We should really look at the financial angle. Would you apply for a search warrant and then start the process with the bank? They always take their time in responding. When you say running out, what was the last balance?"

"Less than a thousand."

"Local bank or...national."

"Local."

"Do what you can to move this along. Last time we needed a bank's cooperation it took weeks. This could be an important piece in this investigation."

"Yes," she responded.

Jennifer Bidwell looked at the array of gifts Scott Nelson had spread across her kitchen table.

"Chocolate croissants, coffee, roses, you know how to push all the right buttons," she said. "But you caught me sleeping in. I'm desperate for a shower."

"Babes, it's the only time I can probably see you today," said Scott.

"What's happening?" she asked.

"There's the leaving party, rather than the wedding. Ingersolle's on my case, lots to do."

"I'll be there," said Jennifer.

"I didn't think you would be, because of your injury."

But you never asked, thought Jennifer. *You're here with gifts, but you don't really seem to be here.*

"As you can see, I'm able to get around. Linda's going to pick me up and bring me home. She's been so great. She stayed here with me all weekend," she said pointedly. "Anyway, I've been working on this event from the beginning. I want to be there when the final curtain drops. Do you think anyone will show up?"

"I'm not good at predicting," Scott said while fiddling with the roses in their white ceramic vase. "It's a travel day, a good day to get out of here. And given that there's no wedding, I'm not sure a beach party is enticement enough to keep people around."

"How about the bride and groom? Will they show up?"

"I have no idea. I'm not in the loop."

"How did you get here? Catch a ride in with the marine patrol?"

"No, I wanted to get out of there without anyone knowing. I waded across. My sister, Julie, met me on the other side. I've got her car."

Scott wrapped his arms around Jennifer and pulled her close until she jumped and said, "Easy."

"I needed to see you. I've been missing you, Babes."

With her good arm, hand on his chest, she pushed him back and then slipped out of his embrace.

"Yeah, I've been missing you, too," Jennifer said.

"There's something I need to ask you," said Scott.

"Okay," she responded, noting a change in his demeanor.

"The old guy, Gerhard Talmadge, I don't know if I ever told you the whole story. My boss hates him. I'd get fired if she knew all the stuff I did for him. If anyone asks, don't say anything, please."

"Yeah, you said that at the beginning. But who's going to ask? Ms. Ingersolle? I've never met the woman."

"Well, you never know. Maybe the police?"

"That's silly, Scott. Why would I ever talk to them?"

"Yeah, you're right. But if they ever do ask, mum's the word. Listen, I've got to scoot. See you at the party. I'll be the one in the crowd making eyes at you." He slung his arm around her shoulders, and she winced again and ducked out of his grasp.

"I'm sorry," he said. "It's just that I've been really missing you." He embraced her again, gently this time, and kissed her forehead. "This nightmare will soon be behind us, Babes. You'll be done with this job, and we won't have to keep our relationship on the down low anymore. We can start planning our life together."

35

"Thank you for coming in. I'm Detective Sergeant Sue Lawrence."

"No problem," said Jennifer Bidwell. "We were coming this way. You said this will only take a few minutes?"

Sue studied the tall, long-limbed woman in her twenties with an open, friendly face and a sling on her arm. "This is my boss, Linda Wetherbee. She's doing the driving," she explained, gesturing with her good arm.

"What's this all about?" Ms. Wetherbee asked Sue in an officious tone.

"We're following up on a couple of things that happened Friday night at Gull Point. We're questioning a few people who might have witnessed the incident we're looking into. If you wait for us here, I'll have Ms. Bidwell back to you in a few minutes. And please help yourself to the coffee, if you like. It's fresh."

"Everything smells new here," Jennifer Bidwell observed as Sue led her down a hallway to an interview room.

"It is, pretty much. We've only been back in our offices for a few months," said Sue.

"I remember seeing footage on the news," Jennifer said. "Lots of fire damage, I imagine."

"Yes, that and the water damage that followed," explained Sue. "The sprinkler system soaked everything. The interior of this part of the building had to be gutted and rebuilt. If you'll come in here please," Sue said, directing Bidwell into an interview room and gesturing toward a chair.

"This room looks like what you see on TV crime shows," Jennifer said as she sat down.

"I'm not quite sure how it all works," Sue admitted. "We're starting to video record most of our interviews to make sure we get an accurate written transcript." She opened her laptop and pushed it to the side, leaving her view of Jennifer Bidwell across the table unobstructed.

Jennifer shifted uncomfortably in her chair. "Are you filming me right now?"

"With your permission," answered Sue. Jennifer's answer came slowly. "Okay, I guess. So what is it you want to ask me? I'm really not sure why I'm here."

"Unfortunately, I can't share any information about our ongoing investigation, but you might have seen something that could help us when you were at Gull Point. We believe you were there from late in the afternoon on Friday until the time you were evacuated from the scene and transported to the hospital. Is that true?"

"Yes. How do you know that?"

"Your car was left at the scene. Scott Nelson identified the vehicle as belonging to you and told us a little about you."

Sue watched Jennifer Bidwell closely. She thought the young woman seemed to relax a bit at the mention of Nelson's name.

"What can I tell you?" Bidwell asked.

"Just tell me about Friday evening. You work for an event planner, right?"

"Yes. Linda Wetherbee, who brought me here, owns and manages Simply Romantic."

"You and Linda planned the Friday evening events at Gull Point?"

"Sort of. This wedding isn't our normal kind of event," Jennifer said. "We usually do everything, but on this job we were just doing bits and pieces. For the Friday party, we hired a local caterer and contracted for the shuttle busses. My job was to make sure everything went smoothly with the busses and to greet the guests. So I got there...I don't know...maybe a half-hour before the first shuttle was scheduled to arrive at around five."

"So you got there, parked your car, then what?"

Sue had reviewed the video clips of Bidwell from Friday afternoon and evening. On a pad in front of her she had an outline of Bidwell's actions, with the time stamps. She watched the woman closely as Bidwell's narrative departed from the documented sequence of events.

"I just sort of hung out and looked at the lake until I got a text that the first bus was on the way. Then I stood at the circular drive at the side of the mansion and met the busses."

"And how long did you stay there?"

"Until all the guests had been dropped off. The last shuttle was supposed to arrive at 6:15, but of course it was later, because nothing ever runs on time. The busses went back to a staging area near the highway. The plan was that I'd call them back when people wanted to leave. Because of the storm, that never happened." Jennifer cradled her injured arm protectively for a few seconds.

"So what did you do once you weren't needed to coordinate the shuttles and do the greeting?" Sue asked. "What had you planned on doing for the rest of the evening?"

"I walked down and got some food. Then I sat on the hill and watched all the activity. It was quite a show. We've done a lot of events, but I've never seen anything like this."

"What do you mean?"

"Apparently there's a good happy hour at Manitou Shores, because many of the guests arrived happier than usual, and as the night went on, some of them were getting out of hand, screaming, getting physical with the staff, running into the water and into the woods."

"Did you ever see Ms. Ingersolle's private security staff intervene with any of the guests?"

Jennifer shook her head. "I never met the security staff, and I didn't see anyone intervene in any way."

"Okay, good to know," Sue said. "You've been working with Scott Nelson on this project?"

"Yes, there have been a lot of details to coordinate."

"How is he to work with?"

"Very professional."

"Did you see Scott during the evening?"

"Briefly. He seemed to be everywhere."

"There was an elderly man who lived at Gull Point, Gerhard Talmadge. He lived in the smaller house on the property. Did you know the man?"

Bidwell raised her head and looked up toward the ceiling, a gesture that suggested she was thinking, and Sue had no doubt she was. "I don't believe so," Jennifer said. "The name is slightly familiar. Maybe Scott mentioned that he lived in the smaller house."

"So not knowing Gerhard Talmadge, you wouldn't have recognized him if you saw him at the party?"

Jennifer nodded. "Correct."

"I want to show you a few video clips," Sue said, positioning her laptop so they both could see the screen. "They're from the security cameras at Gull Point. After viewing this footage, you might want to adjust some of your answers, and that's just fine. For example, you said that when you arrived, you were a bit early and hung out and looked at the lake. So here is a short clip showing your arrival." Sue tapped the play button.

After the clip had run, Sue said, "The footage shows that the first thing you did was go up to Scott Nelson's apartment."

"I guess I forgot that," Jennifer said, her smooth brow furrowing. "You know, the whole evening was so traumatic, it's a miracle I remember anything at all."

"I understand. I was out in the storm, too." Sue paused for a moment, then continued. "You also said during the evening you only saw Scott Nelson briefly?"

"Yes." Her answer, one word, was little more than a whisper.

"Jennifer, here's a clip of you and Scott walking up toward the garage. It appears you're sipping champagne."

Sue ran the clip, looking steadily at Bidwell. "Yes," she answered, briefly making eye contact.

"Note the time that you go up to Scott's apartment together," said Sue, pointing to the time stamp at the bottom of the screen.

"And now we have a short clip of Scott exiting the building. Please note the time when Scott leaves."

Sue paced herself, letting the information soak in. "And, last, here is a clip of you leaving. Please note the time there."

"Okay, okay," Jennifer said, the register of her voice rising nervously. "This is my personal business. I'm not sure what it has to do with whatever you're investigating."

"You told me you hardly know Scott Nelson. Why would you lie about that?" Sue asked calmly.

"We should not have become involved. That was unprofessional. We both knew it. It just happened. He was afraid he would lose his job, and I didn't want Linda to know. We planned to go public once the wedding was over. It only had to be a secret for three more days."

Sue nodded. "All right. But you also told me that you didn't know Gerhard Talmadge."

Jennifer Bidwell's only response was to glare at Sue.

"Here's the last video clip," Sue said. She started the footage, her eyes fixed on Bidwell.

"It looks like you did know Mr. Talmadge," she said once the clip had ended. "You had a conversation with him and his assistant. Then you brought them plates of food. And a few minutes later you're there with glasses of beer. Why would you tell me that you didn't know him?"

"Okay, okay," she said, distraught. "I knew Mr. Talmadge. He was a lovely old man. He was going blind. Scott wasn't supposed to have anything to do with him because Ms. Ingersolle wouldn't stand for it. But Scott kept risking his job to help him. I don't understand what's going on!" Her face contorted, and she began to cry.

"Jennifer, all I want is the truth," Sue said, rising and placing a box of tissues in front of her. "Gerhard Talmadge was found dead on Saturday morning."

"I know, I know!" Jennifer sobbed. "A tree fell on him. I got hit by a tree, too. I could have died, too!"

"It was more than a tree, Jennifer."

The young woman went perfectly still, a tissue poised below her nose. "What are you saying?"

"It's a suspicious death. Someone might have done something to hurt Mr. Talmadge. Did you see anyone other than his healthcare aide with him on Friday evening?"

"No. I just saw him and his helper at the edge of the crowd. They seemed lost. I went up and talked with them, then I brought them some food. That's exactly what happened, the honest truth."

"I know, that's what the video shows. What did you talk about? Did he seem at all fearful?"

"The music was so loud, we could hardly hear each other. You can see in the video that I'm yelling in his ear. I just asked him if he was having fun and if he wanted me to get him something to eat. He seemed happy to be there."

"And before Friday night, you spent time with Mr. Talmadge?"

"Yes, I was doing it to help Scott. I would take Mr. Talmadge to, you know, some of his doctor's appointments, to the drug store, and to the grocery store. Not all the time. Just when Scott couldn't do it. Mr. Talmadge needed help—he shouldn't have been living alone. And we were doing it on the sly. Scott said Ms. Ingersolle would fire him straight up if she knew. My boss wouldn't have been pleased either. I was running errands for Mr. Talmadge when I was supposed to be working."

"During the time you spent with Talmadge, was there any suggestion that he was frightened or fearful?"

"Fearful of what?"

"People who might want to harm him."

"No, he never said anything like that. I felt sorry for him. He wanted to be independent, but it was obvious that the way of life he was so used to would have to come to an end. I think he was doing his best to hide what was really going on. But I could see it. I was there up close. I was happy see there was a young caregiver with him. Someone had obviously figured out the man needed help." Jennifer took a tissue from the box and blew her nose. "Why did you put me through this?" she asked accusingly.

"Would you have told me the truth about your relationship with Mr. Talmadge if I hadn't shown you the clips?" Sue let the question hang. When she didn't get a response, she asked,

"Did Scott Nelson ask you not to answer questions about Gerhard Talmadge?"

Jennifer stared down at the tabletop in front of her.

"The truth, Ms. Bidwell," Sue said.

Without looking up from the table, Jennifer nodded.

"I need you to answer that out loud. A yes or a no."

"Yes."

"And the event you're going to today, is it part of the Ingersolle wedding events?"

"Yes," Jennifer said.

"Will Scott Nelson be there?"

"I don't know."

"Where's the party taking place?"

"On the beach at Good Harbor. We've got a use permit from the NPS."

"I'm sure you do," said Sue, standing. "Thank you for coming in."

Jennifer Bidwell gripped the table with her good hand and stood shakily. Then she rushed past Sue, opened the door, and headed down the hallway. Sue stood at the door and watched her retreat. She wondered how much influence Scott had over this young woman. She had a feeling that before this was all over, Jennifer Bidwell would be sorry she'd ever met Scott Nelson—if she wasn't already.

36

"This place smells new," said Sal Abato as Ray led him toward the interview room.

"We've done some redecorating," explained Ray.

"Oh yeah, yeah, Scott told me there was a shootout and a fire here last year. You got wounded, right?"

Ray nodded. It wasn't something he was ready to talk about, not now, perhaps not ever. "You get to see one of our updated interview rooms," said Ray, opening a door and directing Sal toward a chair.

"Wow, look at this. You got it all, don't you? Mics, cameras, one-way glass. It makes me feel old, Sheriff. The stuff we had in the city—steel table, steel chairs, you know, cement block walls with ten layers of paint, tile floors. The recorder was right there," he said, pointing to the side of the table that butted against the wall. "And that was before everything became smoke-free. The interview rooms always reeked of cigarette smoke and fear. Perps got the truth sweated out of them."

"I remember the old interrogation rooms from back in the day," said Ray.

"So why am I here?" asked Sal, placing both hands palms down on the table.

"Sal, it's all about the world in which we live. You know— dash cams, body cams, all the technology. Everyone wants a video record—prosecutors, defense attorneys, and your average John Doe. When I did the initial interview with you, I was making notes with pen and paper, and I also had my body cam turned on."

"Yeah, I remember. After a long, long night without sleep, that's not how you want to end up on candid camera."

"We were both exhausted," said Ray. "And in truth, the video collected from body and car cams is often of marginal quality: jerky, poorly lit, plagued by wind noise. So when we need a further conversation with someone connected to an incident under investigation, we like to have them come in, especially now that we have all this new technology."

"Yeah, I can understand that," Sal said, his response flat and without enthusiasm.

"We're just getting the system up and running, and we're struggling with some bugs. And we're in the process of going paperless. Instead of having to sort through big case books, everything related to an open case goes into a computer file. Then there's a series of hyperlinks that connects all the relevant information. You can go online and find everything: video, reports, scene of the crime photos, autopsy reports, the whole nine yards. I think this will save us a lot of time and help us do a better job."

"Impressive," Sal responded.

Ray opened his laptop and placed it on the table so they could both see the screen.

"Here's the main menu. Scrolling down to open cases, arranged by date and subject, I can get to the burglary or suspicious death investigation at Gull Point. When I click here, we see the names of everyone with whom we've had contact in alpha order. And Sal, 'Abato' puts you at the top of the list. And under your name, you can see all the written reports and videos that are currently in the file."

"Yeah, that's pretty cool," said Sal.

"And here's some video you may not be familiar with. Using facial recognition software, we've looked through CCTV video on the flash drives you gave me. Here are several clips of you and Helio on Friday evening. You'll see the time stamps on the bottom of the screen."

Ray started the first video clip. It showed Sal and Helio, each holding and drinking from champagne bottles. Then he ran several more clips of the two men drinking and talking. In each successive clip, Sal appeared to be more and more intoxicated, while Helio appeared to remain sober. Then Ray showed three clips of Helio getting bottles of champagne from the bar near the beach.

After the screen went blank, Ray said, "Looks like you were having quite a time."

"Yeah," said Sal, appearing abashed. "Forgot how quickly the bubbly does its magic. I think we got a bit carried away." Sal paused for a moment. "Well, fortunately, we were safe deep in the woods. We didn't do anything that would have gotten us thrown in the local hoosegow. That would have been a hard one to explain to Ms. Ingersolle. I'd probably be looking for a new job." He paused again and looked at Ray. "Hell, if she saw this video, Helio and me, we'd both probably be looking for work." Sal paused for a beat or two. "Yeah, I'm embarrassed, Sheriff. We should have been better than that. Ms. Ingersolle has every right to be pissed. We let her down. We didn't protect her property."

Then Ray asked, "Has drinking ever been a problem for you?"

"That's none of your business," Sal responded with a sneer. "I came in voluntarily to help with your investigation. Now I'm getting the third degree. You're asking the question because you've got the answer already. You and your computer genius have done the research. Okay, so I got a few DUIs back in the day, before I worked for Ingersolle. If you ever had to do real cop work—"

"Sal that was just a guess on my part, an informed guess. And you've seen the same data as I have over the years. Police officers have alcoholism rates at 20 or 30 percent. Some studies suggest even higher, especially in urban areas."

"Well it's tough work, isn't it, Sheriff?"

"It is, Sal. And Sal, I think we want the same things. We want to find the possible murderer, and we want to recover the stolen artwork."

"Exactly."

"The video, you're having a good time. And by the last clip, you're way beyond the good time. Right?"

Sal exhaled loudly. "Yeah."

"Watching the video got me wondering how much of what you

told me about checking the place over after midnight was true. My guess is that you were off sleeping somewhere. Maybe Helio was sleeping, too, or perhaps not. We developed a timeline for Friday evening and Saturday morning and we placed the forced entry and theft of the prints from the gallery sometime after midnight, based on what you told us. But maybe you didn't do the walk-through after midnight. If you two weren't checking, that artwork could have been stolen earlier in the evening, possibly during the height of the party. Or it could have occurred during or just after the storm, when no one would have noticed the sound of a door being popped. Who knows, the perpetrators might have made their getaway on one of our department boats as we were doing the evacuation.

"And how well do you know Helio?" Ray continued. "In the video, he looks like he was doing his best to get you drunk. Did he put you to bed? Then he could have pulled off the burglary at his leisure."

"Shit," said Abato. "I've never been on this side of the table before. Have we moved from a citizen interview to suspect interrogation? If so, I want a lawyer before we go any further."

"That certainly is your right," said Ray. "I'm just wondering about how much of the first story you gave me is true?" Ray's question hung in the air for a long moment. He and Sal stared at each other, and Ray began to wonder if the man was going to respond.

Then Sal looked away and slumped in his chair. "Okay, okay, we were partying too much," he said. "I was pretty wasted when the storm hit. But then I was wide awake. You know, standing there in the wind and rain, lightning striking near us. And then all those hurt people. The adrenalin kicked in. I was suddenly wide awake and totally sober. I knew exactly what to do, because that's what I've been trained to do—help people. Me and Helio, we were a team. And then when it was all over, I crashed. I thought Helio did, too."

"And where did you crash?"

"We have a two-bedroom suite just down the hall from our office."

"Was Helio with you?"

"Yeah, I think so. Some parts are more a blur than others."

"And in the morning?"

"I was up first. I needed coffee real bad. Helio found me in the kitchen. He was looking worse for wear, too. These young guys, they just don't have the stamina…"

"Other than when Helio went down to the bar, you two were together all evening?"

"Well, not exactly," Sal sighed. "Helio, he always talks like he's a real ass bandit. He was down there doing some dancing, hoping to get some action. He knows Piper a little bit from the store. She's nice to him, so he thinks he can get a bit of that before she gets married. I said, 'She's nice to everyone, idiot,' and I said, 'In your dreams.' And he says, 'Like mother, like daughter.' You know how some young guys brag. You know it's all total BS."

"So what are you telling me?" asked Ray.

"I'm just saying he was coming and going. But not long enough for any action. Truth be told, Sheriff, these women were way out of his league, you know?"

"You told me you recommended that Ms. Ingersolle do background checks on all prospective employees. Did Helio go through that process?"

Sal clasped his hands but couldn't keep his fingers from fidgeting. "Well, in his case," he said, "we waived some of the pre-employment stuff. In fact, we created a position for him."

"Why's that?"

"Boss's order."

"What did you think about that?"

"I wasn't happy, but I kept that to myself. Ms. Ingersolle is not someone to tangle with, especially on something like this. Since I was going to be Helio's supervisor, I figured I could watch his every move and make sure he didn't get into trouble. I'm pretty sure I have the authority to fire his sorry ass if he makes a wrong move. Of course, I'd have to document it all carefully. Wouldn't want to give him a wrongful dismissal case."

"So what do you think now? Was he minding his p's and q's when you were sleeping it off, or was he into a bit of larceny?"

When an answer didn't appear to be forthcoming, Ray asked, "Do you have an estimate of the value of the stolen works yet?"

Sal moved his head from side to side and pulled his phone out of his pocket. "I've checked the gallery database. There's an inventory number. A description something like '5 prints, early 20th century. The artist's name is left blank, so is the source, so is the price, so is the code we use to tell where the work is either stored or on display. This database is usually meticulously maintained. I've never seen an entry like this before. Don't bother to ask me to explain why because I don't have an answer."

Ray raised his hands, palms out, a gesture of resignation. "Okay. Understood. Just a couple of more questions, Sal. As you moved among the guests on Friday evening, did you see anyone who looked out of place? Maybe crashers, or someone from the area simply attracted by the light and the music? I'm talking about people who weren't invited. It would have been easy for anyone to walk down the road or arrive by boat or canoe and join the party."

Sal thought about it. "That would be a real experience for some high school kids, sneaking into a party like that," he said. "But I got kids that age, so I know what they look like. I didn't see anyone like that. The partiers, they mostly looked about Piper's age, late twenties early thirties, maybe. And they were Piper's kind of people, you know what I'm saying? I didn't see anyone that looked like they ended up on the wrong beach."

"And you were circulating a lot?"

"Yeah, especially at the beginning of the night. I was walking around, trying to get a sense of the crowd. Anything else, Sheriff?"

"Yeah, just one thing more. The security system, you say the one at the New York location is state-of-the-art. Why was the system at the mansion so outdated? You're the director of security. How did you allow that to happen?"

"I just couldn't get Ingersolle's ear. Her brain's locked crime in

New York. I couldn't convince her that we needed a similar setup here. Come back in a month or two, and we'll have a state-of-the-art system. I guess it's just human nature, isn't it? What's the old saying…something like we shut the barn door after the horse has bolted?"

Ray stood. "Thank you for coming in, Sal. Will you be staying in the area?"

"Scheduled to be here for another eight or nine days."

"Don't leave town without talking to me first," Ray said. "You're one of our key witnesses."

37

Barbara Sinclair was already working in the technology room when Ray and Sue arrived. Unwinding her long legs from beneath the desk, she stood, and Ray, not used to looking up to many people when he spoke to them, considered this new perspective.

"Don't you ever go home?" asked Sue.

"I got some sleep. But hey, these toys are so fantastic. I'm like a kid in a candy store."

"Where do you want to start?" asked Ray as they all sat down at the conference table.

"Jennifer Bidwell," responded Sue.

A few seconds after the words were out of her mouth, Barbara made a few keystrokes and Jennifer's face appeared on a large screen on the wall.

"Here's a text copy of Sue's interview," said Barbara, passing a small bundle of stapled sheets to Ray and Sue. "I used the speech-to-text feature in the program, then separated out Sue and Bidwell's dialogue."

"It looks like a script for a play," Ray said. "How accurate is the conversion software?"

"The company advertises it to be about 98 percent. That is probably under ideal conditions. It's less than that but still amazing. I think I've corrected most of the errors. But the great thing here is that we have both the audio and video if there are ever any questions about the accuracy of the written copy."

Turning to Ray, Sue asked, "Do you want to read the text copy first, or is it okay if I just hit the highlights for now?"

"Given the press of time, just the highlights."

"Well, as you can see, Bidwell initially tells me that she and Scott Nelson have a professional relationship—she represents the event planner, he represents the client. After she and I looked at the first few of the clips she appears in last Friday, Bidwell amended her story.

Barbara ran the clips recorded Friday night of Jennifer Bidwell.

Ray watched the video, then read through the last few pages of the text copy of the interview. Sue waited until he looked up.

"Without this video, Jennifer probably would have continued to withhold the truth from you in loyalty to Scott."

"Yes," agreed Sue. "Obviously, the most crucial information here is Scott Nelson's friendship with Gerhard Talmadge," said Sue. "Nelson was more or less looking after Talmadge and enlisting Bidwell's help as well. In our earlier conversations, Nelson was doing his best to convince us that he had limited contact with the man. Why?"

"If the relationship between Ingersolle and Talmadge is as toxic as we've been led to believe," said Ray, "Nelson was just looking to keep his job."

"Yes," said Sue, "but it's difficult to believe that he was helping Talmadge out of the goodness of his heart. What was in it for him? What was worth risking his well-paying job for?"

"Okay, your point is well taken. We don't know much about Scott Nelson. And he clearly had the means and opportunity for these crimes. But more than 200 people had the means and opportunity Friday night. But what motive? As far as we know, he has no criminal history. He's got a cushy nest here…" "Do you have other clips with Scott Nelson?" Sue asked Barbara.

"Lots. He shows up on the video all evening," Barbara said. "On most of them Nelson was doing exactly the kind of things someone with his job would be doing. He's helping out at the bar, bringing supplies to the caterers. There are several places where he seems to be answering questions or directing people. You can see his hand gestures, his leaning in to hear or be heard with all the racket. He was mostly out of range of the on-camera mics, but you can make a reasonably reliable guess what he was communicating."

"Okay, we need to bring Nelson in," said Ray. "And that interview needs to be carefully scripted."

"Agreed," said Sue. "I'll start working on it after we're finished here. And I think both of us should be in the room."

"Yes," said Ray.

"We need to look again at the clips of Sal Abato and Helio Lopez," said Sue. "Barbara, run those clip again, please."

After they had viewed the clips, Ray asked, "What do you think?"

"Okay," Sue responded, "the first time through, I was convinced that Lopez was trying to get Abato drunk. I'm not sure about that anymore."

Barbara Sinclair's rich laughter filled the room. "Hey, girl, I'm with you. And I didn't catch on to that the first time, either. But the second time, I got suspicious. I was wondering who was gaming whom. The third time through, I was ready to give the Oscar to Abato."

"What if they were trying to get each other drunk and they both ended up smashed?" asked Ray.

"There's that," said Sue.

38

As they drove toward the Ingersolle beach party, Sue asked, "What's with the music?"

"Renaissance dances," Ray responded, seemingly intent on the music. "Michael Praetorius," he added.

"What goes on in your head when you hear that kind of music?"

Ray took a moment to think about her question, then said, "The sound is very pleasing. I feel transported to another time. When you asked me the question, I was focusing on the underlying rhythm. I could almost see the dancers moving."

Sue remained silent until the piece ended. Then she asked, "What do you hear from Hanna?"

"I haven't talked to her in a couple of weeks. She's clearly found her niche and is busy all the time."

"How do you feel about that? Are you hurt, lonely?"

Ray focused on the road but cocked his head as if listening to an internal voice. "Well, I'm sad. We had a good thing for a while. But she was ready to move on professionally. It was something she needed to do. I went to Palo Alto with an open mind, but I soon realized that California isn't where I want to be."

"So it is over, the relationship?"

"Yes, I think so. There will always be great affection on my part. Hanna got me through a tough time. But the day-to-day relationship is over."

"And you did the same for her, Ray. That time she went with me to Mayo, we had some real heart-to-heart conversations. She said you were the anchor she needed to work through her PTSD and face her alcohol dependence."

"I didn't do anything special."

"Says the guy who would hop in a kayak and paddle out with her in any weather when she was fighting her demons. The guy who was calm under tense circumstances, supportive, and could cook."

"It wasn't all one-sided, Sue. Twice she helped me recover from injuries. And then she put her life on hold and got fired from her job because I was the priority."

Ray went silent for a bit, then said, "I have this theory that people come into your life when you need them. I don't know why it happens, divine intervention or something...it just seems to happen. She was there for me; I was there for her. Now she needed to move on. She's doing important work."

Lost in thought, Sue peered out of the side window, taking little note of the world flashing by. She wanted to tell Ray she hadn't liked Hanna, at least initially. Now, as she thought about her animus toward Hanna, she realized it was all about jealousy.

"I feel uncomfortable crashing this party," she said.

Ray smiled slightly. "I know, but I can't think of anything else to do at the moment. Depending on who shows up, we'll see some or all of the likely cast of characters in this little drama."

"Are you hoping to see those two Moldovan beauties again?" Sue asked in a teasing tone.

Ray's smile broadened, but he didn't say anything.

Alice Ingersolle, standing near the shore with her back to the lake, looked toward the crowd clustered near the food trucks and picnic tables at the end of the sandy cul-de-sac as she grilled Scott Nelson and Sal Abato about the two police investigations focused on Gull Point.

Suddenly, her attention shifted to two newcomers standing on a rise, looking down on the activity. The two men followed her eyes. "Sal," she ordered, "find out what they want. And try to get them out of here."

The two men scurried away. The last thing she wanted today was a police presence. Over the previous several near-sleepless nights she had worried about the rumors circulating about the catastrophic weekend.

Jennifer Bidwell, standing with Linda Wetherbee near the food trucks, caught a glimpse of Scott hurrying along the beach, but not in her direction. Then she noticed the sheriff and the female sergeant, the woman who had tricked her into saying more than she should have. She flushed and shuddered as they approached.

Linda noticed Jennifer's reaction. "Are you okay?" she asked. "I think the sun's getting to you. Maybe we should sit down." She urged Jennifer toward an empty picnic table. Then she followed Jennifer's fixed stare. "You stay here," she instructed. "I'll see what's happening."

Ray watched Sal, Scott, and Linda Wetherbee coming in their direction. "A receiving line," he quipped. "Not our usual greeting."

"Happy to see you, Sheriff," said Sal, his geniality restored after their last tense encounter in the interview room. "I hope you're not here on official business."

"Just normal holiday weekend patrol work," said Ray. "These events sometimes attract crashers, usually teens. Just the appearance of an officer is enough to send them on their way."

"No problem, here," said Sal. "We've been watching things closely."

Linda Wetherbee closed the circle and extended her hand. "Hi, Ray."

"Linda, it's been a while."

"Yes. Your people have been amazing over the last few days. I was planning to send you a note when things slowed down."

"And you've all met Detective Sergeant Sue Lawrence," said Ray. "We're only here for a few minutes and we'll be gone."

"We appreciate your stopping," said Linda Wetherbee. "The party is winding down," she added. "People are already drifting away."

"And Ms. Ingersolle?" inquired Sue.

"She's out near the water, chatting with some of her guests. Do you need a word with her?" Scott asked.

"No," answered Sue. "No reason to bother her. But please let her know that if she has any questions or concerns, she should contact us. We will do our best to keep her up-to-date on the progress of our investigation."

"I'll tell her that," said Nelson.

"And I'll keep my eyes peeled for crashers," added Sal.

Ray and Sue both found Alice Ingersolle's firewall amusing. They couldn't look at each other while walking back to the parking lot, and they were both on the verge of laughter by the time they got back to the truck.

"We quickly attracted a crowd, didn't we?" Ray said.

"We did," agreed Sue. "I think they wish this whole thing would just go away. I can't say I don't wish the same thing."

"Yes, get Talmadge buried or urned and get the carpenters and decorators in for a few days. A new coat of paint and this will all be in the past."

"Did you want to talk to Ms. Ingersolle?" asked Sue.

"I don't really have anything new to tell her. And she's in no rush to talk to us. Curious, isn't it? A burglary, valuable artworks missing, you'd think she'd be all over us, wanting to know why the place wasn't swarming with FBI agents."

"Yes, that seems to be her style," Sue agreed. "Let's get some lunch, then head back to Gull Point."

"Okay," said Ray, his tone flat and distant.

"You heard me about lunch?" she asked.

"Yes," he answered.

"Ray, what are you thinking?"

"While the search for the murder weapon is going on in the area in the lake, I want to take some time to explore the rest of the island. I want to get a sense of the other buildings on the property." He paused for a beat, then said, "Motive, means, opportunity."

"Fill in some of the blanks for me?" asked Sue, mild irritation in her voice.

Ray talked about the murder and the theft of the artwork. Focusing on the artwork, he said the motive was obviously money and noted that while the estate might have been jammed with people on Friday night, none of the invited guests probably knew there was a gallery in the house. While he was cautious about totally discounting the possibility of a perpetrator from the outside coming in to do a heist, his best guess was that Scott, Helio, and Sal, individually or as a pair or a threesome, were responsible for the theft. In addition to their own living quarters at the estate, there were endless places they could stash the artwork until things cooled down.

"What do you think?" he asked Sue. "We usually arrive at about the same conclusions, but you know I do my best thinking with a full stomach."

39

Later in the day, Ray and Sue returned to Gull Point after hearing that a possible murder weapon been recovered. They found Brett Carty waiting at the harbor. He led them to a picnic table near the beach.

Sue stood looking at the battered faces of the mini-sledge hammer standing on a piece of plastic at the center of a picnic table near Gull Point's small harbor. The once square-edged head of the possible murder weapon was deformed by years of pounding, leaving the metal faces almost circular rather than square.

"Where was it found?" Sue asked Brett.

"Just offshore from the place where the body was recovered. And when I say just offshore, I'm talking about five feet at the most. I was just wading out when I spotted it. There's a steep drop-off close in, but the hammer wasn't even tossed that far."

"What are you thinking?"

"I don't know what to think."

"How did you retrieve it?" she asked.

"SOP, with a gloved hand. Then I walked back here with it."

"Any chance of a latent print?" asked Ray.

Sue examined the hammer, walking around the table to get a view from multiple perspectives. "I'm not optimistic," she finally said, pointing to the handle of the hammer, which was swollen by being submerged for nearly three days. "If it was a handgun tossed into the lake, probably some chance. This, I don't know. But I'll check. The pathologists might be able to confirm that it's the likely weapon."

"What does this tell us about the perp?" Ray asked.

"Not particularly skilled at tossing hammers," Sue said.

"How about just being weak?" Brett Carty offered.

"Yeah, that, too," said Sue. "Get this in an evidence bag and have it transported back to the office and secured. I'll check it later."

"Anything else you want us to do while I've got the team here?" Brett asked Ray.

Ray thought for a moment and looked over at Sue. She nodded.

"Remember, there was a tennis shoe with human bones found here earlier this spring. That shoe washed up on the lawn right over there." Ray pointed. "Since you guys have all your gear here, would you check the area immediately beyond the drop-off at the front of the harbor? See if there's anything on the bottom, like a body."

"Yeah, we can do that. The water is always very clear at this time of year. But we might not get done today," Brett said.

"Do what you can. You can finish up tomorrow if necessary."

Ray and Sue walked away from the beach, up the meandering path of pea gravel that had been carefully designed to fit the topography of the slope. Halfway up from the beach, the path forked, the right branch running up toward the main lakeside entrance of the mansion, and the left branch winding up to the circular drive. They followed the path to the left, past the mansion and garage. The four double doors on the side of the garage facing the blacktop drive were closed, as was the service door in the center. Ray and Sue each shouldered a backpack in which Sue had packed photographic gear and evidence collection supplies.

"I don't think Nelson and Abato and the muscle beach guy will be back from the wedding party, or the non-wedding party, for a couple of hours," Sue said.

"Lopez, he appeals to you?" Ray asked.

"I didn't say that. What I said was he has great definition, you know, arms and chest. I mean, he's ripped. But the tattoos, for me, that's a real turnoff. Can you imagine having to look at the same damn pictures day after day, year after year? And a fire breathing dragon, I mean…. And then when the guy gets old and his skin gets thin and gravity starts pulling everything down, yuck. Good thing you don't have tatts, Elkins."

"Maybe I do."

"You don't."

He regarded her with raised eyebrows.

"I checked you out when you were in the hospital. You know, when you were wearing more tubes and wires than clothes."

"That's sort of kinky and intrusive of you."

"Not really. You were just lying there not saying anything. I had to give my brain something to chew on." Her cheeks turned pink, and she started laughing.

"What's so funny?" asked Ray.

"I feel like I got caught in the act. Where are we going, anyway?"

Ray explained that during the Friday night search for Gerhard Talmadge he had quickly checked around the exteriors of several old buildings in the woods way beyond the cottage by flashlight. Now he wanted to take a second look because the buildings might be easy places to hide the missing artwork.

"Where should we start?" asked Sue as they moved off the road into the woods.

Pointing as he talked, Ray said, "There's a quaint little potting shed over there at the bottom of the garden. Then there's that decrepit looking barn, and finally the old garage."

"Let's do quaint first," said Sue.

Following the path toward the small building, they paused far enough out to take in the whole structure. The shed was constructed in much the same style and manner as the cottage.

"Oh, Elkins," said Sue, "what a charming place. There's even a chimney pot. I could live here."

"You might want to check the interior before making an offer," he responded, moving toward the building. He pushed the door open and stepped onto the dirt floor. The odor of soil, water, and vegetation filled his nostrils. "Smells like a greenhouse," he said.

Galvanized watering cans, cracked and crumbling terra-cotta pots, and vintage gardening tools—trowels, scoops, and shears, mostly rusted, some with a few vestiges of faded paint—had been piled on the floor along the wall near the door. An extended counter constructed of rough lumber was attached to the south-facing wall just below the rows of wood-framed windows that ran the length of the building.

"Look at this," said Sue, moving along the counter where she had spotted tubes of paint, brushes, artist charcoal, and drawing pencils. "Someone was working in here. All the art supplies are partially or mostly consumed. Yet everything is perfectly organized. There's not a hint of the usual studio mess."

"It doesn't look like Talmadge's studio," Ray observed.

"You got that right," agreed Sue. "Yes, this was someone else's workspace."

"I wonder who?" said Ray.

Sue eyed the art materials carefully. "The whole lot is covered with a thick coat of dust and grime." One at a time, she picked up some of the paint tubes with a gloved hand and scrutinized them. "I can see some partials, especially on the paper labels. These tubes don't appear to have been touched in years. It looks like the painter just walked away. Let's package these up and take them with us just in case I ever want to run the prints. And let me make a photographic record of this space. Why don't you step outside for a few and enjoy the spring air? This will just take a couple of minutes."

Next they moved down a two track to the front of the old barn.

A large door covering the front of the building was suspended on an overhead track. Ray tried to push the door open, but it didn't budge. He followed a narrow path along the left side of the barn to a weathered entry door. He turned the doorknob, then he struggled to push the door open. Gradually, the rusted hinges gave just enough to allow him to slip into the building.

The dark interior was only lit by the ribbons of light seeping in around the edges of the main door. The air was redolent of mildew and decay. Ray allowed his eyes to adjust to the dull light and then used his hands to help guide his way past the vehicles and equipment to the building's front, where he struggled to unfasten the crude locking hardware that secured the door to the framing. Finally, he pushed the door open, flooding the interior with light.

"I don't think anyone has been in here for a long time," said Ray as he took in the collection of old vehicles and machinery. "This barn was someone's man cave," Ray said. "And no trash allowed. It's a museum of old machinery."

He and Sue circled a large tractor with a crudely fabricated snowplow attached to the front. Chains were wrapped around one of the tractor's two huge tires.

"What's the deal with the chains?" Sue asked.

"Traction, Sue. All the rage before snow tires and all-wheel drive."

When Sue noted that the chains were missing from the other drive wheel, Ray explained that chains breaking and then falling off was common at the time.

"Look at this, Elkins," said Sue.

She had discovered an old sports car on four long-deflated tires. The canvas top had rotted away in places, exposing the interior. Ray ran his gloved finger along the front fender, removing a dense layer of dust and grime and revealing the dark green lacquer paint. "It needs some love," he said.

"What is it?" she asked.

"Something British," he answered, then added after a closer look, "a Jaguar."

"New York plates, 1953," said Sue as she walked around the rear of the vehicle. "Looks like the mice had their way with the leather seats years ago."

"Yes," he answered, taking time to carefully inspect the old car.

"There's an old speedboat, too," Sue said, moving to the back of the building. "But no place to do art. Too dark and too damp. Looks like a long forgotten place," she said as she moved out into the sunshine. Ray agreed as he started to close the place up again.

"Two down, one to go," said Sue as they headed to their last destination.

40

The garage behind Gerhard Talmadge's cottage was constructed in the same style as the potting shed and cottage.

"Look at that door. How could you get a car in there?" asked Sue as they stood in front of the old building.

"Model Ts and Model As weren't very wide. And after cars got wider, why tear down a perfectly good building when you can fill it with junk?"

She looked up at the window over the doors. "There's a second story."

Ray pulled at the handle on the garage door. The door didn't budge. Then he marched around the building and tried the entry door at the center of the rear wall. He looked around and picked up a terracotta pot on the left side of the door. A key, brass and corroded, was in the saucer.

"Great deduction, Elkins."

"A 50/50 chance. Half the people in this county keep a spare door key under a flower pot near the door." As he pushed the door open, the hinges complained.

"Great sound effects," said Sue.

Ray reached around the dark interior until he found an old-fashioned light switch, a round ceramic mechanism. He twisted the switch, then laughed.

"What's going on?" asked Sue.

"I tried to turn the lights on. I keep forgetting about the electricity."

"A mind is a terrible thing to lose," she said.

"I'll get the main door open. That will give us a lot of light."

Ray navigated the crowded interior to the front of the building and soon had the doors open. The garage was populated with rusting bicycles and lawnmowers, several outboard motors on stands, a canoe, oars and paddles, water skis, and a collection of cardboard boxes, rotting and spilling their contents onto the floor.

Sue scanned the scattered tools and toys of a hundred summers.

"Where should we start?" she asked archly. "Bicycles or water skis?"

"Don't be sarcastic," he responded, then he pointed to a narrow stairway running along the left wall and said, "Let's check the upstairs."

"You first," said Sue.

Ray negotiated his way through the detritus and climbed the steep stairs to a small landing. A door blocked his way. He tried the handle; the door was locked. Taking one step back, he gave the door a sharp kick with the flat of his foot near the handle. The door popped open.

"Elkins, I don't…believe what I just saw," said Sue as she started to mount the stairs.

Ray entered the attic-like room. Sunlight streamed in from the small west-facing window, illuminating the gloomy interior. He surveyed the sparsely furnished space. A toilet, sink, and a metal shower stall stood along one wall. On the opposite side of the room a single bed covered with a thin mattress was pushed close to the wall. A dresser and a desk stood next to the bed.

"Nothing much up here," said Sue, coming to his side. Then she asked, "Where's all the junk?"

"It really makes you think something must be wrong," he responded.

Ray ran the beam of his small flashlight around the perimeter of the room, finally focusing his attention on the scant furnishings. He checked the drawers in the desk and the dresser. They were empty. He piled them, upside down, on the top of the desk.

Pulling the flimsy piece of bedding up from the frame, he checked the top, one side, and one end of the mattress both with his eyes and his hands. Then he passed the flashlight to Sue and pulled the mattress around to look at the bottom, the other side, and end.

"What are you finding?" asked Sue.

"Do you have a knife?"

"Yes," she answered, pulling a multi-tool from her utility belt and passing it to him.

As Ray carefully ran his fingers over the end of the mattress, Sue kept the beam of light on the area he was exploring. He paused, opened the knife, then adroitly started pulling at a carefully stitched seam, cutting off a knot and then pulling a thin nylon thread out of the surrounding material.

"Twenty-pound monofilament," he said after he removed the last of the stitching. Then Ray fished around the interior of the mattress, pushing his fingers into the thick batting, most of his forearm disappearing into the interior. Then he paused briefly and slowly extracted his arm, clutching a small red folder with his fingers. He passed the object to Sue.

"What have we got?" he asked as he flopped the mattress back on the bed.

"A passport, Peoples Republic of China, issued to Yuan Zheng Hong; 26 years old. Profession listed as student. He had entered Canada on June 6 of 2015. But there is no stamp indicating when he had entered the US. I wonder how long he was here. A year, less or more? How did you know to search the mattress?" she asked.

"Pure luck. There wasn't anything else to search. And something was wrong here. The place wasn't filled with junk. Something happened here and not in the too distant past."

"This isn't going to have a happy ending, is it?" Sue said.

"No, I don't think so," Ray said. "It looks like a young man named Yuan Zheng Hong once lived here. Now he's gone. Someone did an almost perfect job of removing all traces of this man."

"Why did Yuan Zheng Hong hide his passport?" asked Sue.

"I'm wondering the same thing. Think you can find a fingerprint on the passport? A match with the ones on the paint tubes would give us some direction."

"Maybe, but if I don't, I think this is a biometric passport. There's a chip imbedded in the document. If I can't get a match of the document itself, I can get one from the chip. The Bureau can help me or at least point me in the right direction. Ray, I wonder what other secrets we'll uncover."

Ray looked around the room one last time. "Okay, I think we're done for today. Let's come back tomorrow morning with some extra lights. I want to thoroughly check this room over a second time—walls, floor, ceiling, the whole nine yards—on the off chance something else was hidden by…"

"Yuan Zheng Hong."

"Yuan Zheng Hong," Ray repeated. "Thank you."

"Good plan. Elkins, I'm starving, and I want to see my dog."

"How about the Last Chance?" said Ray.

"Why do I get the feeling the workday isn't quite over?"

"Which local eatery is closest to Gull Point?"

"The Last Chance."

"Exactly, and while the seemingly ageless barkeeper, Jack Grochowski, isn't as good with names as he used to be, he never seems to forget a face. I'm sure he knows all the local kids like Scott Nelson. And I'll bet he's seen a lot of Gerhard Talmadge over the years. Let's see if he remembers either or both of them being in the company of a young Chinese man a few years back."

41

Ray was sitting at the conference table yawning and stretching his arms over his head.

"Short night, boss?" Barbara Sinclair asked, settling across from him.

"Way too short," he answered.

Sue joined them, following her usual ritual of arranging her computer, coffee mug, and legal pad and pencils on the table before dropping into a chair.

After Sue and Barbara briefly exchanged pleasantries, Ray said, "Barbara, I'd like you to do some searches. The names will sound familiar. They're people you've already identified in the surveillance videos."

He pointed to the list he had added to one side of the whiteboard. "Please do a search in the National Crime Information Center on these individuals. And there's one more name I want you to check."

Ray moved to the board and wrote Yuan Zheng Hong at the bottom of the list.

"We found his passport yesterday. He might show up as a missing person. It appears he entered Canada legally from China four years ago. That was the final stamp on his passport."

"The passport is already in the evidence room," added Sue. "I can help you with this. We need to find out what the appropriate protocol is for reporting a missing foreign national. This is something that will involve the FBI."

"Good. The others on the list, do you want to limit my search to NCIC?"

"I don't understand," said Ray.

"The summer before I completed my degree, I did an internship doing background checks for an HR recruiting firm. First, we checked to see if the applicant had any arrests or convictions, the kinds of things that would automatically trigger an extensive background check and probably exclude the person from any further consideration. If nothing was alarming in that first scan, we'd then look at the applicant's social media. You'd be surprised what turns up there."

"What do you mean?" asked Ray. "Give me an example."

"LinkedIn, you're familiar with that?" she asked in a teasing manner.

"Yes," said Ray.

"Some people pad their profiles. And by that I mean seriously puff up their credentials. They list schools they didn't attend, degrees they never earned, honors they were never awarded, publications they never authored, and jobs they never had. That kind of thing."

"How did you know where to begin?" Ray asked.

"The firm had a terrific training program. We spent lots of hours comparing truthful and fraudulent portfolios. After you've looked through scores of LinkedIn pages, you get an eye for what the firm called the ABCs. The A profiles were mostly honest. The B profiles were somewhat padded. And the C profiles were mostly BS. The mostly BS profiles were the easiest to spot. They were just over the top. You've got to wonder what these people were thinking. The C profiles from our LinkedIn scan triggered an intense review of a job candidate's résumé and application."

"Would you look at anything other than LinkedIn?" asked Sue.

"Facebook, Twitter, Instagram…I'm not talking about a lot of time."

"This seems invasive…"

"Not in any way. This is the person's public face. It's their brag, something they choose to publish online. In a hiring situation, a Facebook page might tell you more about someone than their résumé or even an interview. You know what I'm saying. The people on your list, I'd like to do a quick scan of their social media, in addition to just an arrest records check," Sinclair said.

"Okay," said Ray. "Can you get it done quickly? I want to bring in all these individuals for formal interviews. The information you gather might be useful."

"Absolutely," said Sinclair as she pushed back her chair and stood.

"Wait a bit," said Ray. "Sit, please. There's something I want you to hear. I've already added a note on this in the case file if you want to reference it again. Sue, why don't you fill Barbara in on our conversation at the Last Chance."

"After we got off the island last night…why am I thinking of that as an island?"

"Because it is," Sinclair interjected, "at least at the moment."

"Elkins insisted that we stop at the Last Chance."

"I remember the place. You took me there for lunch when I came up for an interview. Remember, you were giving me the grand tour of the county. Good burgers."

"The barman there, Jack…"

"Yeah, that super-geezer…"

"Well, Ray chatted him up about Scott Nelson. And Jack had a story about how Scott's father carried his one and only son in shortly after Scott was born and passed out cigars. Then he told us how Scott showed up one night when he was in high school and tried to buy a six-pack. And Jack reminded Scott he was only seventeen. Jack's memory, long-term that is, is impressive. At this point in the conversation, Ray puts Yuan Zheng Hong's passport on the bar. It's in a plastic bag and open to the first page. Jack carries it down the bar where he holds it under a bright light. When he comes back, he says, and I'm paraphrasing here, 'Now I know why you mentioned Scott Nelson, that's his friend Mike. A few years back, they were in here all the time. Mike liked beer, especially the hoppy local brew I keep on tap. Mike, he never said much. He mostly just smiled when you talked to him. I'm not sure how much English he had. And then Mike disappeared. I asked Scott what happened to his friend, and he said Mike went back to China.'"

"Interesting. Anything else?"

"Jack said that Scott came in with Gerhard Talmadge all the time, and over a lot of years."

Sinclair looked over at Ray. "Should I start with Scott Nelson?"

"Yes, perfect."

"Anything else?"

"Yes, this is something else Sue and I talked about last night."

"Are you guys ever off the clock?"

Not responding to Sinclair's comment, Ray said, "We've been told that there was a drawn-out battle between Alice Ingersolle and her stepfather, Gerhardt Talmadge, over ownership of the Gull Point property. This battle probably involves the will of Irene Ingersolle. Would you see what's out there?"

"Motive or motives?" said Sue, not moving from the conference table. "Yuan Zheng Hong, why was he here? What happened to him? Should we be searching for a body, and if so, where? Obviously, Scott Nelson is up to his eyeballs in all of this," she continued. "And he's consistently lied to us. Should we pull him in for an interview, two on one, laying out all the misinformation he's given us? And maybe at some point slide Yuan Zheng Hong's passport in front of him?"

"Let's wait and turn up the heat a bit. Nelson is probably around today. We know he's been keeping us under surveillance, so let's put on a parade of sorts. We show up with our backpacks and some extra battery powered lights. And Barbara, why don't you come with us. We could use an extra pair of eyes…and more importantly I want to make sure we attract Scott's attention. We want him to know we're working on the second floor of the garage."

"And in the process of doing that, if we can manage to introduce Barbara to Scott Nelson…?" said Sue.

"Exactly. Put some flesh on the bones."

"I'm sure he's running multiple scenarios in his head of how he's going keep professing his innocence," said Ray. "Let's give him some more things to be anxious about."

"So I'm supposed to make a cameo appearance in this little drama?" asked Barbara.

"Yes," Ray answered. "Arrive with us. Help us check out the apartment in the garage. Then you can come back here and continue with your work. We'll catch up over a late lunch. I'm buying. What should we bring you?"

"I'll have what she's having," said Barbara, pointing to Sue.

42

Ray walked out to the end of the dock and peered off into the mist. The hot, humid weather of the last few days, more typical of midsummer than late spring, had been pushed out of the area by a cold front moving down the Great Lakes from Canada.

"I just messaged the boat crew to pick us up," said Sue, coming to his side. "What a beautiful morning." She looked at Ray and followed his eyes. "You want to be out there, don't you? Out in your kayak heading toward the Manitou Islands."

Ray nodded.

"What's it like?"

"Magical. Especially on a morning like this. I like to launch early, just after first light. If there's no wave or wind action, it's mostly silent—just the sound of paddle strokes and my breathing, a couple of steady rhythms. And then there's a gentle gurgling sound as the bow cuts through the water.

"The mist usually burns off before I reach the islands. When it lifts, it's a Brigadoon moment. South Manitou's an enchanted world frozen more than a century ago, the houses, outbuildings, and the lighthouse. I walk around the village like the last person left on the planet. And when I look back at the mainland, it's just the topography —the dunes, Alligator Hill, Pyramid Point. Eight miles out, there's no sound coming from the mainland, and you can't see anything moving. I linger a bit before starting back, sit on the shore near the lighthouse, drink some coffee and watch the waves start to build in the passage as the day warms and the wind picks up."

"Back to reality, Elkins. Here comes our ride," said Sue.

Ray gave himself a mental shake. "Where's Barbara?"

"She's sitting in her car working on her laptop. I'll get her."

Fifteen minutes later, they had docked at Gull Point and were walking up the slope toward the old garage behind Gerhard Talmadge's cottage, Ray leading the way, Sue and Barbara following a few steps back. Ray was listening to their conversation with one ear. They seemed to be talking shop.

"Sheriff, any new developments?" asked Scott Nelson. He stood in the middle of the trail as if he had been waiting for them, effectively blocking their way.

Ray moved in close, then said, "Good morning, Scott," without answering his question. Then he turned and did the introductions. "You know Detective Sue Lawrence, and this is Officer Barbara Sinclair."

"So," started Scott, looking down on them from his slightly elevated position, "What are you up to today?"

"Continuing with the investigation, Scott. And I'm glad you're here because I have a question for you."

"I'm always happy to help, Sheriff."

Right words, wrong tone, thought Ray. "Yesterday, Scott, we were looking through the old garage, the one behind the cottage. It appears that there's a small apartment on the second story."

"Really?"

"And," continued Ray, "I was wondering if anyone had been living there recently."

"Lots of people coming and going," said Scott, "but I find it hard to believe anyone might have stayed in the garage. Once years ago, I peeked in one day when the doors were standing open. The place was just crammed with junk."

"Did you know there was an apartment on the second floor?" said Ray.

"An apartment, really? I can't imagine anyone living there."

"So you never saw any lights in the garage at night or anything else that might have drawn your attention?"

"If I had, I would have probably thought that Gerhard was in there looking for something. Anyway, it never registered."

"The comings and goings, Scott, who are you talking about?"

"Hard to say, Sheriff. I just saw people around. I mean, I wasn't looking. I just assumed they were connected with Gerhard's art business. So, you know, I'm thinking gallery people, or maybe collectors coming directly to Gerhard. I can't tell you much more. Like I was never introduced to any of them. I just saw them in passing."

"Young, old, American, or foreign? Scott, anything you can add might help us."

"Again, Sheriff, I wasn't paying attention. I'd guess they were mostly middle age or older. Probably the kind of people who can afford to buy art. I can't tell you much more."

"And of these many visitors, there was never anyone around for an extended period of time who might have camped out in the apartment in the garage?"

"Never say never, but I think it's unlikely. I wasn't keeping watch over Talmadge. That wasn't in my job description."

"I understand, Scott. Thanks." Ray started to move past, stopping when they were at eye level. "One more thing, Scott. Are Sal and Helio here? I want to talk with them."

"They spent the night on the *Hermes*. They're not back yet. Ms. Ingersolle wanted to go over some things with them."

"Thanks. If you see them, let them know I need to talk with them."

"Will do."

The threesome moved on in silence until they reached the old garage. Standing outside the building, Sue said to Barbara, "Now you've seen Scott Nelson both on video and in the flesh."

"Yes, indeed. Almost feeling kind of guilty. Is voyeurism a crime in Michigan or just a personal failing?"

"Personal failing, mostly," quipped Sue.

"Help us here for a bit, then you can head back while we recheck another building. I'm willing to bet Nelson will be watching for you, and he'll do his best to start a conversation. Don't tell him anything. Just be your usual pleasant self."

"He can be charming," added Sue. "He will do his best to chat you up. Probably even hit on you."

"Come on," said Barbara. "He's going to hit on a person of color who's a head taller than him and a cop, too?"

"You're young, female, and attractive," said Sue. "And while that won't be lost on him, his real interest in you is to find out where we are in the investigation."

43

Ray and Sue, with Barbara's assistance, carefully checked the apartment above the garage, searching for any other place where documents or personal items might have been secreted. There were none. Then they parted ways, Barbara returning to the office, Ray and Sue going back to the potting shed for a second, more systematic search. Returning to the beach, they encountered Brett Carty.

"How is the search going?" asked Ray.

"No bodies," answered Carty in a jocular tone. "We have harvested an interesting collection of junk, including the proverbial kitchen sink. Nothing is particularly suspicious. I've marked out the area we've covered," Brett said, passing Ray an iPad. "I was wondering if you want us to continue. And if so, do you want to change the perimeters of the search?"

Ray looked at the screen showing an outline of the Gull Point peninsula. The landmass was gray, the area that had been searched highlighted in light blue, the rest of the water in dark blue.

"We've worked most of the relatively shallow water. As we move out, it gets a lot deeper, colder, and darker. Our progress will be slower. Do you want us to continue tomorrow, if we can't finish today?"

Ray looked back at the screen. Using his finger, he said, "I'd like you to keep going a bit farther. Do this whole area in front of the marina. "

"You've got to see what we've collected so far," said Carty, leading the way. He stopped on a gentle slope near the shore and gestured toward the array of discarded items that the dive team had pulled from the lake.

"You will find a list in my report," he added. "But in summary from left to right: one cast iron kitchen sink, one rusty lawn chair, a large Zenith radio, the kind with tubes, and lots of small junk: sunglasses, bottles, cans, and a rusty minnow pail. I hope this isn't typical of junk along the whole shoreline."

"Frightening thought, but it probably is." Ray pointed to a pile off to the side. "What's over there?"

"Two very bald car tires, and a battery from a boat or car. What are we looking for?"

"A man went missing from this place about four years ago. I'm wondering if he ended up in the lake. Wouldn't be much left. Maybe some clothing with something to hold it down."

"The old cement boots story."

"Yeah, something like that. Do what you can safely do today. And come back tomorrow if necessary."

44

As they were eating lunch around the conference table, Ray asked, "Barbara, have you had a chance to do any of the background checks?"

Barbara nodded, holding her burger and chewing furiously. Finally, she said, "Scott Nelson."

"How about a five-minute duty-free lunch?" pleaded Sue. She took a bite of her burger.

"Is this SOP, working through lunch?" asked Barbara, directing her question to Sue.

Sue went on to explain that Ray was always on task, including mealtimes. The only exception to the rule was when he was having one of his favorite meals, like rack of lamb or wild-caught salmon from the Bay of Fundy. Then he was all about perfect preparation and presentation. "And," she added, "he's a great cook."

"Scott Nelson?" said Ray, looking at Barbara.

She balled up the empty wrapper from her burger and tossed a perfect hook shot to the wastebasket in the far corner of the room. From a stack of papers, she took individual sheets and arranged them around a yellow legal pad. Then she began, "Scott Nelson. No hint of crime on the NCIC. No felonies, no speeding tickets, no nothing. A regular Eagle Scout, literally."

"Did he get your phone number?" asked Sue.

"He tried," she said, bursting into a peal of laughter. "He looked quite pleased when I gave him my business card. The dude didn't understand that number is for the general switchboard."

She took a sip of her Diet Coke, "When I first reviewed the video, I skipped the early material on the flash drives and focused on the events of last Friday. Today, I started looking through the video recorded on Wednesday. Here's the first segment of video in which Piper makes an appearance." They watched as Piper Ingersolle approached the mansion garage and opened the door leading to the stairway to Scott's apartment. As she moved past the camera, she could be heard calling Scott's name.

Sinclair paused the feed and said, "Notice the time stamp, 10:09 p.m."

She started the video again. They heard the sound of footsteps on the garage stairway and then saw Piper emerge from the building, her back to the camera. She stopped abruptly, then turned back toward the camera, unbuttoned her blouse, realigned the buttons, and fastened them again.

"And notice this time stamp, 11:20 p.m."

"I did," said Sue. "Ray's overcoming the shock of seeing a wholesome young woman's bra without her consent."

"I'm in no way suggesting what might have gone down during that hour and eleven minutes," Sinclair said. "As for the thing with the buttons, maybe they were just comparing their tans. I hear white folk do that."

"So you're warning us about the pitfalls of voyeurism?" asked Sue, trying to control her giggling.

"You got it. And here's the grand finale, sort of the dessert course," said Barbara.

Ray saw the clip he had seen before of Scott and Piper standing together on Friday night outside the tent. They were talking and laughing. Then Sinclair zoomed in on them and the image became grainier and filled the screen. Ray watched as Scott leaned forward and Piper ducked away and feigned a slapping motion. Piper turned and started to walk away, and Scott gave her a parting pat on the rear. She turned back in his direction and blew him a kiss before finally moving away.

"I can see why you guys warned me about that man," said Barbara. "He must have some kind of mojo. He seems to know his way around a woman."

"Maybe you should have given him your cell number," said Sue.

"I'm reconsidering," Sinclair retorted. "And now I'm going to move on to social media. First, LinkedIn. There are a lot of Scott Nelsons on LinkedIn, but I did find our Scott."

She clicked the remote, and Scott's LinkedIn page appeared on the screen, which listed Harvard as his undergraduate alma mater.

"Here's where I ran into my first red flag. I couldn't find his name on the list for his stated graduation year at Harvard. I talked with someone in the registrar's office, a woman who did her best not to tell me anything. I eventually ended up with her supervisor. Mind, I wasn't asking for grades or anything. All I wanted to know was did our Scott Nelson from Cedar County, Michigan, attend Harvard and I gave the possible range of years. The two of us finally got to the point where we agreed that we were talking about the same Scott Nelson. And what I learned was that, no, he didn't graduate from Harvard. He was there for four semesters, end of story."

"Wow," Sue said. "He's cockier than I thought."

"So then I moved on to the University of Minnesota, where Scott supposedly went to graduate school. And I discovered that there is no record of his enrollment in any school or college at that university. I did find a Scott Nelson who lived in Minneapolis during the time he claims to have been a student there. It appears to be our Scott Nelson. Maybe he just lived there and worked. There are a lot of hangers-on around large universities.

"And then I moved on to his publications. Check out the citations, they're very impressive. The problem is I couldn't find any of the articles, and some of the journals didn't even exist. And I'm not saying the journals ceased publishing; they never existed. But I've got to hand it to him, if you're not familiar with his area of study and you're just glancing through, it looks impressive."

"So, there's essentially…what? Five years pass from the time Scott disappears after his second year at Harvard," said Sue.

"Exactly," Sinclair said.

"We need to bring him in," said Ray. "And after we question him, put him under surveillance so he doesn't do a runner. How about Sal and Helio?"

"Sal is who he says he is. Nothing in NCIC. He does have a couple of DUIs about ten years ago, nothing more. Helio Lopez was not easy. Lots of people with that name, primarily in the southwest but scattered across the country. Several hits on NCIC, but not the right age, not our guy. I need to do some more digging. Hard to believe, but some people don't have a presence on social media. Get some ID from this man."

"On my list," said Sue.

"Did you guys find anything interesting after I left the scene?" asked Sinclair.

"Nothing," answered Sue. Turning to Ray, she asked, "How do you want to deal with Scott?"

"Let's start with a friendly conversation. We'll tell Scott he's our expert on Gull Point and we need his assistance. We'll listen politely and only lightly challenge anything he tells us. And we'll end the interview before anything gets too threatening. I want him to leave this interview feeling that he's in control of the situation."

"You want me to make the call?" asked Sue.

"Yes. Tell him we need his help in our inquires. See if he's available now. Tell him we'll get the transportation in place."

45

"Scott, thanks for coming in on short notice. We needed a conversation with you because when it comes to Gull Point, you're the most well informed person we have. You know the terrain, the people, the history, and the night of the storm, you were there," said Sue.

"Scott," said Ray, "there are a few inconsistencies in some of the things you've told us. And we understand how that might have happened. We've all been overwhelmed by the events of the last few days."

"We just need to clarify a few things," added Sue.

"I'm happy to help," Scott said. "It has been a crazy time. I'm sure we can sort it all out."

"Remember when we told you that we had found the apartment in the old garage behind the Talmadge cottage? You seemed surprised at the suggestion that someone might have been living there. Is that correct?"

"That's right."

"Scott, we recently had a chat with an individual who has known you for many years," Sue said. "And that person told us that they often saw you in the company of a young Asian man."

"Really," Scott said. "Did they give you a time?"

"This would have been about four years ago," Ray said.

Scott looked up at the ceiling, slowly bringing his eyes back to Ray's. "I can think of one possibility. We had a gardener from Central America a few years ago. Guatemala as I remember it. Native stock, you know what I'm saying. Little or no European blood. His looks…it was difficult to guess his ethnicity. You know, up here people think anyone who's brown with black hair is Mexican. They don't seem to know there's anything below Mexico. And if your face doesn't quite fit the Mexican stereotype, you might be Tibetan or Chinese or something else. The Bering Land Bridge theory isn't part of school curriculum around here. At least it wasn't when I was in school."

"Did this gardener have a name?" asked Sue.

"Miguel, as I remember it."

"What was his last name?" said Sue.

"I wouldn't know that."

"So this Miguel, he worked for you? You're in charge of grounds, right?"

"He worked for our landscaping contractor at the time. Miguel was assigned here for the summer to look after the flower beds and shrubbery."

"Did he stay here, like in the apartment in the garage?"

"No, absolutely not. He stayed with his people. You know, there were pockets of Spanish speaking farm workers back then before immigration became such a big deal. I don't know where he stayed. All I know is he arrived in an old black pickup truck. I think it had Arizona plates."

"Would you have payroll information on this man?" asked Sue.

"No. Like I said, he worked for our landscaping contractor. Miguel would have been a line item on my monthly bill. I imagine his boss paid him in cash. Those people, they don't have bank accounts or anything."

"Did you ever have a meal with this Miguel?" Ray asked.

"Yes, probably. I tried to do things for him. He was a hard worker."

"Any chance you, Miguel, and Gerhard Talmadge might have had dinner out somewhere?" he asked.

"Miguel, he stayed around in the evenings sometimes, did some gardening for Talmadge. So, yeah, that might have happened."

"I'm confused," said Sue. "You told us you avoided Mr. Talmadge. You suggested that your employer might fire you if you were friendly with Mr. Talmadge."

"Look, if anyone ever asked me if I was friends with Gerhard Talmadge, I'd tell them what I told you. But Mr. Talmadge and I were neighbors, so through sheer proximity, we often couldn't avoid being together. And he was getting on in years. He often needed some help."

"But you chose to go out to a public venue with Mr. Talmadge," pressed Ray.

"I never did that when Ms. Ingersolle was around, and that was less than two months a year."

Just then, after a knock on the interview room door, Barbara Sinclair poked her head inside. "Excuse me, Sheriff, Detective Lawrence," she said. "You're needed to handle an emergency situation."

Ray and Sue stood, picking up laptops and legal pads. "Someone will be back in a few minutes to finish up. If you need anything in the interim, just knock on the door. There's an officer posted outside."

Ray looked at the camera. "Interview interrupted as Elkins and Lawrence leave the room."

The threesome moved down the hall to the conference room. "How was my timing?" asked Barbara Sinclair as she dropped into a chair.

"Perfect," said Ray. "What do you think?"

"He's good," she said.

"I know," Sue said. "I found myself wanting to believe him at times."

"You both need to take a few minutes to watch this conversation from the outside," Sinclair said. "Nelson's focus was intense, and was mostly looking at you, Sheriff."

Ray looked up at the screen and observed the live feed from the interview room. Nelson was sitting at the metal table, his hands resting on the surface, fingers interlocked.

"Look at him evaluating his own performance," Sinclair said with mock warmth. "He's a creative storyteller, a smart guy. But his hubris might do him in."

"That's what I'm thinking, too, the hubris piece," said Ray. "If I can put myself in his head for a minute, I bet he'd like to take the Miguel story back. It just leads to other possible questions. He's worried that we'll ask for the name and address of the landscaping company, and he'll be just painting himself into a corner. He's thinking about better lies, like Talmadge often had guests and invited him along. He never really knew who the people were. He'd only see them once or twice."

"Should we confront him with the information Sinclair has uncovered and try to start breaking him down?"

Ray was slow to answer. Finally, he said, "I don't think so. At this point, he's in no legal jeopardy. Let's stop while this is still a friendly conversation. We have suspicions, we have possible scenarios, but only circumstantial evidence. And what motive might he have had…?"

"For either or both crimes?" offered Sue, completing the sentence. "And if we confront him with what we currently have, he's going to understand his possible peril, get a lawyer, and go silent."

"Yes. Let's be cordial, thank him for his time, and get him transported back to Gull Point."

46

Ray and Sue encountered Brett Carty as soon as they arrived at Gull Point in the morning.

"How's it going?" Ray asked.

"We've completed checking the area you wanted searched."

"And?"

"More debris, much like we found earlier—a rusty sand pail, a shovel head, a few beer cans, one jam jar. What were you hoping to find?"

"How about snow chains, big ones for a tractor tire, sort of tied together with a skeleton inside."

"Or at least one Air Jordon," added Sue.

"Sorry," said Brett, "nothing that interesting."

They found Sal sitting at a small table outside the mansion, a coffee mug in one hand, a cigarette in the other.

"Hi, Sal," said Ray, standing across from him.

"Morning, Sheriff, morning, Sergeant," Sal responded. "What's going on?"

"We have a few questions for you. Do you have a minute?"

"I suspect it's going to be more than a minute. And that I don't have much choice. So why don't you two sit down and make yourselves comfortable."

"Right," said Ray. "And, with your permission, we're going to record this conversation."

"And if I don't give you my permission, you're going to take me in, Mirandize me, and interrogate me in your new, high-tech room."

"Yes."

"I guess you have a deal," he said. "Make sure your recording app is working so we don't have to do this again. Fire away."

"Friday night, after the evacuation, there were only the three of you up here, right?"

"Yes. We've been over this before, Sheriff. And I've been spending most of my time thinking about what happened and who might be responsible. Of course you're suspicious of us three. And I'm suspicious, too. Up here I'm wondering about Scott and Helio. At the gallery in New York I'm leery of everyone—the customers, the staff, anyone who might want to walk out of the gallery with a little piece of something worth more than you'll make in your whole career."

"Tell me about Scott. Has he been stealing from the company?"

"Sheriff, there are things I can't talk about. Let's just say I keep an eye on him."

"Well, if he's stealing from the company and—"

"Look, Sheriff, it's more complex than that. Let's see, how do I explain it delicately? He's more than an employee; he's a special friend of the CEO."

Ray sensed Sue looking at him out of the corner of her eye. Scott Nelson certainly did get around.

"If I had my way," Sal said, "he'd be gone."

"Because?"

Sal hesitated, shifting in his chair. Finally, he said, "When I contracted the HR firm to do background checks of job applicants, I also had them go through the personnel files of all currently employed staff members. Scott has sometimes lorded his Harvard pedigree...as if he's a superior species."

Sal ground out his cigarette on the sole of his shoe and dropped the butt in the coffee cup.

"Sheriff, the only bits of truth on his job application were his birthdate and his gender. I guess I should add that he has no criminal record. At least he didn't when we checked. Hell, anyone who doesn't keep an eye on a guy like that is a fool."

"Have you caught him at anything?" asked Sue.

"No," he said. "But like I've said, I'm not here that much. As far as I can tell, Scott hasn't walked with anything or cooked books for the estate. There's no evidence that he's ever padded an expense report or taken a kickback from a contractor. That said, I question his competence."

"What are you talking about?" asked Sue.

"Scott, he's so convincing. Anytime something isn't right around the estate, it's never his fault. There's always an excuse—a contractor didn't show up, a supplier didn't deliver, or Ingersolle didn't give him enough funds. But times, they are a changing."

"Explain, please?"

"Ms. Ingersolle is increasingly unhappy with the man. And I've watched her around the store over the years—once you're on her shit list, you're on your way out."

"Did you know about a death here at the estate about four years ago?" asked Ray.

"Not four years ago, not ever."

"Did you or anyone else come out here to get rid of a body?"

"No, never."

"Including Helio?"

"He's only been with us a couple of years."

"Friday night. Any chance Helio did the break-in?"

"I don't think so. After the storm, we got busy doing first aid. We were both maxed on adrenaline. Then we helped you guys do the evacuation. And then we shared guard duty till dawn. We were both crashed out. I don't think so."

"You reported a burglary, Sal, but your employer has failed thus far to provide any images or description of the stolen art. Any insights as to why she's refusing to cooperate with our investigation?"

"No idea, Sheriff. That's one mind I definitely cannot read. And I don't think I'd want to even if I could."

"You don't happen be Ms. Ingersolle's fixer, are you?" asked Ray. "You know, when there's a problem it's your job to make it go away."

"Absolutely not. Listen, when I was a cop, I never had Internal Affairs on my ass, not once. You know why? I've stayed clean. With this company, I look after the security for the organization. That's all. That's my job description. I'm not going to do anything illegal, like getting rid of a body, or heisting some prints just because my boss tells me to. You get what I'm saying?"

"Why are you telling us this?" asked Ray.

"Because I can't say everything about the Ingersolle Galleries is on the up-and-up, just like I couldn't honestly tell people some of my cop buddies weren't on the take. You get my drift. There's a lot of money at stake in this business. That doesn't bring out the best in people."

"Okay, so help me with the drift."

"Some of my cop friends are tight with Bureau people. Word is they're watching the high-end art market. And it's not like the feds are trying to get cultured. It's more like some people aren't paying their taxes. Maybe they're committing fraud, too. Who knows? It's not just Ingersolle Galleries. It's the whole industry." Sal looked from Ray to Sue and back again. "Now is this good enough, or do you want to take me in?"

"It's good enough for now, Sal. Just don't leave town without talking to me first."

"Okay."

"One more thing," Sue said. "Friday night, during the big party, who had access to this house?"

"Ms. Ingersolle wanted the mansion off limits as much as possible. So other than Piper and her bridesmaids, no one had access. Piper and her friends used some guest rooms as a staging area before their grand entrance. They weren't staying here. The kitchen was closed off. The caterers for Friday's party had to bring their own equipment. There were toilet units in place down close to the party area so no one would wander up here looking for a john. You get what I'm saying. There was no reason for anyone to come here during the party."

"And after the storm?"

"You know what it looked like. Most of the glass on the side of the great room facing the pool was missing. After that initial blast people were looking for help. They could see some light up here. We had flashlights and then some candles."

"So at that time, after the storm, would it have been easy to gain access the gallery?" asked Sue.

Sal chewed on a lip for a few seconds, then answered. "Well, it shouldn't have been. The stairway to the gallery would have been closed off."

"I'm not following," said Ray.

"Let me show you," Sal said, pushing himself out of his chair and leading them into the mansion. Looking back at them as he walked, he said, "This place is set up like a hotel or a conference center." He paused where the hallway widened into the front entrance and said, "You can change the layout by opening and closing different sets of doors. The doors leading to the stairway giving access to the gallery were closed and locked before the party started. And long before Piper and her friends arrived."

A bit farther on, Sal paused again and pointed. "Look, on each side, pocket doors." He pulled a metal tab, and the door on his right side slid into view.

Ray looked at Sue, then back at Sal. "You didn't mention these doors when we first came here to investigate the break-in."

"We must have opened them when we did our walkthrough that night, after the storm. They're usually left locked if there is anything on display in the gallery."

"So you're telling us that to the best of your knowledge at the time of the break-in, this set of doors and another set doors at the other end were locked, and there was no evidence that either set of doors had been tampered with?" asked Ray.

"Yes. You have to understand that we entered the hallway through the other set of doors. We unlocked those doors to enter, relocked them, then came down the hall and discovered the damaged doors that open to the gallery. After looking around the gallery and seeing the missing prints, we came down these stairs and..." Sal went silent, then said, "Shit, I don't remember these doors being closed. But I probably didn't think anything about it at the time. I mean, I probably thought Scott opened the doors. He was running around like a madman making a list of all the damage. In the process, he was opening everything we had closed off for the party."

"Sal, do me a favor," Ray said. "Close these the doors. Let's see if there's any damage."

Ray and Sue stepped back, and Sal closed the doors. Then he looked at Ray. "Well, as you can see…"

"No hint the doors have been forced," said Ray. "Who has access to the key that opens these doors?"

"The master opens these. Scott has a master. I do, too. In fact Scott, he probably has several. He lends master keys to tradesmen who have to work in different parts of the estate. Ms. Ingersolle probably has one, too."

"Sal, you got your key?"

The man fished around in his pants pocket, retrieving a red identification tag with a key attached to it.

"I need that key," Ray said. "Can you do without it for a couple of hours?"

"Sure," Sal said.

"Sal, guide us to your apartment. We need to have a look."

"I know you do. The beds aren't made. That might make things easier."

"Is Scott around?"

"I haven't seen him. But you've got a master key. I don't think he ever locks."

47

"Let's find a place to talk." said Sue.

"Actually, I was going to propose that," said Ray. "How about in the shade?"

They settled into two teak Adirondack chairs under an ancient oak. They sat in silence as they took in the view, the expansive lawn and then the big lake, flat and quiet under a blazing noon sun.

"You want a protein bar?" Sue asked.

"What kind?"

"A date/nut combo."

"Sure."

"That search was a waste of time," said Sue, "but we had to do it." She went on to comment that the suite shared by Sal and Helio had all the charm of a budget motel, while Scott's apartment was bright and spacious, and the second floor location provided great views of the lake and woods.

"A view of the bay and decent pay. Scott has a nicely feathered nest," agreed Ray. "Going back to Sal, was he telling us the truth?"

"I think so," said Sue. "But that 'internal affairs' spiel was playing at the brotherhood of cops and the thin blue line stuff a bit too much. My crap detector was starting to ring. That said, I think Sal is exactly what he shows to the world."

"How about Helio?" asked Ray.

"Well, we don't know much about him—other than the great pecs and six-pack, the T-shirts a few sizes too small, and his past work history as Ms. Ingersolle's personal trainer. I almost buy Sal's story that Helio, rather than focusing on his job responsibilities, was mostly hoping to get lucky Friday evening. You know, all that stuff with the champagne bottles. If he could get his boss beyond caring, he'd be free to mingle with the crowd. And given how much everyone was probably drinking, he might have gotten lucky. I mean, when people are smashed, they're looking at bodies, not checking for Mensa membership cards. But that's beside the point."

"What exactly is your point?" asked Ray, amused by her riff.

"If Sal or Helio had pulled an art theft or walked with Ingersolle's silver—I mean she's got to have some serious sterling in a joint like this—they wouldn't have stuck around with the stolen goods in their duffel bags. They would have been gone before sunrise. Neither one seems to be in a particular hurry to leave."

"Three minus two."

"Scott Nelson," said Sue. "But he didn't leave town, either."

"Where does he have to go?" asked Ray.

"There's that. Given what we learned from Sinclair's research on Scott supported by the background check Sal had done…"

Sue stopped mid-sentence. "You know, I think initially we both bought into one of Scott's early stories about his limited knowledge of what went on at Gull Point, his 'need to know' line. The reality probably is that he's aware of everything that happens here. I mean, Scott's got the keys to the place and is mostly unsupervised. We've seen him in action. He's very attuned to the world around him. He may not be sharing much with us, but I doubt that anything gets past him. Look at the way he checked me out early on."

"You got a home-cooked dinner out of it," said Ray.

"True. But now, I wonder what his real motivations were. The tennis shoe incident put us on his radar. If he had knowledge of Yuan Zheng Hong's disappearance…" Sue left the thought hanging.

"Exactly," said Ray. "And think about the tales he's had to weave for more than a decade to keep the phony narrative of his life story afloat. What does he do now? Something like, 'Hey, Mom and Dad, the reason I didn't invite you to come out to Cambridge for graduation was I left Harvard after only four semesters.' Sue, we know liars. They are part of the stock-in-trade of our profession. But Scott, he takes lying to a different level."

"Okay, so is Scott involved with: a. the missing artwork, b. the bashing in of Talmadge's head, c. the Yuan Zheng Hong mystery?"

"Interesting question," said Ray. "And if so, what were his motives?

And what about Jennifer Bidwell? Girlfriend *du jour* or perhaps the new love of his life?"

"You think he wanted to hide the relationship for some reason beyond protecting his job?" Ray asked.

"What if the relationship is more serious than it appears to be? What if he is thinking about running away with her? Maybe he's thinking about creating a new life somewhere else. If he left this place, he'd need some serious money. He's bright, he's got good social skills. He could probably build a new life without a résumé."

"Here's my speculation," said Ray. "Scott's not running because he's got nowhere to run to. He's got a beautiful place to live and a good income. He's going to have a hard time duplicating what he has here. And there's one more thing. I don't think he's that excited about Jennifer."

"Okay, let's say you're right about that," Sue said. "But Sal suggested that Scott has been providing Ms. Ingersolle with… additional services? And what if that relationship is coming to an end? If that's true, Scott's job could be in jeopardy."

"Heisting some valuable prints might be a way of insuring his financial future. Scott takes the prints, he hides them somewhere, waits till things cool down, and then…he's got to find a buyer. Probably not easy to do without the right connections."

"We've searched his apartment and, of course, he wouldn't hide them there," Sue said. "So where would he hide them? Maybe we should check out that old Jaguar again, just so you can get another look? I've never seen you so smitten," said Sue.

"That's interesting."

"What is?"

"Vehicles," Ray answered. "Let's start with Scott Nelson's truck. Then let's check out Jennifer Bidwell's Subaru."

He pushed himself out of the chair and stretched, slowly turning from side to side.

"You okay?" asked Sue.

"Back hurts. I've been sitting too much. I need a long walk on the beach."

"That sounds good. But right now, you look uncomfortable. Why not stretch out on the lawn while I search the cars?"

"Tempting, but no," he said and set out at a good pace across the lawn toward the area where the cars were parked.

48

Ray dropped the hood on Scott Nelson's Toyota pickup, then gave it a tug with his fingers to make sure the latch had caught.

"Nothing," he said to Sue as she backed out of the truck's cab.

"Same here," she said. "The front seat is clean, but the glove box, console, and area behind the seats are filled with all kinds of junk. I'm talking about fast food wrappers, paper cups, and assorted other trash. It's like his life."

"I don't get your metaphor, Sue."

"At first glance, everything looks tidy. If you dig a little deeper, you discover all the trash."

Ray smiled. "That's quite clever. Did you look through all the stuff in the back?"

"It's too much of a mess. But I can assure you there is no two-foot mailing tube or thirty-six-inch flat package. I'll bag a couple of the cups for possible DNA sampling."

"I'll check out the Subaru while you do that."

Ray walked around the exterior of the small SUV and checked the doors. They were unlocked. One by one he opened the doors and inspected the interior. With the exception of some sand on the floor mats and a snowbrush on the back seat, the car was empty. He walked around to the rear and popped the hatch. "Why are you looking in my car? What's going on, Sheriff?"

Ray turned and saw Jennifer Bidwell striding toward him across the grass, presumably having come from the dock. In a few seconds, she was at his side, her eyes blazing with anger.

"We have search warrants for all the buildings and vehicles on the property, Ms. Bidwell," Ray said. "We're looking for the artwork that was stolen from Ms. Ingersolle's gallery."

"But why my car?" she asked.

"On the off chance that the stolen property might still be somewhere on the estate. We've searched all of the buildings. Now we're checking all of the vehicles."

"How did you get the doors unlocked?"

"They were open," Ray said.

She abruptly gave up her protest, and her focus shifted toward the garage and Scott Nelson's apartment. "Have you seen Scott?" she asked.

"Not since we've been here this afternoon," Ray said.

"Are you done with my car?"

"Your car was easy, mostly empty and very organized. One glance was enough. All I have yet to do is look in the tire compartment," he explained. Then he lifted the panel.

"You seem to be missing a spare," he said.

"That's impossible," said Jennifer.

Ray lifted a cardboard mailer out of the tire well with a gloved hand and held it up in her direction.

"Is this yours?" he asked her before passing the tube to Sue.

"I've never seen it before. Honest," Jennifer said, moving closer to her car. "Where the hell's my spare tire. Someone stole my tire."

She focused on Ray. "I don't know anything. Where the fuck is Scott?" Turning, she ran toward the garage, and when she reached it, she pulled open the door and disappeared up the stairway leading to Scott's apartment.

"See what's in the tube," said Ray.

Sue carefully cut the packing tape that secured one end of the tube and removed a coil of paper. Pulling the roll partially open, she revealed a delicately drawn ballet slipper and part of a lower calf, the leading edge of the point shoe was flattened as if bearing the weight of the dancer.

"That's enough," said Ray. "Secure them back in the tube. I'll call for backup." He stepped away and made the call, then returned to Sue's side.

As he watched Sue push the roll of prints back into the container, he became aware of rising voices, the sound of an argument escalating. Three voices—two women's, one man's—came through the open windows of Scott Nelson's apartment.

"Brace yourself," said Sue. "We're going to be dealing with a domestic momentarily." She put the tube back into Jennifer Bidwell's car and closed the hatch.

"Got your camera on?" said Ray.

Sue nodded. They started across the drive toward the building, only to be stopped in their tracks by the roar of gunfire. A window in the apartment above them exploded outward. Glass sprayed across the driveway in front of Ray and Sue. Seconds later, Piper Ingersolle sprinted from the doorway, crying, trying to hold an unbuttoned blouse closed.

"She's crazy!" Piper shouted. "She's going to kill us all!"

Scott burst out of the stairwell next, clearing the doorway just before another blast of gunfire reverberated behind him. He screamed and tumbled forward.

Ray came in from an oblique angle and tackled Bidwell's midsection as she emerged from the building, knocking her off her feet, the shotgun flying from her grasp. She struggled to free herself, tearing at his arms with claw-like fingers.

Sue joined the fray, trying to help pin down Jennifer's flailing arms and legs. Finally, together, they managed to cuff Jennifer's hands behind her. They were still on the ground, trying to restrain her when the other officers arrived.

Ray pushed himself up, then pulled Jennifer to her feet.

"Scott's your thief!" she shouted at Ray.

"I'm wounded!" Scott yelled from the ground. His legs were covered in blood.

Ray knelt at Scott's side and inspected the wounds. "Birdshot," said Ray, "just a few hits. You'll live."

"He was dead anyway," Jennifer yelled at Scott. "Dead," she repeated.

"Who was dead?" asked Ray.

Jennifer closed her mouth.

"Ray," said Sue.

He looked at her. She was holding her right wrist in a guarded position close to her chest.

"Again?" he asked with dismay.

She nodded.

He looked over at Brett Carty, the first arriving officer. "Get this man medical care, then hold him for questioning. And these two women, hold them for questioning, too. I'll take Sergeant Lawrence to the ER."

49

Ray settled on a chair in the waiting area near the emergency room, glanced around at the sparsely populated area, and looked up at a cable news talking head on an overhead screen. Pulling out his phone, he first read the headlines in the *Times* and then the *Post*, briefly dropping into stories but mostly moving on before he got to the end.

Then he started thumbing through a book of poetry he had carried in with him from the car. He jumped from page to page until he was pulled into a line about water. Slowing, he took in the next line, read it a second time, and then move on to the next stanza, becoming lost in the images and the emotions they evoked.

"Sheriff."

Ray stood and stepped to meet the man dressed in blue scrubs. "How is she?" he asked.

"I've put her in a cast. This break is worse than the last one. It's in the same area again. This woman needs time to heal, Sheriff," he said sternly. "Just because she's out of a cast doesn't mean she can return to normal duty."

"I understand, Doctor."

"Yes, you probably do," he said, his manner softening. "But Sergeant Lawrence doesn't. She's still at that indestructible age. I don't want any complications. After the cast comes off, she must wear a protective splint. She will need PT, also. She's admitted to the fact that she didn't do the PT I prescribed for her last fracture."

"I'll make sure that happens," said Ray.

The surgeon nodded and continued. "And when I say normal duties, that doesn't include physical confrontations and wrestling suspects to the ground. Normal will be office duties. Nothing more physical than using a stapler."

"I'll do my best," said Ray.

"Does she live with someone? She's going need some help caring for herself."

"She lives on her own. I'll see what I can get in place."

"Good. Ms. Lawrence will need assistance with day-to-day activities. And Sheriff, I want this fracture to heal properly. I don't want her to have a wrist filled with arthritis when she's middle-aged."

"How was it?" asked Ray as he reached across Sue to fasten her seatbelt.

"It was uncomfortable. But after the doctor pumped me full of pain meds, it was a piece of cake."

"The drugs, they wear off," said Ray.

"There's always a downside," she said, flashing a sardonic smile.

"Sue, the doctor says you're going to need some help."

"Yeah, I know. I got a lecture."

"Maybe we could get Barbara Sinclair to stay with you for a few weeks. You two seem to have a great rapport."

"We do. Barbara's smart, funny, and a great cook. And her desserts are to die for, but..."

"But what?"

"Elkins. You've recently been letting me bunk in your guest room occasionally. It's so much easier to look after Simone when I stay with you."

Ray didn't respond.

"Did you hear what I said?" Sue finally asked.

"Yes, it is easier. I like it when you're there. It seems natural."

"Your relationship with the doc is over, right?"

"Yes," answered Ray."

"So Elkins, how many of your women have come and gone during my tenure in the department?"

"A few," answered Ray, keeping his eyes on the road ahead.

"Of all of them, I really thought Hanna was a keeper," Sue said.

"I was starting to think that, too."

"In the beginning, I didn't like her very much. And then I began to really admire her. You know what I didn't like about her?"

Ray looked her way and then back at the road.

"I didn't like her because she had you. It took me a long time to figure that out. When she went with me to Mayo, I don't know how it came up, but she said something like, 'You're in love with Ray, aren't you?' She forced me to confront my feelings."

"Before we split up, Hanna asked me a similar question. I explained to her why a relationship between us was impossible."

"Why?" asked Sue.

"Well, first, I'm your boss. We have a professional relationship. And then, I'm almost as old as your father."

"Only if you started impregnating girls when you were twelve," she laughed. Then she said, "Ray, a couple of hours ago, I watched you tackle a crazy woman with a shotgun. In December, I knelt at your side on that snow-covered slope when you were critically wounded. I held you, praying you wouldn't die."

"Where are you going with this?" he asked, his voice tight with discomfort.

"I want to be with you, Ray. I hope you feel the same way."

"Sue, I've been attracted to you for a long time. But one, we work together. And two, I'm not good at relationships. Like you said, women come and go. And what we have now is so good, I'm afraid I'd make a mess of things."

"Are you willing to give it a try?"

After a long silence, Ray said, "Do you have a plan?"

"Kind of, at least the beginning of a plan. Tonight, after we finish these interviews and after we pick up Simone, I want to go home with you. We'll drink champagne while you're cooking, maybe open a second bottle to go with the meal. Then I want to fall asleep in your arms and wake up next to you in the morning."

"What if I roll on your wrist during the night?"

"Elkins, all relationships are dangerous. I'm willing to take the risk."

Ray wondered if he was willing to take the risk. He didn't think he could bear to lose her.

50

"Why am I being held?" asked Piper. "Are you charging me?"

"No, you're not being charged," Ray said. "But you were involved in a domestic dispute, and we have a few questions. Maybe you can help us understand what just happened."

"What do you want to know?" asked Piper.

"Please tell us what happened from your perspective."

"Scott and I, we go back a lot of years," Piper said. "As you know, my grandfather just died, and my wedding has been postponed, and I needed a friend. So, when I came over here from the hotel today to pick up some things, I stopped by to see him. I knew he was seeing someone, but he said it was casual, and neither one of us had any idea that she was at Gull Point."

Piper reddened a bit. "Alas, we were caught *in flagrante delicto*. I mean, suddenly this woman came crashing into the room, screaming. So then I was screaming, and Scott was yelling, and then she found Scott's shotgun somewhere. She was crying hysterically, so I couldn't understand what she was saying. There is obviously a lot of stuff between Scott and her that I know nothing about. I really didn't understand half of what was going down. I gather she felt they had an exclusive relationship."

"Can you remember anything else?" asked Sue.

Piper kneaded her forehead. "Just bits and pieces, lots of obscenities, something about all of Scott's promises, something about how they would be rich, and then a whole litany of what she had done for Scott. You've got to know I wasn't listening very carefully. I was just trying to grab my clothes and get out of there."

"How well do you know Scott?" Sue asked.

"What are you asking, exactly?"

"We've been finding some inconsistencies between—"

Piper looked at Sue. "You mean his making things up?" she said. "That was always Scott. Even as a kid. He was always telling grandiose stories, stories where he was always the hero. You know, like escaping from a pirate ship. He had this rich imagination. I've always liked him anyway. He's always been kind of lost, but he has a good heart."

"Do you know the extent of his, to use your phrase, making things up?" asked Sue.

"Yes. Sal Abato called it to my attention after he had a background check run on Scott. I told him I didn't want to know."

"Who was Jennifer Bidwell aiming the shotgun at?" asked Ray.

"Well, I assumed Scott, but maybe it was both of us. She didn't seem to know what she was doing. She was waving the gun back and forth, yelling and crying. Then it went off, and she looked like she was going to fall down. I don't know if she was trying to kill us or was just making a point. I don't think she's ever shot a gun before. Either way, I've never been so scared."

Piper's eyes welled up, and she wiped at them with her hand. Sue passed her a box of tissues.

After a long silence, Ray asked, "Is there anything else you can add to your account?"

"No, that's sort of it. I have no sense of time, but I think we're only talking about three or four minutes. Once the woman had that gun in her hands, I really thought I was going to die." She paused. "Can I ask you a question?"

"Go ahead," said Ray.

"You mentioned that something set this woman off. Can you tell me what that was all about?"

"Do you know about the theft of some prints from the gallery in the main building?" asked Ray. "It happened Friday night or early Saturday morning."

"My mother said something about it on the phone—she was irate about it—but I really wasn't listening. I can't say I care about her stupid art right now. I've been distraught over my grandfather's death and by Mother's absolute crap attitude about it."

"We discovered a mailing tube in Jennifer's car," explained Ray. "It was hidden in the spare tire well. There were art prints in the mailer, perhaps the ones that were stolen."

"Prints, what do they look like?" asked Piper.

"We've only just glanced at them. The prints and mailing tube are being logged into our properties department."

"The prints, are you talking about flowers, a bowl of fruit, a horse, a series of nudes?"

Sue answered, "Nothing like that. They're ballet themed."

Piper leaned to one side to retrieve her phone from the back pocket of her jeans. Then her fingers raced across the touchscreen. She regarded the screen for a long moment, then held the phone toward Ray and Sue.

"Did they look like this?" Piper asked as she passed the phone to Ray.

Ray nodded as he showed Sue the image. "That isn't the exact one, but it's a variation on the theme. Right?" he asked, addressing Sue.

"A different image, but it's very much in the same style," agreed Sue.

"There are five sketches. Just look through them," said Piper.

Ray shared the screen with Sue as he flipped from sketch to sketch.

"That's the one," said Sue. "I remember the pose. Why don't you get the prints so we can see if the others match?"

After Ray left the room, Piper said, "Maybe I do need an attorney."

"What's going on?" asked Sue.

"Why are these prints so important?" Piper asked.

"You know about the theft of artwork on Friday night. Are these prints we just found in Bidwell's vehicle the missing artwork and, if so, who stole them?" Sue asked.

Moments later, Ray entered the room holding the roll of prints, his hands covered with light-blue latex gloves.

"I'll spread these out one at a time. Piper, see if you can match each one to your pictures."

Standing at the end of the table, Ray stretched out each print one at a time. The two women stood at either side.

"That didn't take long. The images appear to be exactly the same or very close," said Sue as soon as they completed the process. "Piper, maybe you can help us understand what this is all about."

"I have a confession of sorts to make," Piper began. "I didn't tell you the truth when I told you that my grandfather had given me a series of photographs of me and my grandmother from my childhood."

"He gave you something else?" said Ray.

Piper nodded. "Grandfather was intent on giving me a special wedding present: the five sketches that had been hanging in the cottage for as long as I can remember. He told me that he had gifted them to my grandmother at the time of their marriage. I was greatly moved by this gesture. I was thinking about the lovely symmetry of the gift. I could feel the connection of love and relationships moving across generations. Then Grandfather sort of shattered my romantic view of these sketches."

"What did he say?" asked Sue.

"He told me the prints might be stolen art from the Nazi era." After pausing to let that information sink in, Piper continued, "The sketches of young girls in different poses, they were part of a game my grandmother and I played when I was a girl. I didn't want to tell you the truth about them, Sheriff, because I was afraid of losing them."

"Were you telling the truth when you said you sent them to your office in New York by FedEx?" asked Ray.

"Yes," she said.

"This set of prints and the ones you mailed, are they similar?" asked Ray.

"The images seem exactly the same, but these are copies,

photographic or Xerox. This paper is off-white, but it looks and feels new. The prints Grandfather gave to me are on paper that seemed quite old. The texture of this paper is very smooth, whereas the paper on Grandfather's prints is rougher. You can see a shadow effect—the area covered by the frame was lighter than the rest of the print. And probably the biggest difference is the smell. I noticed that the prints Grandfather gave me have a musty smell."

"Let me make sure I understand what you're saying," Ray said. "To you, the drawings appear to be similar, but the ones given to you by Gerhard Talmadge appear to be much older than the ones we found earlier today."

"Exactly. I mean, I'm sort of freaked out. What the hell is going on here?"

"I wish we knew," said Ray. "Might you have any explanations?"

"I can only think that someone is trying to pass off these copies as the real Degas sketches, but I can't even think about the implications of such an idea right now. Between getting shot at and this, I'm sort of in shock."

"Maybe with your cooperation, we could get to the bottom of this."

"Sheriff, just say the word. I want to understand it."

"Okay," said Ray. "If we can arrange something with the FBI, would you be willing to transfer custody of your sketches to the Bureau until we get this whole thing sorted out? I have to warn you, if these prints are on a stolen art list, you will lose them."

"I'm aware of that. In fact, I'm starting to think I would prefer it."

"Why don't you go with Sue, and she'll get the paperwork started. Are you going to stay in the area?"

"Yes. I'll be here at least until my grandfather's body is released. After he's buried, I'll start thinking about going home and getting back to work."

"Make sure we have your correct contact information," Ray said. "And please check with me before you leave the area. There will probably be loose ends you can help us with."

Piper and Sue rose and turned toward the door of the interview room.

"And Piper, one more thing," Ray said, and she turned back toward him. "Did you tell anyone about the prints you had sent to your office in New York? Scott, for example?"

"No. Nobody. Not Scott, not my mother, not Sal, not Trevor. It was sort of a secret between Grandfather and me. It was sort of like when I was a kid. We'd have little secrets just between us."

51

Sue sat across from Scott Nelson in the interview room and read from the laminated sheet:

You have the right to remain silent. Anything you say can and will be used against you in a court of law. You have the right to an attorney. If you cannot afford an attorney, one will be provided for you. Do you understand the rights I have just read to you? With these rights in mind, do you wish to speak to me?

"No problem, Sue, or should I call you Detective Sergeant Lawrence?" he asked, tossing her a coy smile.

"Mr. Nelson, you're looking at some serious charges. This is not a game."

"I did nothing wrong. As soon as you hear my side of the story, I'll be walking out of here. I don't need any damn attorney. I can defend myself."

Ray entered the interview room and sat at Sue's left side.

"I was just telling your sergeant here, this is all a big mistake. Some crazy woman breaks into my house and attacks me, and I get hauled off to jail. I mean, this is just totally bizarre. Sheriff, I've got work to do. Let's get this over with so I can get on with my life."

"How are your wounds?" asked Ray.

"It looked worse than it was. The docs removed three pellets from one calf, gave me a shot and scripts for antibiotics and pain pills."

"It could have been a lot worse, Scott," said Ray.

"Yeah, I was lucky."

"Scott, we were in the drive just across from your building this afternoon when all this chaos erupted. Why don't you tell us what took place from your point of view?" said Ray.

"Jennifer, she's crazy. I mean, I sort of knew she was a bit strange, but I didn't have any idea of the extent of her problems."

"How long have you known Jennifer Bidwell?" asked Sue.

"Only a few months."

"What's the nature of your relationship with Ms. Bidwell?" asked Sue.

"Professional. I was coordinating things between the wedding planner and Ms. Ingersolle."

"So this woman, Jennifer Bidwell, with whom you have a professional relationship, out of the blue runs into your apartment, finds a loaded shotgun, and starts shooting at you?" asked Ray.

"Exactly, perfect, now you understand why I said Jennifer is totally crazy. I guess I should be more politically correct. The woman has serious emotional problems."

"And your relationship was totally professional. You never met with Jennifer Bidwell socially?" asked Ray.

"We shared a beer once or twice and went out for a burger from time to time. It was all work-related. People must eat. You can accomplish a lot over a meal."

"The shotgun that Jennifer was firing, does that weapon belong to you?" asked Ray.

"Yes, I'm a duck hunter. And I like to go skeet shooting every once in a while."

"How is it that Ms. Bidwell knew about the gun? Was it just lying there out in the open?" Sue asked.

"I keep it in a closet in the bedroom. Jennifer must have seen me put it away. She expressed an interest in guns, so I took her skeet shooting a few weeks ago."

"Scott," said Ray. "We've got video evidence that Jennifer was in and out of your apartment on several occasions recently at times outside regular working hours. How do you explain that?"

"Well, I did see her socially a few times. Our workday often goes way beyond the eight-to-five schedule. And sometimes we've just ended up hanging out." Scott paused for a moment and looked away. Then brought his focus back to Ray. "I mean, maybe in her delusional world, she was reading more into our occasional.... You know what I'm trying to say?"

"It appears to me," said Sue, "again based on video data, that your relationship involved more than an occasional bite to eat. I mean, sharing a bottle of champagne, then disappearing up into your apartment for an extended amount of time during Friday evening's party? By all appearances, you've been having a physical relationship with this woman."

Scott looked away, pulled at his chin a few times, then looked at Sue. "Ahh, involved? What do you mean involved? We worked together, maybe a little bit more. Things happen between consenting adults. But there were no promises, stated or implied."

"Might Ms. Bidwell have seen your relationship differently?" asked Sue.

"I'm not responsible for what Ms. Bidwell sees or thinks or does. I exercise no control over her—thought control or otherwise."

"That's not what I asked you."

"Look, I see it now. She's crazy. I mean—well, I shouldn't tell you this...but it just shows her mental state. She confessed to me that on Friday night, after the big storm, she found Gerhard trapped under a tree. You know what she did? She clubbed him over the head! She's the one who should be sitting here answering your questions."

"You're telling us that she told you she killed Gerhard?" asked Sue.

"Yes."

"Did you ask her why?"

"Yes. Jennifer said she did it for us. But there is no us!" Scott said, his voice rising. "There never was an us. There never will be an us. That woman lives in a fantasy world."

"Why didn't you tell us immediately?" asked Ray.

"Because the morning after the storm when you asked me to identify the body, you said that Gerhard was killed by a falling tree. I thought Jennifer's story was just one more of her delusions. She needs a psychiatrist, not a cop. Can I go now?" He looked directly into the camera. "The painkillers are making me awfully tired."

"I have one more question, Scott," Ray said. "Jennifer Bidwell arrived when we were inspecting her car, the Subaru you identified as belonging to her earlier. As you know, we've been looking for the artwork you reported missing from Ms. Ingersolle's gallery. When Sue and I checked Jennifer's car, we found a large cardboard mailing tube in her spare tire well. We peeled back the tape and pulled out some sketches of young ballerinas. Seeing that mailing tube really set Jennifer off. That's when she dashed toward your apartment. Any idea why?"

"I don't know anything about a mailer," he said, taking a deep breath. "She appeared to be so innocent, but maybe she was using me to get to Ms. Ingersolle's art collection. There's clearly more to her dark side than I ever imagined."

"That's funny," Sue said, "because the tube was sealed at each end with packing tape. When I checked the tape for prints, I found yours all over it. That kind of tape is great for collecting and preserving accurate prints."

"She found the packing tape in my apartment. Of course, it would have my prints on it."

"Scott," said Sue, "we also found your prints on Gerhard Talmadge's basement door. The window had been broken to gain entrance. Your prints were on the door handle. Why were you breaking into Mr. Talmadge's house?"

"I would like to call my lawyer now. If you have any more questions, you know where to find me."

"We do, Scott," Sue said. "We're going to put you back in a cell and let you think about your answers. If you decide you would like to talk to your attorney or need a public defender, the deputy will give you access to a phone."

52

After Sue finished reading the Miranda warning, she looked across the table at Jennifer Bidwell and her attorney, Agnes Hathaway. The lawyer looked at her client over the top of her half-frame reading glasses. "My instructions to you are to say nothing."

"What time did you arrive at Gull Point?" asked Sue.

"It was after 2:00," Jennifer Bidwell answered.

"You are not listening," Hathaway hissed at her client.

"Transportation, how did you get there?"

"One of your officers gave me a ride in one of your boats."

"How did you make that happen?" Ray asked.

"I told him who I was, that I worked for the wedding planner. When he asked me my reason for wanting to go to Gull Point, I told him with the road being out, my Subaru was being held captive, and there were some papers in it that I needed. So he gave me a ride over and said he would wait for me. I assured him I'd only be about ten minutes."

"You were not truthful with the officer," said Sue.

"It wasn't much of a lie. I needed to see Scott."

Ms. Hathaway cleared her throat. "I need to speak with my client privately. She obviously doesn't comprehend that she's putting herself in jeopardy."

"How much time, counselor?" asked Sue.

"Ten minutes. And I want to be in another room. I don't like these cameras and mics."

"We will turn them off."

"That's not good enough. Another room, I insist."

Sue led them across the hall to a small, unoccupied office.

"We will be waiting for you in the interview room. I'll have a deputy outside this door in case you need anything."

Sue noted that Jennifer Bidwell appeared even more agitated when the deputy escorted the two women back to the interview room almost a half an hour later.

"When we left off, I had just asked you when you arrived at Gull Point," Sue said. "You answered that it was mid-afternoon. Is that correct?"

"Yes."

"You said you were coming to Gull Point to see Scott?"

"Yes."

"You're talking about Scott Nelson, correct?"

"There's no need to say anything further, Jennifer," Ms. Hathaway said. "We should end this right now."

"I don't need you. I don't want you here. I didn't hire you," Jennifer said, directing her attention at her lawyer. "My boss wants you here to protect her, not me."

"What was your question?" Jennifer asked, turning back to Sue.

"I was trying to establish that you came to Gull Point to see Scott Nelson."

"Yes, Scott Nelson."

"Why did you need to see Scott?" Sue probed.

"Stop now," urged Hathaway.

"We had plans. At least I thought we had plans. Suddenly, Scott wasn't answering my calls or texts. I needed to see him face-to-face."

"Then what happened?"

"You know what happened," Jennifer snarled. "You guys were searching my car, and you found those drawings. They shouldn't have been there. I knew that bastard had been using me. But stealing something and stashing it in my car. I just lost it. And then I went to confront…" Her face contorted. Then she began to sob uncontrollably. Sue slid a tissue box in her direction.

"Bastard, bastard, bastard. Scott's just been using me. Everything he said is a lie."

They waited several long minutes until Jennifer had regained control of her emotions. As they waited, Agnes Hathaway said, "You're a foolish, stupid girl. This will all be used against you in court."

"Then what happened?" asked Sue.

"I ran to confront Scott, up the stairs and into the apartment. I found him in bed with that woman. I wanted to kill him. I was yelling at him. I think I was hitting him with my fists. And then I grabbed the shotgun."

"Where was the shotgun?" asked Ray.

"In the corner near the bed, like always. I grabbed it. By then, Scott and the woman, they were running toward the stairway. I followed them. When I got to the stairs, the gun suddenly went off."

"Were you trying to kill Scott, the woman, or both of them?" Ray asked.

"I don't know. I don't think so. It just happened. All I know is when you guys had me on the ground, I was glad it was over. This isn't me. Scott has turned my life upside down in just a few weeks."

"Gerhard Talmadge, did you know him?" Ray asked.

"Yes, briefly. He needed a lot of help with transportation. Doctors' appointments, stuff like that. Grocery shopping, too. And trips to the drug store. Scott had been helping Talmadge out. He got me to take over. Scott was so busy getting things done for the wedding."

"Did you see Mr. Talmadge the night of the party?"

"Yes."

"Did you have any contact with him."

"Yes, I saw him standing there watching the party. I took him some food."

"Was that the only time you saw him."

"You must stop now," ordered Agnes Hathaway.

"They need to know the truth," countered Jennifer Bidwell, tears streaming down her face again.

"The truth can come out at trial," said Ms. Hathaway.

"I saw Mr. Talmadge again when it was really storming. He was running. The man is almost blind. I followed him. I wanted to help him. I was close to him when I got flattened by a falling tree. Eventually, I crawled out. He was almost next to me. The tree trunk was across his back. He was dead, not breathing. No pulse."

"How did you know?" asked Ray.

"I felt around his neck like I learned in CPR class. There was no pulse. None."

"Then what did you do?"

"I was hurt. I needed to get help."

"Is there anything else you want to tell us. Now is the time to get it all out," Sue said gently.

"No, nothing else."

"Scott Nelson said you told him you hit Mr. Talmadge in the head to make sure he was dead."

"Bastard, that isn't the way it happened. Mr. Talmadge was dead. I knew that. When I got near the tent, I stumbled over some tools. There was a hammer."

"That's enough," said Hathaway.

"Get it over with," urged Sue. "Tell us everything and be done with it."

"I took the hammer and went back to Mr. Talmadge. He was so close. I just gave him a tap."

"Why, Jennifer? Why would you do that?" Sue asked.

"Scott, he said Mr. Talmadge had promised to leave him some valuable art. Scott said we'd be rich then. He promised to take me away. We'd get married and have a family. I knew Mr. Talmadge was dead. I was going to tell Scott I made sure Mr. Talmadge was dead. I thought Scott would love me more, but he didn't. He was in bed with that woman."

53

Scott Nelson looked off into the distance as Sue read the Miranda warning.

"Scott, when we last left off questioning you, we were asking you about the presence of your fingerprints on Gerhard Talmadge's basement door. The window in that door had been broken to gain entrance into the building. How do you explain your fingerprints being there?" asked Ray.

"Let no good deed go unpunished," Scott said sourly.

"I'm not following," said Ray.

"Gerhard, poor old Gerhard. In addition to being almost blind, he was losing it. He was convinced that people were trying to break into his cottage and steal things, especially his wallet. He was absolutely OCD about keeping his place locked up. The problem was, Gerhard was always locking himself out. He never remembered to take his key with him. And then he'd come and find me. I had a key to his cottage. Sometime in the last few weeks, he borrowed the key and then didn't bring it back. A few days later, he locked himself out again. I popped the window in the basement door. I picked that door so the broken window wouldn't be obvious to people passing by. That's why my prints are there. So if it's a crime to help an old guy into his house, I'm guilty as hell. Drag me to the gallows."

"Did you arrange to have the window replaced?"

"Yeah, well, I was going to get to that and a whole lot of other things around there as soon as the wedding was history. And you know how that worked out."

"Scott, let's go back to the mailing tube, the one with your fingerprints on it. I wonder how the mailing tube got in Jennifer Bidwell's trunk?"

"That's not so hard to understand. If those were the prints stolen from the gallery, the thief was probably just looking for a place to stash them until they could retrieve them later."

"Good theory," said Ray. "A couple days ago, when you saw me checking vehicles…"

"Yeah, I remember. I told you the Subaru might be hers."

"Yes, as if you didn't really know for sure the car parked directly across from the entrance to your apartment belonged to Jennifer Bidwell. During our conversation, I checked to see if the vehicle was locked. It was, and I duly noted that it was. But earlier today, when I tried the doors to that vehicle, they were unlocked. I should add, Scott, when we searched your apartment earlier, Bidwell's purse was sitting on the table just inside the door, the table that you seem to toss mail on when you come up the stairs. Her wallet and keys were in the purse."

"I can't remember seeing her purse, but she might have stashed it there Friday night. Women are always doing that, you know, putting their purse somewhere so they don't have to carry it. So if she did, maybe the real thief went into my apartment and got the keys. I mean, I never lock the door."

"Sergeant Lawrence and I have studied all the security video. We've talked with Sal Abato and Helio Lopez. Several things are fishy about the robbery you reported to me Saturday morning.

"When Sal walked us through the area, he pointed out the pocket doors at the ends of the hallways that provide access to the gallery door. He said those doors were locked before the party. Later, when we checked those doors, neither showed any evidence of being forced." Ray paused for a moment, then continued, "Scott, you had the means and the opportunity, and the keys to open those doors."

"Yeah, sure, but what motive could I have had. I mean, stealing some worthless copies from my employer. Come on."

Ray smiled. "Scott, when you reported the robbery, you told me the prints were valuable. Now, suddenly, they are worthless. What changed?"

"You have nothing, Sheriff, just some circumstantial junk."

"Yes, circumstantial junk. And failure to report a death in the case of Gerhard Talmadge. Breaking and entering and robbery of Ms. Ingersolle's artworks. Breaking and entering the home of Gerhard Talmadge. In Michigan, lying to police is also a crime. Scott, the list goes on and on. The prosecutor will be able to pick and choose. This is not going to go well for you."

"It's all circumstantial. You've got nothing."

"I don't know," said Sue. "At trial, all the prosecution has to do is point out the discrepancies in your LinkedIn profile. Once the prosecution establishes your lack of credibility…"

"To put it in plain English, Scott, it looks like you lie about everything. Maybe you can't differentiate anymore between what is true and what's a lie," said Ray.

"What if I did this on the instructions of my employer?"

"What are you talking about, Scott?" asked Ray.

"The robbery."

"You're going to tell us that Ms. Ingersolle instructed you to stage a break-in and steal some fake drawings."

"Well, not exactly."

"We are all ears, Scott, but if this is just another wild story, spare us. It's been a long day," said Ray.

"The prints in the gallery were just copies that were staged—you know positioned with the right width of matting and proper framing to best show off the work. She did the staging herself on Friday morning. And the potential buyer for the prints was coming in next week. And then everything went wrong."

"What are you talking about?" Sue asked.

"Gerhard had the originals. He was in need of money and he and Ms. Ingersolle worked out an arrangement where she would find a buyer for the work. I was supposed to swap them out, with his knowledge, of course. He was going to be paid handsomely. But he died. The prints, his prints needed to be moved. After Jennifer told me he was dead, I went over to his house. It was locked, and yes, I broke the window. I got in there. It was dark, so dark. All I had was my phone for light. And then, when I finally made it to the hallway, they were gone. The walls were empty. I thought the best thing to do was fake a robbery in the gallery. And I needed to tell the police, you guys, right away. You know, make it official. That way Ms. Ingersolle could explain to her clients why she didn't have the prints. I mean, she said a very wealthy collector was coming to look at them. I saved her a lot of embarrassment. And I thought it wouldn't matter."

"Scott, do you know that lying to police is a crime?" asked Ray.

"Well, it wasn't really a lie. I mean, once things were worked out I'm sure we could have reached an understanding."

Ray was having trouble withholding his impatience.

"Didn't you wonder what had happened to the real prints?"

"Yes. First, I thought it was Helio or maybe Sal. Then it occurred to me that Piper might be involved. But I honestly don't know what happened to them."

"That, I believe," said Ray.

"You said you did the robbery on instructions from Ms. Ingersolle."

"Well, not exactly. I had to do something. She expects me to take care of things."

"How much does she know?"

"She knows about the robbery, my faked robbery. She knows about Gerhard's prints going missing. I was told to leave it alone for a while. She was going to make inquiries."

After a short pause, Scott asked, "Is there anything else, Sheriff?"

"Yes," he answered. He locked eyes with Scott. "What can you tell us about Yuan Zheng Hong."

Scott flinched. Then he put his head on the table.

"Scott, you need a lawyer, a criminal lawyer."

54

Ray carried the bags of groceries into the house. Sue followed, giving Simone a brief walk before she went in. Ray stood at the counter and started to empty the bags, separating and grouping the items by category and moving them to the cupboard or refrigerator. Sue slid onto a stool and watched briefly, her attention diverted by a sharp bark from Simone.

"She wants her dinner," said Ray, not looking away from his tasks.

Sue started to giggle.

Ray looked up. "What's so funny?" he asked.

"Does she always do that when she wants food?"

"Yes," said Ray. "Doesn't she do that with you?"

"Never, not once. That's why I'm laughing."

"Why would she want to bark for prescription diet?

"Elkins."

"Well, how does she get your attention?

"If I'm standing, Simone rubs against my legs in an almost catlike manner. If that doesn't work, she plops her body on my feet and grrrs. If I'm sitting, Simone does her best to crawl into my lap and give little kisses."

"So, what are you trying to tell me?" asked Ray.

"We have co-parented this little dog for a couple of years, and she mastered different ways to communicate with us. And I'm learning an important lesson."

"What are you talking about?"

"Oh, Elkins," she said, coming around the counter and wrapping her arms around his neck. She pulled him close and kissed him as he wrapped his arms around her. Sue then slowly ran the tip her tongue over his lips. Nuzzling close to his chest, she emitted a guttural growl, followed a few seconds later by a sharp bark.

"You want to be fed, too?"

"Elkins, forget about putting the groceries away. I want a glass of champagne. Then I want to fall asleep in your arms."

"I was just trying to do what you told me earlier. You said you wanted to drink champagne and watch me cook dinner and then…"

"Look at the time. It's too late for all that. How about a fast grilled cheese sandwich? I'll feed and walk Simone while you do that. But first, before anything else, pop a cork and kiss me some more."

55

Ray turned off M22 onto the sand trail that led west toward Gull Point.

"Are we going to have to swim?" asked Sue.

"Piper said the temporary bridge is in place," he responded."

"Just look how lush everything is," said Sue. "By the time you get way into June, you forget all about the winter. Suddenly everything is green and vigorous and winter is way out there in the future. Elkins, when were we first here? It seems like eons ago."

"Yeah, it does. I still want to tie that Nike Air Jordon to Yuan Zheng Hong."

"It doesn't work, sorry. The body once connected to that Air Jordon had only been in the water a year, maybe two. Why do you want to connect them?" asked Sue.

"My need for closure, perhaps. I still wonder about Yuan Zheng Hong and the Air Jordon guy, too. Lots of broken lives."

"Scott Nelson did a lot of damage, and he's probably going to walk from most of it," said Sue.

"Yeah, beware of narcissists."

"You grew to like Abato, didn't you?" said Sue.

"Yes. Sal's a working stiff trying to provide for his family. In the process, he's not about to sacrifice his integrity, which has to be damn hard to do in that smoke and mirrors environment. For the most part, he was candid with us."

"And Abato is Nelson's replacement at Gull Point, at least for the near term?"

"That's what Piper told me. He's bringing his family out for the summer. Piper also said her mother popped for Scott Nelson's bail and she's committed to covering his legal expenses. That's probably enough to keep Scott's silence. He knows way too much about things that have happened at Gull Point over the years."

Ray slowed and carefully rolled up the steel ramp onto the surface of the temporary bridge over the washed-out roadway. "No swimming today," he said when he reached the other side.

He pulled to the side of the road near the old cottage. A large dumpster, piled high, occupied part of the parking area, sharing the space with dozens of flats of flowers. Piper, in jeans, a faded blue work shirt, and worn running shoes, put down the flowers she was carrying and came to greet them.

"Thank you for coming," she said, greeting them warmly.

"It looks like you're fixing up the old cottage," said Ray, more than a hint of disbelief in his tone as he looked at the long neglected building.

"Yes, lots of changes. I even surprised myself. There were a lot of things I wanted to tell you on the phone, but I didn't want to talk your ear off. After Mother relented on bulldozing the place, well, one thing led to another. The cottage is mine as long as I want it. My first goal is to get the place cleaned out and restore the gardens. I want the cottage to look like it did when I was a kid. I'm probably chasing ghosts, but why not?"

"What happened to New York?" asked Ray.

"It's on hold. I need to slow down my life. I need to grieve, for both Grandfather and for Gram, too. I also want to understand why my memories of this place are so unique, so happy. I can stay here and try to figure that out on my own, or I can go back to the city and pay some shrink a pile of money to help me figure things out. At the moment I think here is better. But enough about me. There's something I want to show you."

Piper led them through the gate—past cultivated flower beds, some already planted—and up the front steps into the central hall of the cottage. She gestured toward five prints, newly framed and carefully hung along one wall.

"There they are after spending a few weeks in New York,

including time in the custody of the FBI. They're back where they should be, just as I remember them."

"They're lovely," said Sue, slowly moving from print to print. "Degas?"

"So it would seem, but they're on paper that didn't come into the market until the late '20s, about a decade after Degas's death."

"So they become even more mysterious," said Ray.

"Exactly. Grandfather's wedding present to Gram was a forgery, whatever you want to call it. Which brings up another interesting question. Gram was extremely knowledgeable, especially of work from that period. She would have known those sketches were not original. Was the subject ever broached? Was it a private joke between the two of them? I've heard that Grandfather was a skilled forger himself, back in the day. Maybe she knew but enjoyed them for what they were, forgeries done by the man she loved, the guy who brought her lots of joy in the autumn of her life."

"How about your mother?" asked Ray.

"My mother, I'll never know for sure what she believed. But my guess is she thought they were original. If this was all a joke on Grandfather's part, he's having the last laugh."

"Yuan Zheng Hong, the man I told you about on the phone, anything come to mind about him?" asked Ray.

"No, I never knew of anyone like that. And Grandfather, he never mentioned it. There is one thing, though. The apartment above the garage that you talked about on the phone, I was up there when I was a kid. The place was filled with a lot of old junk. They didn't want me playing anywhere in the garage. My memory is that they told me it had been the maid's apartment when the cottage was just a summer place." Piper looked over at Ray.

"I've got a couple of questions for you."

"Okay."

"Jennifer Bidwell, what's happening with her?" asked Piper.

"Everything is in the prosecutor's hands. Bidwell could be charged with multiple felonies. It goes without saying that her life has been turned upside down. The one good thing, her employer, Linda Wetherbee, is providing financial and moral support."

"How about Scott?"

"We've provided the prosecutor all the evidence we've gathered. At this point, it's all circumstantial. I wouldn't hazard a guess as to what the prosecutor might do. On the question of Yuan Zheng Hong, Scott's been interviewed by the FBI several times. Their investigation is continuing. At this point there is just the passport and some prints. There's no body and no other evidence. Nelson isn't talking, and your grandfather is dead. I'm not optimistic that we will ever know anything more."

"And my questions about my grandfather's finances?"

"You speeded up things by giving us access to your grandfather's bank accounts. The forensic accountant is working through that material. I can't tell you much more at this time."

"Yes, I know you can't say anything, but I can. Suddenly, Grandfather was taking $1,000 in cash out of his account every month. That went on for over three years. It continued till last month when his balance dropped below a thousand. Where did that cash go? He wasn't spending that kind of money. He was being extorted. Over what? Yuan Zheng Hong?"

"All I can tell you is that investigation is still ongoing," Ray answered.

"So you're back here alone," said Sue.

"Yes. Trevor left on the Tuesday after that disastrous weekend. When I finally got back to New York, he had moved out of our apartment. I called his cell, the number was no longer in service. I called his office. They said he was on leave. So I guess he's off pursuing his life, and I'm doing the same."

Piper looked at Sue and smiled. "How's the wrist? Will you be in a cast much longer?"

"Hopefully, just a week more. Thank you for asking."

"You two, you're quite the team. Are you a couple?"

Sue blushed and looked over at Ray. The ball had been lobbed into his court.

He looked back at Sue, then over to Piper. He put his arm over Sue's shoulder and gently pulled her to his side. "We're spending time together."

"Good. You two look like a good fit."

Author's Note

Destination Wedding was written in the months just before and during the year of the pandemic. It was a time when I was mostly cut off from face-to-face contact with our immediate family, friends, and colleagues. I had been thinking about this book and doing some preliminary re-search for more than a year before I began to write. After the pandemic hit, emails and Zoom meetings replaced more enjoyable information gathering conversations over coffee.

Special thanks to my writing group—Peter Marabell, Winifred Simpson, and Marietta Hamady, veteran Zoomers all—for their continued support and thoughtful suggestions.

Special thanks to Heather Shaw: editor, book designer, and marketing guru. For almost two decades, I've benefited from Heather's friendship, support, and wise counsel.

And to my readers, thank you for all the emails over the last year. Your support and encouragement keep at the keyboard.

Finally, my thanks to my wife, Mary K, who spent so many hours reading and commenting on the early drafts of this book.

Books in the Ray Elkins Series:

CPSIA information can be obtained
at www.ICGtesting.com
Printed in the USA
LVHW041330081220
673640LV00034B/196